I0690917

Heart's Compass

THE EARL'S SPARK

ALIYAH BURKE

Kemet Uncovered
Talios
Devi
Linc
Saffron
Taber
Ashia

Heart's Compass
The Princess and the Marquess
Flight of the Hawk
The Earl's Spark

Keeper of the Stars
Part One
Part Two
Part Three
Part Four
Part Five

Astral Guardians
Chasing the Storm
Highlands at Dawn
Fields of Thunder
Branded by Frost
Driven by Night
Moon of Fire

Family Forever
Don't You Wanna Stay?
Love and Moonshine
First You Dream

What's her Secret?
Preconception

A Little Bit Cupid
This Ain't No Love Story

My Bloody Valentine
Perfect Duet

With Taige Crenshaw

Single Title
Unbreakable Bonds

THE EARL'S SPARK

Dedication

To Opal — thank you for being you!

Chapter One

Phillip Vallence, Earl of Edais and current owner of the sugar and tobacco plantation Hawk's Cove, stared at the books on the large mahogany desk he sat behind. The desk was massive even by his standards, and he loved the intricate work on the edges, along with the stamped brass ornamentation.

He sighed and pushed a hand through his hair, curling up his lip at the ever-present feel of sweat on his skin. Something that hadn't been much of an issue most days in England. Blowing out a breath, he tore his attention from everything else that it found and placed it back onto what he needed to focus on.

The books.

Funds.

Money.

Livelihood.

All of it was boring to him. He had a man in England he'd entrusted with his estates there, but here he didn't have anyone of his own yet. Right now he waited to go over the numbers when the man he'd summoned to look over them with him showed up.

This was a working plantation, but he didn't have slaves. He paid a wage to every worker here and was going to continue to do so. More of a wage if he could figure out how to make sense out of the other man's style of ledger keeping.

Otherwise, it looked like he would have to continue to pay the man to keep his books. He'd spoken to shops in the small nearby town and had confirmed he was in good standing with them all. In fact, all he'd heard was praise on how his accounts were never late.

The knock came and he bade them enter without looking away from the intricately neat printing of numbers. Phillip didn't think his London-based steward would be on board for coming down here. Even though the weather was sublime and he had quickly fallen for the allure of this island. The sweat was something he'd had to get used to, still was in some respects, and knowing his man back home, he wouldn't be interested in moving here.

"You requested my presence, my lord?"

He reached for his drink and sipped as he took his time gazing over Elonne. Not overly tall, his dark skin also had a sheen. The man was fit and his clothing had seen better days.

"Come in and sit down. Elonne, was it? Can I call you Elonne?"

"You can call me what you wish, my lord."

Despite the tone and the smooth way the response fell, Phillip felt the undercurrent of tension in the words. He understood it—well, as much as a man of his station and position in life could.

His visitor remained perched on the edge of the chair as if he expected it to move back so he landed on the floor.

Phillip nudged the books toward him, the three of them that were chock full of lines overflowing with numbers and calculations that made his own head spin.

"Your books, my lord." A slow blink as the gaze moved from him down to the books, where it hovered a moment, and back up. Not so much with fear, but with confusion as to what reason he'd had to be summoned. "Is there a problem?"

"No problem. I would just like to learn the method you used to do these so I can follow along without having to ask you to explain it all."

"You're not… I mean, of course, sir. I can come by tomorrow and tell you."

His nose itched. Always had when he smelled a lie or an untruth. Leaning back in his chair, he steepled his fingers.

"Now works best for me." He made sure to hold Elonne's gaze when he spoke.

The man glanced down for a moment, his lips moving before he lifted his head once more. "I'm sorry, my lord. I cannot."

He didn't like being had. Phillip moved his fingertips so they tapped against one another. "Cannot?" he asked silkily. "Or *will* not?"

Knowing full well he baited the man, who seemed much more concerned than when he had first entered the room, Phillip waited. No longer the rash younger man, he'd grown a lot, partially on his own and partially because he'd had to in order to maintain his friendships. The ones that meant a damn to him.

Elonne held his gaze. The man had that much going for him at least. There wasn't any squirming or hemming and hawing to try to buy some additional time. "Cannot, my lord."

"Then I was misinformed when I was advised that you were the one who takes care of the estate's books?" A layer of honey to bring him in closer.

"No, my lord."

He flattened his lips together. "Explain this to me then." His tone had gotten hard and carried the same 'I am above you because of my station in life' character that he had used on a daily basis in England. "I would really like to know how the man I had been led to believe took care of the books on my newest purchase suddenly is informing me he does not know how to teach me his method."

"My sibling Fyre does the books. I needed to spend more time out in the fields to get the harvest in. Fyre took over and added in this new way to keep those who would come and snoop from being able to read your profits."

Who is trying to find out about my business here?

Elonne got to his feet and approached the desk. He reached one hand out to the books but paused before there was actual touching. "May I, my lord?"

"By all means." He waved a hand and continued leaning back in the chair. Phillip had to admit, he *was* intrigued. And impressed. This man was still working in the fields when he was fairly certain what he would be earning as one who took care of the books should provide him with enough.

The man turned one book toward him and placed the tip of a blunt finger along a line.

"I know that this means you are flush, my lord. This symbol means that, but I cannot tell you all the profits from sugar, tobacco or other items that are grown here. I can tell you that when we started growing and selling other items, more people came around to see how much money was being made. The book change came when we found a few visitors snooping around."

"*Snooping around.*" That, he wasn't a fan of hearing. The hardness in his gut took root and grew. It took an effort to keep his sneer contained but he did, waiting to hear what else he would be enlightened about.

There was a way out of this. He could, and *would*, figure it out. The directionless emotion pouring through him pissed him off. That feeling had been part of the reason he had left England. He wanted to do more. *Be* more.

Make something of himself, even if that wasn't a typical urge for a member of the peerage. His friends had, and while he was still included in the circle, he was now the outlier. The one without a woman, without a cause, without *any* direction.

Something he wanted desperately to change.

"Where is Fyre now?"

Unease hit the man's expression. He clearly worked hard to contain his frown, causing his forehead to wrinkle. "In town, working."

"So there is not enough work doing the books here to keep him busy? He is also in town working?"

Something akin to shame kicked free over his features. "The books were my job, my lord. Fyre works at a few other places. I was the one who asked for the assistance in keeping your books. Fyre would never speak of what was seen here."

Phillip thought about this discussion. He knew this island had a different mentality than some of the others he'd visited on his way here. The dynamic wasn't just slave and owner. There were Blacks who had businesses in the port town and some, he had been told, had small farms of their own. That alone had marked this island as one of the odd ones out and he fully expected in the future there might be trouble from the other plantation owners on surrounding islands who still had slaves and were looking to always increase their own holdings.

Right now, he had to figure out this puzzle of his steward's bookkeeping.

"Where is Fyre now?" He repeated his question.

"In town, my lord." The answer hadn't changed and was given without so much as a slight hesitation.

Wouldn't divulge a location. Interesting. "And how soon will he be made available?"

"I am unsure, my lord. There are long hours to be kept."

Regret slashed over Elonne's face the second the words escaped. Phillip let it go. There were times and places for every battle. This wasn't one of them. At least not for the moment.

"Very well then, we shall ride into town."

He'd expected more of a fuss from Elonne, and was both surprised and pleased when the immediate agreement came.

Phillip sent one of his footmen to get their mounts ready and Elonne accompanied him. Once again alone in his study, he stared down at that handwriting. Neat. Precise.

He was sure Fyre kept great books, he just needed to know how to interpret them for himself. Given how scattered this place had been when he'd taken over, he wasn't about to let any portion of this plantation not be overseen by him.

With a heavy sigh, his thoughts turned back to England and the people he'd left there. Friends? Two to three, and they were blissful in their wedded state. When he'd come here to help out a friend of his friends, he had not expected to fall in love with the island. Or her people.

All of them.

The island hummed and vibrated with a life one never saw in London. Or anywhere he'd been in England. Sure, the heat had taken a bit to get used to, but the problem of sleeping with one sheet or none seemed better to him than hoping his heating stones wouldn't die out through the night and he would have to wake someone to tend his fire.

"My lord, your horse is ready."

He looked up to see one of the maids standing in the doorway.

Standing, he nodded. "Very good." He shoved the ledgers into a bag then slung it over his shoulder.

As his feet hit the wood of the veranda, he found Elonne standing by two horses, holding their reins. The worry on his face was unmistakable. No doubt in Phillip's mind that there was a story there, but he would find out soon enough.

Stowing the books behind the saddle, he looked back at his new home while his fingers tied the bag with deft strokes. There was still work to be done, quite a bit, but for the first time in years, he had a thrum of excitement in his chest. A chance here was what had appealed to him, *called* to him. A chance to prove he was more than just a title. To prove he was more than a wastrel who thought of nothing but the next pussy he could sink into or bet he could make.

Pussy, however, was always a nice thought, and since he'd gotten here, he'd kept his dick dry. He was determined to make a name for himself because of what he did with his plantation, not because of the women he fucked.

With ease, he swung up in the saddle and waited for Elonne to follow suit. Together, they turned their horses and made their way to the end of the driveway, heading into town.

* * * *

Four shops later, his frustration had mounted. Fyre hadn't been at any of those places. What kind of man worked at so many different stores? How were things kept in good order if he bounced around from place to place so much?

They entered another and he looked around at the variety of items.

"Elonne. What are you doing here?"

The soft voice jolted through him, causing him to jerk with the shock. Lust slammed him and it took a moment for him to snap from the haze which had settled over his entire body.

Phillip looked up and was mesmerized by the woman standing behind the counter, a pencil in hand hovering over a book. Dark curls had been pulled back from her face and her smooth brown skin, a shade he'd never seen before. The collar of her dress hid most of her neck and that was upsetting to him.

How would someone describe her? Short of breathtaking, I have no words.

Warmth flooded him as the hairs rose on his arms and the nape of his neck. Flushed, he struggled to catch his breath. Never had he had such a visceral reaction to a woman before.

His nerves were on fire and it wouldn't take much more than the slightest of sparks to set him ablaze.

How was it possible for a woman dressed in the drabbest of colors to somehow be the brightest one in the room? He moved his mouth a few times but words didn't and wouldn't come. Who was this woman?

What is wrong with me?

"Looking for you, Fyre." Elonne tugged at his collar. "Lord Edais wants an explanation about his books."

Well, shit. His bookkeeper was a woman.

Gwen, better known as Fyre to the majority of the people on the island, swallowed with deliberate measure. She was going to kill her brother. Assuming this English lord didn't kill the both of them. How dare he bring that man to one of her businesses? And all without giving her a chance to prepare.

She'd managed to avoid him since he'd come in and taken over Hawk's Cove. Grudgingly, she could admit, he looked much better now. He was dressed more like the men who lived here than someone about to attend the opera in London.

Or so I would assume. I have never been to an opera nor seen anyone actually dressed to attend one.

His sandy brown hair had lightened as he'd spent time in the strong sunlight. But it was those eyes, gray and sharp, that got to her. He was thinner than some of the men she knew, but it wasn't because of sickness. She had watched him work.

Every chance she could.

Okay, perhaps a few times.

Remembering herself, she executed a curtsey. "Good day, my lord."

Her hands were slick all of a sudden and she found herself holding her breath. Not advisable.

A low grumble rolled through the room and part of her wanted to lounge in the warmth it gave her, but another part of her wanted to run. Far. Fast. Without looking back.

This man is dangerous.

"Really?" His accent was sharp and yet she found she didn't mind so much how his words fell from his mouth to the air for her to hear. "That is what you say to me? Nothing about how it is the two of you have been deceiving me, doing who knows what with my books?"

Panic flared. The fear of losing her life hadn't lessened. She hadn't been given permission to touch his books. Not only that, but her brother was in danger as well.

Grateful there wasn't anyone else in the building, she made her way from behind the counter.

"Begging your pardon, my lord." She kept her eyes down.

His big feet stepped into view. In her periphery, she watched her brother move as well and she flicked her fingers toward him, holding him off. No matter what the consequences, she knew Elonne would never allow this man to lay hands on her.

In either of the ways her brain was trying to figure out—pain or pleasure.

He snorted in disbelief. "How long have you been doing them?"

She knew better than to tarry with her response. "Since a week after you left. Elonne got ill after picking up more time in the fields to make sure none of your crops went bad and I took over. It is easier for me than him, but please do not punish him for my behavior. I made the choice and decision to do this, not he."

Fyre pushed out a short breath and lifted her gaze to find his gray eyes waiting for her. She couldn't make out what she read in their depths.

Her brother frowned and made another move forward. Again, she waved him off. In the grand scheme of things, he was far more important than she was. He could do the physical labor she couldn't. And he had a wife and children to take care of. For all intents and purposes, she was alone and expendable.

"You have to explain this to me. I cannot make sense of your system."

"Yes, my lord." She nearly held her breath once more. Perhaps she would get out of this with her life intact.

He walked to the door, where he glanced over his shoulder at her and lifted one eyebrow, impatience stamped all over his features.

Funny how that didn't detract from his attractiveness. That hawklike nose took him from perfectly pretty and handsome to rugged and slightly dangerous.

"Why are you still there?"

"I am working, my lord. I am here for another three hours."

He scowled and crossed his arms as he pivoted back to her. "And then?"

It is like he knew I would try to avoid this today.

"And then I will show up at your home to explain my system." *And hope you do not call for my death.*

He grunted and walked out. "Let us return, Elonne."

Her brother shot her a concerned look as he hurried off after the man who had all the power.

The moment the door closed behind her brother, she exhaled and made her way back to the counter, legs wobbling in both relief and for the simple fact that because of her interaction with the earl, they had decided they weren't strong enough to keep her up any longer. She took a few moments to get some stability back, then retreated around the counter once more.

Legs still shaky like she'd been out toiling in the heat all day, she pulled out the stool and sat with a grateful sigh. Rubbing her chest to try to ease the ache that had filled her lungs, she took several deep breaths.

Tears burned the backs of her eyes and she tried to keep them at bay. Her hand only shook a little as she pulled the book she'd been about to start working on when *he* had come in out from beneath the counter.

He even smelled different than the other men she was around. Something deep and earthy had floated from him to her nose.

I do not need to think about that man any more than I already do. Especially since she thought about him a lot.

With a harsh mental reprimand, she put her wavering attention to the work before her and began getting Mr. Larson's books in order. She tended to do his accounting today as his shop was slower aside from people coming in to pick up packages.

Since she only had two packages left to be picked up, she figured she'd get quite a lot done and not have to come back to catch him up. She was newer to his place and had been pushing hard to get his information in order.

* * * *

As she'd predicted, it had been a quiet day. She'd set up a few appointments for some future customers who wanted time with Mr. Larson. Five minutes before she was to lock up, the door opened once more and in walked another of the plantation owners, who also had a shop in town.

Albie Caulfield.

His black hair never had a strand out of place. Despite living on a tropical island, he was disturbingly pale.

Locking the book away, she turned and dipped a curtsey. "Good evening, Mr. Caulfield."

His grin didn't set off the same flock of flutters she'd acquired when the earl leveled his gray eyes on her, but Albie's smile was one that had her skin crawling. Even so, she didn't show her unease.

"Gwen." He swaggered toward her. "You're always such a delightful sight for my eyes. When are you going to come work for me alone? You know I will make room for you in my house."

Seeing his package, she slid to her right and picked it up, her smile never slipping.

"As always, Mr. Caulfield, thank you for your offer, but I will have to continue to decline. I do not have time to take on another set of books full time. I can help a bit here and there until you find a replacement."

His dark blue eyes flashed, hands flexed, and nostrils flared. But like hers, his smile never faltered.

"I will keep asking." He reached for her hand after she had placed the package on the counter between them.

It took a few times before she tugged free. She didn't like being here alone with this man. While he never did anything definitive, every instinct she had demanded she run far and fast from him — and not in the same way that thought had jumped into her mind when she had been around the earl.

"It is an honor to be requested." His gaze burned into her. "Is there something else I could do for you, Mr. Caulfield?"

"When are you going to call me Albie?" He leaned against the counter.

"That isn't proper, sir."

He came closer and she fought not to retreat from how he pushed into her personal space.

"It is only us here, Gwenie. We could have some fun."

"Am I interrupting?"

Mr. Caulfield jumped back, putting more space between them. She flinched on the inside but had been raised not to show anything, so she acted as if the sudden appearance of one Phillip Vallence, Earl of Edais, hadn't shocked the hell out of her.

"Good evening, my lord."

Another curtsey for him.

Albie's eyebrow shot up at that. "You're the new Earl of Edais?"

From below her lowered lids, she watched the cold, condescending expression on the earl's face.

"I've been an earl for a long time. So no, I'm not a *new* earl. I've been one since my birth. Who are you?" The disdain could be tasted in the air it was so thick.

"Albie Caulfield. I have a smaller plantation on the other side of town." He puffed out his chest. "And a shop here in town."

Those gray eyes didn't soften one bit. "And you are here for what reason?"

In fact, there was a thicker slather of arrogance on the earl's words.

Albie swallowed but didn't back down. "I came to pick up a package and catch up with this woman."

Flint-hard eyes pushed into her, searching for something. "You will be the reason she is late to my home. We have business to conduct."

Her entire body flushed at his words, even though she knew there wasn't anything remotely sexual about them.

Albie didn't move away. He instead looked at her. "Gwen?"

"I am helping his lordship out with some of his books. I said I would be by tonight after I finished here."

The man stepped closer and gripped her arm. "I do not like this. It is not proper for you to be alone with him. And how is it you have time to do his books but cannot be bothered to assist me full time?"

She pulled on her arm but he didn't let go. At least, not until the earl spoke up once more.

"Release her."

Two words. Issued with cold efficiency. Two words that were followed without hesitation. Jaw clenched, Albie picked up his package and walked to the door. Once there, he turned back.

"I will see you tomorrow, Gwen." His gaze hardened. "My lord."

Then they were alone, and unlike when it had been her and Albie, this time her body wasn't letting her forget it had been too long since a man had touched her in a good way. Or in any way.

"I do not appreciate being kept waiting so you can have some rendezvous with a man."

His words snapped her head up, instant rage washing over her as his meaning sank in. She forgot his title and station, which hovered so far above her own she couldn't even see them when she looked up, and stepped around the counter and into his personal space, stabbing him in the chest with her finger.

"You know *nothing* about me so you should keep your uninformed and incorrect assumptions to yourself." She bared her teeth and wanted to snap them in his direction.

"I know you told me you would be on your way after you finished work and yet, when I walk in here, what I find is you *not* working but getting cozy with a man. What should I think?"

"That not all of us are like you Englanders. I do *not* throw myself at every man who crosses my path. Not to mention, I had not closed yet. He was the last customer I had to give a package to. Now, I am done."

"I never said you threw yourself at *every* man. I know that is not true." He stepped closer. His torso was hard beneath her finger and she had this strangest urge to settle her entire hand against him and stroke. Pet. Indulge. "Because if it was, we would be having a very different conversation, Fyre."

Her knees wobbled at the way he said her name— low and drawn out with a distinctly sexual timbre.

Being unable to begin to quantify how this man, this outsider, had affected her made her nervous. *He* made her nervous.

Like he could see beneath the shell she put around herself before she ever left the house. Heck, even at home she maintained it. But this man, the way his gray eyes bore into her, like he alone could see beneath it and to the true heart of her being...

What was he discovering? Lust? Desire? Longing? All of them, for sure.

"I will be along shortly, my lord."

"I will escort you there and after we go over the books, I'll take you"—the slightest of pauses—"home."

"I do not require such a thing."

His grin twisted her gut into knots. "Lucky for all involved, I did not ask." He tipped his head. "I will wait for you outside. Do *not* tarry."

The arrogant earl was gone before she could begin to form an argument as to why she would not be riding to his home with him.

Chapter Two

Phillip reclined in his chair, making damn sure he kept his eyes on the ledger before him. It worked.

He was most certainly *not* staring at and ogling the woman on the other side of the desk — a large expanse of solid wood that could handle him laying her across it and allowing himself the indulgence of her body.

Shifting in his chair, he subtly adjusted his hardness. He'd not been this attracted to anyone in a long while. Had he been a monk?

Certainly not, but he wasn't often close to forgetting his sense because of a woman being near to him. And the shit part about this, she was only here because he'd insisted. Not because she wanted to be, or was attracted to him.

The drink on his left wasn't going to be enough to quench the thirst that Fyre had aroused within him.

Thank God his determination to *not* look at her was working.

She sat there in utter silence. Not fidgeting or moving in any way to make him think she wasn't comfortable or had to get somewhere else. She was, well, a statue.

Truthfully, he didn't need to have her here for the moment—she had been crisp and clear in her breakdown of his money and her notations. He just lingered, not wanting to be apart from her.

"Do you have a copy of the books from when you first took over?"

Without a sound, she rose and walked across the room to a closed cupboard. He bit his lower lip as she opened it only to push up on her toes, reaching over her head. The thrust of her breasts against the thin material of her dress wasn't helping the rod in his breeches.

Eyes locked on her figure, lingering over the swell of her ass that made his hands itch to grab it as he sank between her legs, he rubbed the heel of one hand over his erection, a low moan slipping from his lips.

He could *not look* later.

If she heard him, she didn't take any notice of it. Just carried the book back to him and turned it so the pages would be the correct way once she placed it down. The moment it was on the desktop she retreated to her chair.

"Thank you."

"Of course, my lord."

The door was open and many staff members moved around, occasionally peeking in to see if they needed anything.

He wasn't a fool, well aware that part of the reason for their constant visits was they looked for gossip to spread, but more was they looked out for Fyre. He saw the affection many of those on his staff had for the young woman.

Because he wanted to keep her around, he ground down on the feverish sensations she created in him and made sure all behavior was above board. No matter how much he wanted to brush his lips along her skin. Stroke those curves. Sweep her hair away from her neck, exposing the small space where it met her shoulder and kiss it, push his tongue there and taste her.

He longed for her to tremble in his arms as he whispered what he was going to do to her after she came for him, around his fingers, which would be deep in her wetness.

Phillip coughed and reached for his drink, needing something because he was about to burst free of his breeches. She looked up from the book she'd been going through and making notations in.

"Everything okay, my lord?"

"Phillip."

She lifted her eyebrows. Not one but both of them.

"Call me Phillip."

"I cannot, my lord. That would not be proper." She dropped her gaze back to the pages before her.

You can and you will. Maybe not tonight, but you will scream my name, Fyre.

His housekeeper walked in, a tray of food in hand. Fyre turned her head to see who it was, then went back to the book and—because he'd not been able to pull his gaze from her yet—he saw some scarred skin along her neck ever so briefly before her hair covered it once more. He blinked and took another look at the ledger before him.

"Your meal, my lord." The tray was set beside him.

He grunted as he tried to make sense of the numbers from before she'd taken over. Pinching the bridge of his nose, he looked over to the items waiting for him and scowled.

"What is this?"

"The food you had requested be brought to you this evening, my lord."

Lifting his head, he stared at the woman. Her blue eyes held his but only for a tick of time.

"Where is food for her?" He stabbed a finger in Fyre's direction.

The woman bumbled and blinked a few times before squaring her shoulders. "You did not say you wished to eat with your guest."

Phillip bit back, barely, the snarl that shot from his throat as fast as his own horse had unseated him the first time he'd met Ciara and her big cat.

"I should not have to say it. We are in here working and for you to bring me food but nothing for her does not make me happy."

The housekeeper turned her eyes to Fyre. "What can I bring you?"

Fyre closed the book she'd been working in and rose. "Nothing, thank you. I have to get heading home." She gave the housekeeper a small nod, one he noticed wasn't returned, before she glanced back to him. "I can be by in two days, my lord, if you would still like me to be of assistance."

"Do you not typically do the books daily?"

"No, my lord. If you would like that to change, I can do them daily, starting in two days."

There was a bite to her words, like she dared him to defy her. He longed to nibble on that plump lower lip, tug it and suck it into his mouth.

He laced his fingers and took his time in looking over her. "Two days then." The moment she nodded, he added, "In the morning. I will feed you breakfast so be here early. There will be a lot to cover."

He watched it, in her eyes, the desire to snip back at him. She wasn't a fan of being told what to do. God, she was magnificent.

"Very good, my lord. I will see you in two days." She curtsied and walked out.

The housekeeper stood there, watching their interaction.

"You can leave," he said without looking at her again. He wanted to get up and go after Fyre, take her home.

Shit, it was dark out. He couldn't have her walk.

Shooting to his feet, he was striding to the door before the housekeeper even made it from the room. He called for a footman and sent them after Fyre, to detain her while the carriage was readied.

She was off to the side when he was able to lay eyes on her once more, as he stepped outside. Phillip didn't appreciate her expression, which he saw in the flickering torchlight.

He knew she saw him and he didn't bother calling out her name, just held his hand out in her direction. Fyre hesitated for a moment before walking toward him.

The carriage rumbled up and the footman got the door. Phillip walked her up and pointed for her to get in.

"I told you I would see you got home. Did you think I would allow you to walk at night?"

"I walk all the time at night."

He took her hand, not giving her the chance to refuse him. She stepped into the carriage and brushed against him, showering him with a scent he'd not smelled before being around this woman. What it was, he didn't know, but he *did* know he longed for more of it. On him. Everywhere.

At the last moment he remembered to have a maid come along. The last thing he wanted to do was ruin her reputation.

I mean, I want it ruined so she will be mine but I will not do it this way.

The coach rocked as he climbed in after the maid and sat across from the women, his back to the horses.

The maid was confused but she didn't say a word. Fyre, however, watched him with suspicion. He didn't blame her, for his wants for this woman were definitely not anything for the faint of heart.

He was a lot of things, but a right bastard wasn't one of them. So he would wait. Bide his time. And wear her down, one tantalizing touch after another.

Then he would be sated from his irrational need for this woman he'd just met today.

God, if his friends could see him now. Rafe and Lucien wouldn't believe this. He'd been the reckless one. The bastard who didn't think of anyone else's needs but his own. Hell, he'd nearly ruined Lucien's happiness because he'd been an ass.

He was lucky they were still speaking to him.

However, as he got older and watched their families grow, it only emphasized how alone *he* was. Usually he would just find a mistress and slake his hunger. But the second he'd laid eyes on Fyre, something else had taken over. His craving for her had been much deeper than simplistic lust. He wanted to be hers. Have her be his. Make his the only touch she craved. The only one she experienced. He wanted to hover over her as she arched into his touch and gasped his name in pleasure. Fuck, he longed to see her swell with his child.

I am in so much trouble.

A fact that was only illustrated further when the driver stuck his head in to ask where they were going.

* * * *

"What happened?"

Fyre groaned and rolled over as her brother repeated his insistent question.

"Elonne, this is my one day to sleep past dawn and you are in here squawking like a chicken. Leave me alone."

"I have a bucket of cold water and I *will* use it."

Coming from her brother, it wasn't an idle threat. With an exaggerated groan, she sat up in bed, rubbing her eyes.

"What is so important that it can't wait until I have coffee?"

The rich, heady scent filled her nostrils and her mouth watered in response. This was a delicacy that she'd become addicted to and she jealously guarded what beans she was able to get her hands on.

"I did not state I only had *cold* water."

She still didn't open her eyes for her brother, just accepted the warm, chipped cup and inhaled the fragrance once more. It curled around her like the warmth of the sea around their home. At first sip, she purred and finally opened her eyes.

Elonne watched her, shaking his head with amusement. Yet she could see the concern in his gaze.

"Everything is fine, Elonne. I explained the system to him. I go back tomorrow and will see if I have lost that account. If so, I am sorry. I never meant for that to happen."

He sat beside her on the narrow bed and nudged her with his shoulder. "It is my fault, Fyre. I should have taken better care in regards to the new owner of Hawk's Cove. It would be a large account to lose, but I can find more work."

She drank in silence for a while before digging her toes into the thick rug by her bed, made by Elonne's wife.

"Albie would be a thought if needed." While she wasn't a fan of working for him more, she would do it.

"No." Her brother's single-word refusal said it all. "Stay away from him, Fyre. He is no good."

"I have no interest in him in such a way, Elonne. I only mentioned it because he has asked me a few times to work on his books." Her brother wasn't going to be happy to learn she already had the man on her schedule.

"He is not thinking books when he looks at you, Fyre. And before you argue with me, the next time he offers, tell him I can fit him in. He will back off and say something about waiting for you."

"Just a thought." Her words were barely above a whisper.

He draped an arm around her and hugged her tight. "I know you are just trying to help, but I worry. *We* worry about you."

"And I tell you all that I am fine. I cannot work the fields like you do, but I can do this."

He tugged on her hair that peeked below the wrap around her head. "You always had a penchant for numbers."

"I hate you feel that you have to take care of me."

Elonne growled. "Listen to me, little sister. I will *always* take care of you. It is not a chore."

She finished her coffee. "It is. You have your wife and children. All I am is another mouth to feed." She ignored that she lied to him, she knew the *real* reason.

"Not up for discussion. You are not a bother."

But she was and she could see it on his wife's face. No, she never said anything in front of Elonne, but the looks were there.

"I want a place of my own. Something small."

"No."

"Elonne, listen, I am three and twenty. I want to move out and I have money to do so. I also found a place." She got off the bed and left the room, her clothes in hand to change into.

Her brother remained in her room when she came back dressed for the day. Braiding her hair, she didn't look at him until she held on to the tip of her braid as she tied a red bow around it. She draped it forward over the left side of her neck, hiding what the collar of her dress could not.

Cup in hand, she left the room again, and this time he was on her heels, arguing with her.

Elonne's wife Cara was in the small kitchen and she looked up, the expression on her features smoothing out when she spied Elonne.

"Morning, Gwen."

Cara refused to call her Fyre.

"Good morning. Maybe you can help me convince Elonne my idea is the right one."

"My wife sides with me, Fyre. She will agree with me, not you."

Her dark eyes moving between the siblings, Cara waited.

"I think," Fyre began.

"She thinks she should move out to her own place," Elonne snapped.

Cara's eyes grew wide. Fyre took advantage and pressed on. "It would be a small place, not too far away, and I would still be able to help out with the children, but they are growing and my room could be better used for one of them."

She very deliberately did not mention assisting them with money anymore. Despite how Cara acted, Fyre more than earned her keep staying in this place with them.

"Tell her she is not going, Cara."

Fyre watched her sister-in-law. For about a minute, she didn't say anything. After she stirred whatever was on the stove, she sighed.

"I think we should support Gwen in this."

As she'd expected, Elonne lost it. Her brother was a large man and could be extremely menacing, but she wasn't going to back down.

Swallowing before she tried to get him to see it her way, Cara waited a moment then spoke again. Where her brother was large and loud, Cara never had to raise her voice to get her point made.

"She is a grown woman, Elonne. Why would she want to live with a married couple and their children?"

"Because we are family, and it is dangerous out there for her."

"I am not leaving the town, Elonne. Just this house. I have never lived alone and you two have never been married without me in the house. At least let me give this a try. If it does not work, then I will come back."

She had no intention of returning to this house.

She watched him think it over, then when his broad shoulders slumped when he looked at his wife, she knew he was caving.

"Fine." He stomped off.

Fyre moved up beside Cara, who had returned her attention to her food.

"I know you did not do that for me, Cara, but thank you anyway."

"Just make sure it works and you never have to come back here again to live."

"Like I want to keep living with you." Irritation rose, as was often the case when she dealt with this woman.

Cara narrowed her beady eyes. "You should be thanking me for letting you stay this long."

"You should be grateful I contributed money to the coffers, given how much you like to spend. You will have to slow that down when I leave."

Fyre walked back to her room and packed her meager belongings. She had somewhere to be and a place to rent.

Not long after, she walked along the dirt road, waving at the occasional passer-by. It was still far too early for most people to be up, well, the people who had servants to take care of things for them. The people she saw were the servants.

Stopping off at the baker's, she knocked and smiled when Georges answered.

"Morning, Fyre."

"Georges. I know it is early but I wanted to see if you were still willing to rent out that small place?"

"I am. Are you sure you want to take it?"

"I am positive."

He smiled at her, the aged wrinkles in his face making her want to hug him. The man never failed to set her at ease.

"Marta was hoping you would be interested. She was not comfortable with having a man rent it as she is alone much of the time."

"I would be happy to keep an eye on her."

He opened the door and gestured. "Come in and we will eat fresh bread while we work out the details."

Chapter Three

Her hands smoothed down his back, short nails digging into his skin as she tugged him closer. She arched her hips, taking him in deeper.

More.

He craved more of her. More of the moans. Groans. Mewls. Begging. Panting. Sweat. The way her slit clamped on his cock while he thrust deep inside her heat.

Dipping his head, he feathered kisses along her cheek until he could once again capture her mouth. Her flavor burst over his tongue as he drove it into her at the same pace as his hips delivered his shaft.

Silvered moonlight surrounded them, making her skin gleam with a softness that could have taken his heart if it hadn't already been given. To her.

Legs high up around his waist, she undulated and rolled her hips, taking him deep and keeping up with every powerful stroke. He flexed the hand buried in her hair, holding her head where he could plunder her mouth as he wanted.

Fast, slow, deep, shallow. He couldn't contain his movement.

Sweat ran down his skin, dropping onto the woman beneath him. Her eyes were nearly closed, but she watched him. He knew this because she made his blood burn when she watched him.

He dragged the hand that wasn't sunk into her thick hair down her side, over the swell of one soft breast, moving along after pinching her nipple – an act that had another sharp gasp leaving her throat as her internal muscles gripped him harder.

Need hummed in his veins, popping and sizzling like lightning in a storm, and he knew he hovered along the edge of losing his control. He dipped his head and nipped at her lower lip after pulling back to stare down at her.

It wasn't fair – her flawless skin, thick lashes. Full, pillowy lips that had enticed him from the moment he'd first met her. Watching them widen as he slid his length between her legs only served to increase the pain of holding his orgasm at bay.

"Phillip!" Her cry came on the heels of her tossing her head back, exposing her delicate throat to his view.

He skimmed his fingers along her hips before pushing between them and finding the little swollen nub there. Phillip flicked it, loving the response she gave. Everything went tighter, and for a woman who was tight anyway, this was another level of torture for him.

He took a little bite of her neck, then kissed away the sting as she bucked beneath him.

"More. Oh God, I need... Phillip..."

"Give it to me." He pinched her bundle of nerves and held on as she squirmed.

Her short fingernails tore into his skin, body arching as a cry exploded from her mouth, filling the night sky. The moment she crested he let go of her clit and she cried out once more, coming hard again.

Slamming his mouth over hers, he ate the remainder of her screams as he thrust once more, gripping her hip, and *released deep inside her. He stayed deep, filling her with his seed, and for the first time in his life hoping he got a woman with child. Not just any woman. Her.*

He longed to see her swollen with his seed. Carrying their child.

Phillip's eyes shot open as he lay in his huge bed. Alone. Except for the hard length of his cock, throbbing and demanding relief. His heart pounded and he struggled to breathe.

"My lord."

It wasn't easy to ignore his thickness but he did, sitting up and making sure the length stayed covered.

"What?"

The servant who had walked in went by the name of Lloyd, but more than that didn't come to mind because all his thoughts were still focused on the erection between his legs and the dream he'd been having.

"You have a visitor, my lord."

Phillip exhaled sharply and pinched the bridge of his nose. He'd not even had his first meal.

"Who is here, Lloyd?"

The man pulled back almost like he'd been struck at the use of his name. But, Phillip had to admit, he recovered quickly.

"Fyre. She states the two of you have an appointment this morning."

His blood burst with pops of pleasure. The struggle to keep his smile contained was a serious battle.

"She is correct. Tell her I will be there momentarily. Put her in my office, bring some food and drink."

"Very good, my lord." A bow and he walked out, as quietly as he'd entered.

Phillip exhaled on a moan and fell back on the bed. He hadn't known that she would show up in the morning. Honestly, he'd figured she would be by later in the day, after completing whatever other work she had to complete.

Then again, I did insist on morning and having breakfast with her.

He thought about how long she had to walk to get to his place. Anger simmered as he imagined her walking without any protection.

With a groan of capitulation, he wrapped his hand around his cock and fisted it. Slowly, he stroked. Up and down, squeezing and pinching to try to prolong his self-inflicted torture.

Then he remembered *she* was waiting for him. After that, it didn't take long before he shot his seed into the sheet around his waist. After regaining his breath, he cleaned up and dressed in record time. By the time he hit the stairs, he'd found a bit more decorum.

Not completely honest, but he was hoping it didn't look like he was a youth on his first trip to a brothel.

Handing out morning greetings to the staff as he passed them, he strode to his office, heart picking up in speed the closer he got.

He didn't know what it was about this woman that made him crazy. If Lucien were not so far away, he would have asked him if this had happened to him with Ciara. However, his best friend was over in England.

Stepping into the room, Phillip scanned it and breathed a bit easier the moment he spied her. She stood by the far couch, hands clasped before her.

Lust knocked him hard, like he'd not just found release less than ten minutes ago.

"Good morning, Fyre."

She didn't jump but turned her head toward him, calm and collected. He hid another smile. She would be running the other way if she knew the thoughts that circled his mind when it came to her.

Her curtsey brought shafts of morning's early light to glance along the purple of her dress.

"Good morning, my lord. I hope this was not too early for you."

He smiled. "Of course not. I was just thinking about you."

She stiffened and swallowed.

He moved closer to her. "Want to know what I was thinking?"

Fyre didn't meet his gaze. "I am sure you will tell me if you feel it important, my lord."

A quick glance around made him aware they were still alone. "It is, very." She finally lifted her gaze to his. "I was thinking of—"

"Excuse me, my lord." The footman held the door as one of the maids carried in food.

"Put the food down on the table and leave us. We can serve ourselves as we work."

"Yes, my lord."

The maid and footman did as he'd ordered and he barely took his eyes off Fyre, even though he walked to his desk and unlocked it to pull out the ledgers they had to finish going over.

The staff were efficient at their jobs and soon enough it was just the two of them once more. The door was not shut all the way, so anyone passing by could see or hear them.

"Help yourself." He lifted the three ledgers and walked back to the sitting area. He was tempted to return to what he'd been telling her before the interruption but held back. It wouldn't do to scare her away.

Fyre hadn't moved.

"Do I need to repeat myself?"

"No, my lord."

He put the books down and fixed himself a plate of finger food, then sat in a single chair on the end. He knew if he were next to her on the couch, there would be a different kind of lesson going on.

"Would you feel more comfortable with a maid in here?"

Her features morphed into shock as her eyebrows rose. "My reputation is of little value. I am not concerned."

Phillip didn't like the sound of that. "What about me?"

She poured some tea and looked up at him with a smile that would have taken out his knees had he been standing.

"If you feel safer with a maid to protect your virtue, by all means, call one in."

Fyre blinked a few times and swallowed back his laughter. He greatly approved of this teasing side of her and he had the feeling it wasn't a side that she chose to share with many. That she would with him was a prize he would never forget.

It also let him know that she, despite some outward appearances, felt comfortable enough to joke with him.

"Just so you know, Fyre. If you wanted my virtue, I would hand it over to you without an argument."

Her chest rose and fell in sharp succession with his admission. "We should get to work."

"Of course, milady, anything you want." Her eyes flew back to him. "Yes, you heard me, *anything* you want."

Fyre took a deep breath and turned the page on her current ledger. She'd been working for close to an hour.

This one had pretty much only her writing in it. A tiny smile crossed her face. She loved the entire process that revolved around keeping books such as these, even the details, which some considered mundane. She enjoyed all of it.

It didn't matter that she did this for people who thought less of her. All she wanted to do was numbers. Pulling her thoughts from anything but what she needed to be focusing on, she sighed.

This man, however, he wasn't easy to forget. Nor were his words.

She didn't understand a lot about men, didn't flirt much, if at all, and didn't exactly need her brother to beat off suitors. Sure, there was Albie Caulfield, but in all honesty she believed he was after her because of the magic she could create with numbers and how organized she was.

The man himself was handsome enough, if she could get past the instinctive aversion she had to him, but she'd not cared about the attention a man paid to her until she'd met this new owner of Hawk's Cove. Lord Edais had quickly made a name for himself, having come here and purchased the plantation after the scandal of a colonel who'd kidnapped a woman in his twisted effort to try to force someone's hand while bringing back slavery to this island.

It had been a lot of ugliness.

She'd not had a part in that but had heard a lot about it from the people around. Slavery wasn't allowed on this island anymore, and while most had accepted it, there were times that issues still cropped up.

It was a legitimate reason her brother wasn't a fan of her doing a lot of what she did. Yet she couldn't do field work and this way, at least, she was helping with the money for the house. Or rather, she had been.

Her lips twitched as she thought about finally being on her own. Out from under their rule. Already she had plans on how to decorate to make the small space hers.

"What are you smiling about?"

That deep voice wove around her and made her think about things she shouldn't. She allowed herself a few breaths before she transferred her gaze from the ledger to the English lord.

"How much I enjoy numbers."

His eyes heated and she fought the need to squirm on her seat. How one man's look could be so powerful she wasn't sure. But it was with this one.

He nodded and stared at her for a moment. "Have you eaten enough?"

The question was odd, and she didn't quite follow his inquiry. What was enough? She'd partaken in some food, but she wasn't going to eat all of it. Had he expected her to? With a small frown, she glanced at the food before her then back to him.

"Fyre?"

It wasn't fair, the way his voice flowed over her and stroked places she wouldn't have given a second thought to before he'd ridden into her life.

"I am fine, my lord." She forced herself to meet his stare, regardless of how brief the glance was. "Thank you."

He grunted and rose. She gulped back her desire, which was making her foolish and not focused. Before she could make sense of what was happening, he had shoved the food to one end of the low-slung table and dropped the books he'd had by her pile. Did it stop there? No, of course not. Then, *then*, he sat beside her, his strong thigh pressing hard into hers.

"Teach me."

She wanted to say the same to him. However, she wouldn't mean anything about work. Curving her fingers into the underside of the leather cover on the book she held, she angled her head toward him.

She wasn't here for anything but showing him her bookkeeping. This was what she did, and this was what she excelled at.

His head, tipped toward her, made it so those gray eyes were directly upon her face. She saw mischief in them along with heat. It was the heat that scared her. So she locked her fear down and took a deep breath.

Mistake.

How this man managed to smell so delicious on a sweltering island, she couldn't say. But he did.

A firm mental reprimand and she took a look down at the stacked books before them. "Was there something specific you were" — she paused, not willing to risk upsetting a rich English lord — "unable to translate from my writing? Or are you inquiring about everything?"

"You are very apt at making me believe you are taking the blame for this."

She lowered her gaze.

He clucked his tongue. "Head up, Fyre, or I will think you're not as strong as I believe you are."

She listened. His lips lifted slightly but it was his eyes and the warmth in them that caught her most.

"To answer your question, I would prefer to know your system, all of it. I am confident I will be able to follow along if you show me what things mean. I want to catch the ones who have been snooping around but I feel a need to protect myself while that is in motion."

Disappointment filled her. It was only work, regardless of the flirting. And this would be a sizeable account she was losing the money from. The hit would hurt but she could do it and survive. After all, that's what she did. Survive.

Yet he did share a bit more personal information with me about looking into the people digging around his place.

Her smile never slipped. She rose and walked over to the small bag she always carried. His eyes were on her but he didn't try to stop her. Fyre crouched by the bag and opened it, then rifled through the things she had in there.

When she'd located the sheet she wanted, she rose and walked back to the seat and retook hers, this time making sure there was a bit more space between her and Phillip.

"I need to make a copy of this first. I apologize I did not have it ready prior to this meeting."

A slow smile turned up the corners of his mouth. Damn it, it was a sexy, impish grin. And the results impacted low in her gut.

He stretched his legs out and laced his hands behind his head. "Take all the time you need. I will just sit here. Watching you. *Imagining* things."

He was a dangerous man. She knew this and wouldn't try to dispute it just to make herself feel better.

Instead, she chose to ignore him. Not an easy feat, especially with a man like him. Even if he were being silent, there was this presence about him that made her mind and heart do crazy things.

Taking a back page of his ledger, a blank one, she began to copy the sheet she had in her possession.

"Are you not curious as to *what* I will be imagining?"

I am. I certainly am.

"Not at all, my lord." She didn't slow in her pencil strokes.

His leg pressed more tightly to hers and she could have sworn there wasn't a single article of clothing between them because of the heat that shot through her. When he'd moved closer, she couldn't even say.

"How did you get into this?"

The abrupt change in the subject threw her for a moment. Flicking her tongue over her lips, she made a few more scratches on her current page before angling her head to gaze at him.

Phillip wasn't doing anything but waiting for her to look at him. Those sharp eyes of his saw far more than she wanted to admit she liked. It wasn't easy to remove her gaze from his. One, she didn't want to. Two, she knew—from somewhere deep inside—she *had* to. Staring at this English lord wasn't going to do anything but put her in danger.

Gaze averted, she began finishing up the final few line items that she needed to copy.

"Matter of necessity."

His long, lean body shifted on the seat beside her. The rasp of his finer clothing against hers stirred something inside her. Fyre bit down on the inside of her cheek.

I do not need to think this way. Just do my job and leave. Find another way to get money.

"You say those three words, Fyre, like that will appease my interest." Another subtle shift of his leg against hers as he leaned forward toward the book she wasn't currently using. "Quite the opposite. I find myself even more intrigued."

She was in big trouble.

Chapter Four

Her scent was driving him fucking insane. Phillip swallowed and exhaled slowly through his mouth. To his ears, it was loud and sounded like a hiss, but she didn't move aside from continuing to make her succinct, perfect strokes on the paper.

As she worked, he kept his mouth clamped shut because this woman rattled him. Unlike any of the women from his past—mistresses, young chits at parties looking for a husband, whores, or wives trying to cuckold their husbands, this woman, Fyre, had him tongue-tied.

Her own musk combined with a light floral scent was playing havoc with his body. The wild curls she had yanked back into a serviceable braid had him longing to release them. He'd seen it down the day in the store, when she'd had her hair drawn behind her loosely. Not like today, where he wondered if she had a headache it was such a tight braid.

Although it was no easy feat, he kept his gaze glued to the book he held in his lap. He stared so long at the page the numbers and symbols all blurred, and when someone cleared their throat across from him he looked up with a glare, not liking that he'd been interrupted. Nor that he'd been off guard.

"What?"

His butler stood there, expression blank.

"Miss Asherford is here to see you."

Exactly the type of woman he'd left behind in England. He should have known that no matter where he ended up, there would be some like her though.

"Tell her I am not available and she can make an appointment for tomorrow at ten. I can see her then."

His butler gave a nod even as his disapproving glance slid to the woman on the furniture beside him and back. So fast he may have imagined it, but he didn't think so.

"Something you would like to add, Keating?"

"No, my lord. I shall inform her." A bow and he left as silently as he'd arrived.

Then again, he may have knocked and I just did not hear him because I am so focused on keeping my hands off the woman beside me.

"Here you are, my lord."

He angled his head to the right and found Fyre holding out a sheet. Taking it, he realized she'd handed it to him so he could read it, not so it faced her.

Neat, tight lettering. Easy to read, just like it was in his book. Had he any lingering doubt that this woman had been keeping his books, that would have been banished.

Scanning the page, he understood it all with ease.

"Thank you."

Fyre started to pack up her bag and he furrowed his brow as he watched her. "What are you doing?"

"Was there something else you needed, my lord?"

So much that he couldn't say to her at the moment. But soon, otherwise he would have the most uncomfortable set of balls on the island.

"Are we finished?"

Concern flashed over her face and he kicked himself mentally for scaring her.

"I mean, I asked you here to help me figure this out. You gave me a sheet and seem to be running away." He rested his arms on his thighs. "Are you scared? Or did you think that once I had your key I would no longer require your services?"

"I thought you no longer required my services."

He admired her refusal to admit to her fear. Phillip crooked a finger at her. She didn't refuse him but he could see suspicion and walls flying up with each step that brought her closer. Hell, the knuckles on her hand holding the bag were nearly white.

"Sit back down," he said in a calm tone. "We still have books to go over and I want to make sure I am still on your schedule to stop by and keep them. We mentioned daily."

It killed him to see her breathe a bit easier as she moved away from him. Could he have been mistaken and she *wasn't* attracted to him? He didn't think so, but he also didn't force women.

Slow down and take it a day at a time.

As she sat beside him once more, he struggled to hide his smile. "Do you have a schedule that shows when you are free? Or could you tell me?"

Fyre flicked the tip of her tongue along those full lips. He bit back a lustful groan and did his best to stay in his seat.

"I am sure that your schedule is fuller than mine, my lord. If you can tell me when you have time, I will let you know what would work."

An unexpected chuckle left him, shocking not just her but also himself. Giving in to his overwhelming need to touch her, he reached out and tipped her chin up so they could see each other's eyes.

"We can go back and forth about this all day, Fyre. I know you are used to people abusing their station. And I would be nothing but a liar if I said I had never done that before. I have. Not a part of my life I am proud of, but it did happen. It is not happening now. I am not trying to lure you into any kind of trap."

A lie. I want to trap her. Above me. Beneath me.

He felt the loss deep in his soul when he removed his fingers from her chin. Who knew simply removing a touch from this woman could create such a vacancy within him? She didn't look away though, and he was pleased by that.

When she gave a tiny nod and reached for her bag once more, he figured he'd made headway. Perhaps a victory.

A short-lived one. When he stared at the schedule she opened, he had to look a few times, making sure he wasn't imagining anything. This woman was jam packed. Sunrise to sundown she had places to be.

The thing that got to him the most was that one more than one of those days, her last spot for her day was with none other than Albie Caulfield. Jealousy rose within him like wildfire and he had to bite his tongue to keep his demands to himself.

I think I know now how Lucien felt about Ciara.

Did he want to push? Fuck yes.

"I have to tell you, end of the day would be the best for me. I do tend to have meetings and things during the day." The struggle to keep his voice calm and not the arrogant way it typically was when he was refused, was great.

Phillip expected trouble and pushback. He didn't get anything more than her reaching out for the book that had her month on its pages.

"What days of the week would be best for you, my lord? Or were you serious about daily?"

Fuck yes, I am serious. He thought about the three days that Albie had. So he gave Fyre four.

Her jaw clenched ever so lightly but she didn't refuse.

"And the time that is best for you?"

That was easy enough. The time he gave was the hour after Albie had her. No way this woman was heading home to end her day after being with Albie. Phillip planned on being the last man she thought about before bed. Give him long enough and he would be the first one she thought of in the morning as well.

Her head remained bowed as she worked on the paper in her lap. Phillip took the time to study her. Was she beautiful? Of course she was, but it was more than that. She had this elegance she carried herself with that was such an intoxicating lure to him. Even that didn't completely explain what it was about her, and he wasn't capable enough to put it into words. All he knew was with this woman, well, special seemed to be too tame of a word.

Until he'd come to this island — and more specifically, Hawk's Cove — to help Trace, where he'd changed his self-centered asshole attitude, he'd still sought out the same type of woman. Shallow. Vapid. In it for the pleasure and money or baubles he could give her.

But here, on this small island, was this woman, Fyre. Aptly named, for she shone bright and caught the eye of those who saw her. Not to mention she burned him, in an incredible way, when she allowed him in to see her true personality — and he had no doubt she could do more, if she let someone close. He wanted to be close enough for that heat to stream all over him.

"Very good, my lord. I have you down for those four days at that time."

"Thank you."

She reached for her items and began repacking her bag.

Phillip didn't want her to go but he had no reason to keep her there longer. She'd given him the sheet he had requested and had put him down on her schedule. Rising when she did, he touched her arm.

Fyre turned to glance at him. "Yes, my lord? Did I make a mistake that you had more to go over now?" She licked her lips. "Or are you good with the key I gave you and we can save any questions you may have for the next time I am here?"

Was it wrong to lie just to keep her around? Yes. Did he want to do it anyway? Hell yes. But this wasn't about him and his base needs. "I will have someone take you home."

She pulled back ever so slightly. "Not necessary, my lord, but thank you."

He shook his head and grinned. "I was not asking for your permission. I was informing you that it is going to happen. Either you allow me to do that, or I will accompany you."

Her pulse kicked up on the side of her neck. "A ride is not necessary, my lord. I am sure your people have more important things to do than see me home."

"Keating," he called out.

"My lord?"

"Have a carriage brought around. I need a maid and a footman to take Ms. Fyre home."

"Very good, my lord."

He looked back down at her. "All taken care of. It is dangerous for you to walk alone."

A spark flashed in her eyes but all she did was smile and curtsey. "Thank you, my lord. I will see you in two days." She turned and walked out, leaving him alone and hard as stone.

Two days of hell before he got to see her again. Instead of following to make sure that she left okay, he retreated to his study and closed the door. Back against the wood, he freed himself from his breeches. Phillip hissed in a mixture of relief and need as he stroked his hard cock. He'd not been this desperate for relief in a long time, but since he had started interacting with Fyre, this state had become more common.

* * * *

Fyre dumped the water and allowed the bucket to fall to the damp ground as she glanced back to the open door of her new place. The one she'd just finished cleaning the floor of. Standing tall, she pressed the heel of her palm to her lower back as she tried to work out the kink there. It only worked a little bit.

Her first night in her new place had been both a blessing and nerve-wracking. While she was grateful for the quiet, it would take some getting used to, she believed. But she'd woken early and just lain in bed for a few moments. There hadn't been anyone else to get up and cook for. Or clean up after.

She grinned and turned in a small circle, head back as she just enjoyed being by herself. Georges had been paid for three months and Fyre had gone shopping for staples earlier in the morning. She'd spent the rest of her time so far this day getting settled in.

The space wasn't big, but for the time being, it was all hers.

While she wasn't the best at sewing, she could wield a needle. She'd made herself a table covering and had put some fabric up in the windows to keep out some light and so that if anyone happened to be going by, they couldn't necessarily see inside to what she was doing.

I wonder if Phillip would like my place?

Resting her shoulder against the window, she hugged herself as she stared out across the vast green she saw.

Phillip. Lord Edais. The Earl of Edais.

A man she had no place thinking about much less calling by his first name. Even the simple act of conjuring up his name caused her to get warm all over. A small smile graced her lips as she thought about the four days a week she would be able to spend with him.

There was something about the way he looked at her, touched her, and overall made her feel. An emotion she couldn't, and wouldn't, ever tell her brother about because he wouldn't understand.

I know nothing can come of us. But I am allowed to dream and think about whomever I wish. Not even my brother can take that away from me.

Knock. Knock.

The reorientation from her imagination to reality was a rough one but she put a smile on her face anyway and walked to the door. Opening it to find her brother there, she stepped back and let him in. His frown didn't bode well for this being a pleasant conversation.

"Can I get you something to eat or drink, Elonne?"

"I do not like the idea of you living here." He ripped his hat off his head and dropped it on the floor.

"One, pick up your hat, this is not your house. Two, I am fine. I have both Marta and Georges keeping an eye on me."

"What happens when the single men in town find out you're living by yourself? Even some married ones who think they have a right to force themselves on a woman. Especially a dark woman."

She cut him a piece of bread and a small piece of cheese then took them to him. After he picked up his hat, he sat at her table and picked at them both.

Most people already know because no one here knows how to keep their mouth shut.

"I will be okay, Elonne. I can do this. I am happy, and while I love you and your kids, I am so excited to be on my own." She reached over and pinched off a piece of bread, popping it in her mouth.

"I am going to check on you every day. Nothing you can do to stop that."

"I expect nothing but that from you. You are my big brother. You cannot help but want to protect me."

"Always, Fyre. I will *always* protect you."

"Just as I will always love you for it. Even if you are a bit overbearing at times."

He flicked the end of her nose just as he had when they were kids and he'd tried to get her to think about anything other than her empty stomach or the fact that they were on their own.

"How does your schedule look for the month?"

She held up a finger before pushing away from the table and heading off to get her papers. When she walked back in, she couldn't help but notice her brother had inhaled the rest of his food. Without slowing, she went to get him more bread and cheese to partake of.

"My schedule is full. I took off the accounts that you typically do so those are all yours again."

"Are you going to have enough work?"

"More than. I have the stores I also work at as well as Albie, and I have Lord Edais on the schedule."

Her brother stilled. "He continues to want you to do his books? And I thought I told you to tell Mr. Caulfield no."

"Yes. And you cannot tell me who I can and cannot work for."

Elonne shook his head. "No. That is not safe. Mr. Caulfield will not respect you."

"I was not asking you for permission, brother. Lord Edais asked me to continue working for him and I intend to do just that."

"I have seen the way he looks at you. No, I forbid it."

She yanked the bread and cheese away from him. "You forbid it? Like I am a child in need of discipline?" Honestly, she wasn't sure which of the two men he was going on about, maybe both. Didn't matter, she wasn't giving up her livelihood.

His dark gaze shot sparks as he glared across the small space at her. "I. Forbid. It. No more discussion on the matter. I will speak with him and inform him you have other obligations."

"You will do *no* such thing. I was with him yesterday and we just went over the dates and times for me to come do the work. Do not make this any more unpleasant, Elonne. I am living on my own and will survive, but I cannot do that if I turn down work."

"So move back home."

"That is *your* home, not mine. Besides, I do not like your wife. Cara and I do not get along and we both know you see it."

He grimaced and skimmed his hands over his head. "She is the mother of my children."

Opinions differed on that between them for sure, but she kept hers private. Unable to comment politely on his statement, she shrugged.

He frowned.

"It is not safe for you here."

"Elonne, I love you, but I do not need your permission to live here. I have work and I have a home to call my own. You are always welcome to swing by and check on me but you should focus on your family."

He stepped closer and gripped both her wrists. "You, *you*, are my family."

Her anger vanished. After all, who was she to be mad that her only living relative was showing concern for her?

Giving him a smile, she nodded. "I love you too, Elonne. I want to do this. I *can* do this and I will be safe. As I said previously, Marta and Georges will keep an eye on me also."

His frown told her everything. He didn't trust them. But then, Elonne didn't trust anyone outside of a very small circle. Some of the men he worked the fields with. But the few people he did books for, they were strictly business.

"I worry." He stepped back and crossed his arms.

"Nothing has changed other than where I lay my head at night. I have the same work, will be around the same people."

"It was fine until that earl started showing interest in you." A deeper scowl. "And you agreed to work for Mr. Caulfield."

Fyre struggled not to expose her brother to how just thinking about the earl affected her—a most difficult feat to be sure. Her body responded like she was close to Phillip.

I should not think of him in such a familiar manner. It is not proper.

Didn't stop her thoughts or dreams. Perhaps fantasies would be a better description.

"You wish for me to tell an earl no, that I will not continue doing for him what I have been doing for months? And because my brother sees it as an issue? When it was not one before?"

Elonne flatted his lips in displeasure. "You are getting impertinent."

"Reprimands aside, brother, it would be foolish for me to turn down money. If that is your concern, I am happy to tell him that my brother needs to take over. But I will not allow you to put me in a difficult financial place purely because you want to control me."

"You are a lone female."

"I am aware of that." She shook her head and held up her hands in silent surrender. "My life, Elonne. Mine."

He narrowed his eyes at her then stomped out of her place, slamming the door behind himself.

Waiting to make sure he wouldn't just fly back in, she finally cleaned up the food from the table then got back to what she'd been doing — making this place her own.

As she unfolded the quilt for her bed, she smiled and thought about Phillip. Would he like it?

Better yet, would he be gentle as a lover or would he push her to the edge until she cried out for release? Her body trembled and she bit her lower lip as she realized she desperately wanted to find out.

Chapter Five

Phillip rode through the town on his way to one of the numerous places to get a drink. No carriage today, just him and a horse.

Did he have an ulterior motive for coming in today? Absolutely. He wanted to catch a glimpse of the woman he'd been unable to get out of his mind.

I have not even been away from her for more than a full day and I am craving the knowledge of her well-being.

It was more than that. This woman, Fyre, had become his obsession. Since the moment he'd found out she was the one who had kept his books with such precision. Sure, others could do the job, but not with her joy.

He'd watched her while she was at his place the last time. While she'd been concentrating on the papers before her, he had been doing the same thing, but on her.

Phillip had cataloged every nuance he could to play later in his mind. When she wasn't there any longer, and nor was her scent.

He'd memorized the way her thick lashes curved up from her eyes, framing them in a sultry manner. How she grabbed the lower left corner of her lip in her teeth as she concentrated. All of it, including the tiny mole below the outside edge of her right eye. There were scars on her and he wanted to know what had happened.

Slowing his mount as he came upon more people milling around the street, he tipped his hat and responded to those calling out to him. Once he reached the tavern, he hopped from the saddle and handed off his mount to a small boy waiting to take him.

Before the kid could go far, he flipped him a coin. Then he strode inside. Definitely not White's back in London. But also not the dingiest place he'd ever gotten a drink.

Once he'd claimed a table and had a mug before him, he stretched out his legs and took a look at the people around him. Mostly white men, but there were some of darker skin tone. All of the women in there flirted with everyone in hopes of more money or perhaps a trip upstairs for even more blunt.

He had no intention of taking any of them up on it and waved away any and all advances.

"Lord Edais."

He glanced up to see Albie Caulfield walking toward him, a smile that was as real as any snake's plastered on his face.

"Mr. Caulfield." He gestured at the chair across from him.

"Thank you, my lord." Albie took the seat and pulled off his gloves.

Phillip didn't rush any conversation. He'd learned a long time ago if you sit there quietly and wait, people will show their hand. Eventually.

And he'd learned to be patient.

Albie licked his lips and took a large drink before clasping his hands on the table. "Forgive me, my lord, if this comes across as impertinent, for I mean no disrespect."

He lifted an eyebrow. "Typically any statement starting as such is going to be impertinent."

"It is a delicate matter I wish to speak to you on."

"Delicate matter that you insist on speaking about inside a tavern? Where you can be assured there are any number of people listening?"

"I was not sure I would be welcome to your home."

The barmaid returned but Phillip waved her off. He was intrigued and wanted to know what this ass was up to.

"Most are welcome to my home."

"This is about Fyre."

Look at that. He *was* capable of jealousy. Funny thing though, it wasn't the kind he had felt when he was the outside man looking in at his friend and his relationship. This was bone-deep, primitive and proprietary. Phillip despised hearing that man speak Fyre's name.

But one didn't grow up in the society he had without learning to retain his composure. Giving a nod, he encouraged him to keep speaking even without saying a thing himself.

Caulfield took the silence as permission to keep running his mouth.

"I know she is working on your books and you are on her schedule. I was hoping that"—he cleared his throat—"you would be okay with an earlier time."

Hell no!

Phillip leaned forward and pressed the tips of his fingers together. "Let me make sure I understand what you are requesting of me. You wish for me, the Earl of Edais, to change *my* prearranged times with the one who keeps my books because you, what, want to be her last customer of the day?"

The color of the man's skin deepened as he flushed.

"Yes, my lord. I was hoping to be walking her home."

His thoughts flashed to seeing the two of them in the shop. The way this man had been so close to Fyre and how she hadn't been receptive. Yeah, he was keeping his times.

"I would not be able to help you with that, Mr. Caulfield. Perhaps you will have to find time to court her outside of working hours."

Anger flashed in the man's gaze but his smile never slipped. "I figured I would ask. Perhaps I will change the dates."

Over my dead body. Or is that going to be over yours?

He shrugged like he didn't have a care in the world. After all, what could this man, not even close to his personal status, offer her that Phillip himself couldn't? Plus, he knew she was attracted to him, not Albie.

Does not change a thing. I still want to punch him in the face.

Phillip finished off his drink and rose. "Was there anything else?"

The man shook his head. "No, my lord. Thank you for your time."

Without responding, Phillip walked out and waited for his mount to be brought back.

"Thanks, kid."

He flipped him another coin. It wasn't going to hurt his coffers any but could mean so much to him. A brilliant grin shone from the darker-skinned child before he touched an imaginary hat.

Hands on the reins, he spun back to the boy. "Kid."

"Yes, my lord?"

He bent closer to the kid. "Do you know Fyre?"

A vigorous nod was his response.

"Good. Where is she right now?"

"I can show you."

Phillip grinned. "Okay, lead the way. Do you have a name, kid?"

"James."

"Strong name. Get a move on now."

Leading his horse as he trailed the boy who was moving fast down the street, he stopped and swung up in the saddle to more easily keep an eye on him. When the child stopped before a mercantile shop, he dismounted.

"There?"

"Yes, milord."

"Want to make some extra money?"

That head bobbed so fast Phillip almost smiled.

"I need you to keep an eye on her if I am not with her."

The eagerness faded and worry filled his expression, accompanied by suspicion.

Phillip held out his hand, paused for a moment, then settled it on James' shoulder. "Listen, James. I think she may be in danger and I am only trying to keep her safe."

"Her brother thinks so too, ever since she moved out on her own."

His heart stuttered. She was living on her own?

"You know where her new place is?"

"No. I can find out though."

"Good. This is between us only, no one else. If they ask, tell them you are working for me and if they have questions, to come to me."

"I have a *job*? With you?"

It was a struggle for Phillip not to smile at his enthusiasm. "Yes. I will pay you every day, okay?" The boy's grin was blinding. "Do you know where my estate is?"

"Yes, milord."

"Any sign of trouble for her, or you, head there. Do you understand?"

He nodded. "I have to go back to my other job now. I will see you tomorrow."

James vanished in a flash.

Tying his horse off, Phillip walked up to the door and entered the mercantile. There were so many different items on the shelves he slowed to look at them all.

"May I help you?"

Lord, just the sound of her voice had his breeches tightening.

He watched her walk out of the back, eyes widening as she realized who he was. She recovered quickly though. A small curtsey.

"Lord Edais."

"Afternoon, Fyre."

Her eyes adopted a softer look at the use of that name.

"Is there something I can assist you with, my lord?"

God, he longed to kiss her. Just pull her right into his arms and indulge.

"I am looking for some children's toys. I have not sent my nieces and nephews gifts in a while."

The suspicion in her gaze didn't vanish completely but it faded. She walked around the corner of the counter and his eyes snapped to the faded blue muslin of her dress as it clung to her. A simple cloth covered her head, protecting part of her hair.

"We have toys in this section over here."

As he followed her, he adjusted his hardness, even while his gaze locked on her ass.

This was foolish. I do not know if I can control my urge to touch her.

Not that it mattered. The moment he'd seen her again, he'd known he wouldn't leave until he'd spent as much time with her as he could.

He is here. Again. Why is he here?

Fyre gestured once more to the section he'd asked her about. Then she stepped back, needing to get to her other tasks. Away from this man.

She didn't want to. Fyre longed to stay by him. There was something about him that called to her. But she wasn't a fool, she knew that this man could not just hurt her on an emotional level, he could also ruin her.

A woman of her station in life had no reason to be thinking she could ever mean anything to a man who carried a title. Hell, most men thought women were beneath them anyway, why would this one be any different?

And yet, she couldn't help thinking he was by the way he treated her.

As well as the way he looks at me.

She enjoyed those nearly hidden looks of heated passion.

However, she hadn't grown up where she had without knowing how to keep herself safe, so she backed away, even though she had no desire to do so.

"If you have any questions, Lord Edais, please let me know."

She bit the inside of her lower lip as she left him there to look for gifts for a niece and nephew. Straightening up on the other side of the mercantile, she returned to the counter when another person came in.

This time it was Mrs. Collier. Not the most pleasant woman in the world. She had definite opinions on where people like Fyre should be.

"Good morning, Mrs. Collier."

The woman sniffed, lifted her nose in the air and looked down at Fyre as if she were shit on the bottom of a foot.

"Where is your boss?"

"Mr. Holmes has stepped out for a while. I would be happy to pass along a message if you would like."

She glared and stepped closer. "If I wanted you to try and give him a message I would have *told* you to do so. I sure as hell do not need any n —"

"I think I have what I want to get." Phillip interrupted the discussion by striding up to the counter and placing down the few things he'd picked up.

The woman couldn't change her disposition fast enough. She blushed and primped right there, even though the man stood beside her.

"Lord Edais," she cooed. "I did not know you were here. How have you come to find our lovely island?"

Fyre wanted to back away. She hated when people near her talked around her as if she didn't even exist.

Was she used to it? Of course, but it didn't mean she particularly enjoyed that aspect of having darker skin here.

His expression was nothing like when he looked at Fyre and she took pleasure in that. He flicked a dismissive gaze over Mrs. Collier before bringing those gray eyes back to her.

"I would like all of these."

"Yes, my lord." It didn't take her long to put them in a box for him. Then she pulled out a book and marked his purchase down.

"I have come to find your island, Mrs. Collier, nice for the most part. There are some behaviors that I find disgusting." His tone grew cold. "I mean, I am the only one on the island who holds rank, and yet there are others" — he pinned her with his gaze — "who still are of the misconception they are better than other people."

Mrs. Collier flushed an angry red. "There are proper places for people in the world, my lord."

His laugh wasn't the slightest bit kind. "I am aware. However, I have worked with a lot of people and have come to learn that the ones who think they are better than others are typically the ones who deserve the least amount of respect." He picked up his box. "The ones who try to shame and embarrass others to make themselves feel better are not the kind of people I interact with. Humility speaks volumes. Something you should think about, Mrs. Collier. Ms. Gwen, thank you for all of your assistance. I will make sure your employer knows how valuable you are."

He walked out, a jaunty whistle on his lips, and her heart twisted as she watched him leave from below lowered lids.

"I never!" Mrs. Collier huffed. Then she too left, however, she didn't purchase anything.

Alone, Fyre sank into the counter, using it to hold herself up. She rubbed the nape of her neck before taking a deep breath and getting back to work. A tingle ran up her spine and she turned toward the door, not having heard it. It hadn't moved and she didn't see anyone there.

Exhaling, she turned back to the shelf she'd been straightening and bit back her scream. Phillip stood before her. He caught her by the upper arms to keep her from falling on the floor and she lost even more breath at the simple touch.

"My lord. You frightened me."

His thumbs moved in small circles on her arms. Fyre couldn't help but wish they were on her bare skin instead of the sleeves of her dress.

"Not my intent, however, I did get to have you in my arms." A fleeting grin. "Therefore, I must say it was worth it, to me."

She dropped her gaze to the floor and stepped free of his touch, mourning the loss immediately.

While he didn't close the distance she'd put between them, neither did he allow it to increase. He held his ground. Fyre swallowed and tried to make sense of these unfamiliar feelings that were wreaking havoc on her.

She wasn't an idiot, she got the concepts of lust and desire. Just like she knew what went on between a man and a woman. Or at least the basics. People talked, she listened, and there was that one time she'd walked by and seen—

"Fyre?"

Phillip's deep tone yanked her off the path she had been heading down. Heart pounding, she flushed as she imagined herself and Phillip doing what she'd seen. By the time she met his gaze, there were troubling sparks there.

"What were you thinking about, Fyre?" He licked his lower lip and smiled. "Because you flushed and moaned, and I am determined to find out what it was that put that expression there."

How bad would it be to just follow the cry of her body?

Extremely.

She was colored and had no place dallying with an earl. No matter how much he pretended to like her.

He scowled. "I am not a fan of that look. What is going on in that head of yours?"

She forced a smile. "I am fine, just lost in thought. Begging your pardon, my lord." A breath. "Was there something else you needed today?"

Phillip opened his mouth but at that moment the door opened once more. She watched him cut his gaze to the door.

"Gwen! I have returned." He pushed the door back. "Gwen?" Watery blue eyes swung over to him. "My lord? Have you been waiting long?" Mr. Holmes' pale skin flushed.

"No, Ms. Gwen is here helping me now."

That mollified the man a tiny bit. Still, he hurried around to peer down the aisle.

It wasn't her fault, she wasn't tall enough to see over the shelves and hadn't heard the door's bell, she'd been too wrapped up in Lord Edais.

"Mr. Holmes." She hoped there was enough space between herself and the earl to be proper.

The man flicked his gaze between the both of them. Then he nodded and moved to the back. Phillip glanced back down at her even as he reached for the item nearest to him.

"Are you going to be okay?"

"Of course, my lord. Is there anything else I can assist you with?"

There went that sparkle in his eyes. The one that made her stomach clench with a raw need. Something that scared her.

More precise would be to say, it made her think of things that scared her.

"So many. However, I will head out now. I will see you tonight." He walked away before she could say anything.

He is not on my calendar for tonight.

At the door, he called out, "Thank you again, Ms. Gwen. I appreciate the assistance in choosing gifts for my family." Then he was gone.

Chapter Six

"My lord?"

"Come in, Keating. What is it?"

Phillip barely looked up from the ledger he was going over. He had some thoughts on what to add to the plantation but was trying to figure out with more clarity how much that would cost and what his return would be if he opted to go that route. Did he need to stare at this ledger? No, but for some reason it made sense in his mind.

"You have a visitor."

Nothing else. He looked up once more and lifted a brow. "Did they provide a card? Or a name?"

Keating's lips were thin and yet, somehow, they flattened more, making them nearly vanish.

"No card, my lord. It is a colored man."

Irritation grew. "It is a *man*, Keating. Learn that. Does he have a name?"

"Of course, my lord. Elonne."

Fyre's brother. "Send him in." He looked back at his work, not pausing until Keating returned with Elonne.

This time Phillip closed the ledger and watched Elonne step in.

"Thank you, Keating. Pour us each a drink then leave us to talk."

"Yes, my lord."

Elonne didn't move much from his position until the drinks had been poured and Keating left. Only after a gesture from Phillip did he take a seat.

"Something I can assist you with, Mr. Elonne? I am sorry, I was not provided a last name."

"Parker, my lord."

Gwen Parker. Personally, he preferred Fyre.

"Mr. Parker, how can I help you?"

"I am here about my sister."

Without realizing it until it had happened, he sat up more at the mention of Fyre.

"What about her?"

"I know you can understand a man's need to protect his family. I want you to tell her you are letting her go. I can do your books or point you in the direction of someone else."

Phillip leaned forward, resting his arms along the top of his desk. He laced his fingers.

"Let me make sure I am understanding you properly. You, who told me when I first asked you about the books that you could not give me the breakdown because you had not done them, want me to fire the person who could?" He shook his head. "A man taking care of his family does not pull money from their mouth to line his own pockets, Mr. Parker. Surely you can see how that style of behavior is not supporting your sister."

"My lord."

Nope, he was cutting this off right now.

"And also, who are you to demand what I do? You cannot walk in my home and tell me how to handle one of my employees."

"I have to protect my sister from herself."

"Seems to me you want to control her. She is amazing at what she does and from the looks of her calendar, she has a lot of other work besides mine. Are you telling all of them to get rid of her as well? Or is that pleasure only for the Earl of Edais?"

Elonne at least had the decency to look embarrassed. Not that it lasted long.

"I can take care of my sister and family."

"If that were the truth, Mr. Parker, you would not have had her working on my books in the first place. Or working at the other places she is." He didn't even begin to disguise the derision in his tone.

"She has always worked. Not only that but she has work that will cover what she gives up from this position. I arranged it with Albie Caulfield. He will give her all the work she needs."

Jealousy unfurled in his chest. And anger, at Fyre's brother. He was selling her off. The urge to yell and rage at this man who under the guise of protecting his sister was doing things to elevate himself rose within him.

Phillip had grown up in a world of cold people, where backstabbing and undercutting was a way of life. It was what people did to get ahead.

He leaned back, as if not completely tense and ready to punch Elonne in the face, and touched his fingers together even as he stared at Fyre's brother.

"I will tell her no such thing. However, since you seem to be so concerned for the amount of work on her shoulders, I will do you one better. I will hire her full time here. So you, Elonne, can do the work she'd been doing and feel better that she is taken care of. I guarantee I pay far better than Mr. Caulfield ever can or will." He rose. "Have a good day."

All I have to do now is find her and explain this before he does. While a wish, it wasn't likely to happen. He shrugged. He could explain it away later.

As if on cue, Keating stepped in and stood by Elonne's chair, clearly waiting for him to rise as well. The man took the unspoken directive and got to his feet. No doubt the expression on his face alerted all that he wanted to say more, but he held his tongue.

After Keating escorted Elonne out of the room, Phillip sank back in his chair. Somehow he didn't think that either Albie or Elonne would give up so quickly.

He worked, sort of, for another hour before tossing down his pen in defeat and calling for his horse, even as he moved through the house. Seated on the back of his chestnut, he touched his heels to him and they shot off. For a while he allowed the horse to pick the speed and just enjoyed the ride. Something he'd not done all that much since he'd arrived here.

Phillip rode back to the house once the horse was winded. He swung down before the stallion stopped and passed the reins over to a groomsman, who took them with a nod. Pulling off his gloves as he jogged up the steps to the door, he smacked them against his leg as he paused to allow the footman to open the door for him.

"Keating, have a bath sent up to my room."

"Very good, my lord."

He paced while he waited, anxious to get clean and soak for a bit. Footmen brought in the tub and maids along with other footmen followed carrying buckets of hot water.

He dismissed them all and stripped down to nothing before stepping into the tub. Despite the weather being hot as Hades here, he loved how the water soothed his muscles. And he needed that today. He'd not ridden like he'd done this afternoon in far too long.

Once he'd cleaned up, he leaned back and rested his head along the edge, eyes closed. Out of the million and one things he could have started thinking about, his mind chose Fyre.

He bit his lower lip and skimmed his hand down to his cock, grasping it and starting to stroke. Shit, this wasn't right. He didn't want to use his own hand. He wanted hers. Wanted her in every way possible.

Tightening his grip, he shortened his motions, making them faster and closer to the swollen head of his dick. He slid his other hand up his chest and pinched a nipple, gasping as lust shot through him.

How hot, tight and wet she would be streamed through his mind. Pinching the head of his shaft so he didn't come so soon, he adjusted in the tub to get more comfortable. He needed this. Wanted it.

But he wanted it with the woman, not just her mental image. Harder he pulled. Faster he tugged, twisting his hand to add more friction. A moan slid free and it took him a bit to realize it had escaped his mouth.

"Fyre," he whispered to the room as he squeezed his sac then pumped his hand like crazy as he came, hard.

It took a few moments to regain control of his breathing and to have legs strong enough to hold him when he got up. This woman was going to wreck him. Hell, perhaps she already had.

He dried off and dressed before calling for them to come take out the tub. As he walked down the steps he heard Keating at the door and paused. He wasn't sure who was there and he was not necessarily ready for company.

However, he heard a familiar voice, a thick English accent, and in seconds changed his mind. Phillip took the rest of the stairs in a few rushed steps.

"I have it, Keating." Phillip walked up along his butler and smiled at the man standing there.

Lucien St. Martin, Marquess of Heartstone.

"Saint," he said with affection as he stepped up to hug his friend. A gesture that was returned. As they separated, Phillip looked behind the marquess. "Where is Ciara?"

"Visiting family in Ireland."

Phillip frowned and sent his friend a look of concern. "Everything all right?"

The man nodded.

"Come on in. Keating, get us some food. We will be in my study. And make up a room for Lord Heartstone."

"Right away, sir."

He led the way to his study and poured them each a drink. Leaning against his desk, he hooked his ankles and took a sip. "How the hell are you, Saint?"

His friend pushed a hand through his dark hair and nodded. "Perfect."

That familiar pang of jealousy hit Phillip, as he knew his friend had found love and was loved. By a woman who was a perfect match for him. Even despite the long road it had taken for them to get back to each other, when he watched them now, he knew there could be no other for either of them.

"The kids? I just purchased some gifts for them but now I can send them back with you." He took another drink. "What are you doing here?"

Lucien walked around the room, his presence larger than the man himself, which was saying a lot.

Phillip couldn't help but remember how they had all been, *before*. Whores, mistresses, no regard for much of anything other than their own pleasure. Then Lucien had met Ciara and his entire world had shifted. Their friend Rafe had fallen for Lucien's sister and soon it had been just Phillip who was on the outside looking in at the happiness his friends embodied.

Not to mention his friends had welcomed their new lives with open arms. He loved the children and looked upon them as his own in a manner. He would protect them without hesitation or fail. He'd come to this island as a favor to assist a man whose son was being threatened. That man, his woman and their children were also included in his circle of protection and friendship. However, he hadn't gone back to England. No, instead he'd stayed. Purchased the house, and hadn't considered returning there.

"You have not come home." Lucien turned to look at him, the sun surrounding him from the window behind him. "I, *we*, have become concerned."

"My lord," Keating interrupted. "Ms. Gwen is insisting on an audience."

"Ms. Gwen is *here*." Her tone was sharp.

She'd never been so angry in her entire life. The nerve of these men. Fyre had passed the point of caring what was proper. No one, either the man she worked for or brother, had the right to try to run her life as these two were doing.

Fyre glared across the room to the man leaning on the front of his desk, drink in position of rest beside one powerful thigh. His expression showed his shock.

But beneath that, what was she spying? Amusement? Yes, that's exactly what that was.

"My lord, while I understand I work for you in a small capacity, that does *not* in any way give you the right to discuss my life or my living habits, or tell people that you are going to be the only person I work for."

His lips twitched. "Spoke to your brother about our discussion, did you?"

"Both of you, so smug. Acting as if you are doing me a favor. I work hard. I am damn good at my job. So what if I am a woman, and a woman of darker skin? It does not hamper the way I work."

He held up his hands, the motion drawing her attention to the strength in his fingers and the way the sun glinted through the crystal he held. "I never said it did. Your brother came to me —"

"I am perfectly aware of my brother's actions with you earlier in the day. Both of you are out of line. I think it will be best for all involved for me to stop working for you as well as Mr. Caulfield, and I will make my money elsewhere."

"No!"

She stepped back at the fervent refusal that burst from his mouth.

Fyre propped her hands on her hips. "Contrary to how people view you, *my lord*, you do not control this island. Or me. I work for who I want. He wanted me to quit working for Mr. Caulfield, now he is all about me quitting here, or being let go and working only for Mr. Caulfield."

"Can you say that with any more disdain, Fyre?" He pushed up from the desk and moved toward her. Prowling. Exuding danger on a level she wasn't positive she could deal with. "I get it, you have no use for my title."

"Do not put words in my mouth, Lord Edais. I have no problem with your title. I have an issue with men in my life trying to tell me what is best for me. Like you and my brother."

His lips twitched as he stopped so close to her the smell of his freshly bathed body reached her and she latched on like a starving animal.

Phillip blinked and those gray eyes deepened as he stared down at her. "Am I?"

"Are you what?"

"A man in your life?"

Such decadence lined that question. She swallowed and licked her lips. His gaze darkened further.

However, a clearing throat jarred her and she jumped. By the window stood a man she'd not seen before. Tall, muscular. Jet-black hair and beautiful lake-blue eyes. Golden skin.

Heart thundering for a completely different reason than being so close to Phillip, she gulped and dropped to a curtsey.

How could I have been so foolish?

Not only had she burst in on an earl, but the man had company.

"Forgive me, my lord. I was not aware you were entertaining."

"Chin up, Fyre. This is my best friend, Lucien."

Unsure how much anger and disgust she would witness when she lifted her head, she did so slowly. Those blue eyes sparkled with humor and something else she couldn't quite identify, but if she had to guess, it would be understanding or realization.

He gave her a little bow. "Lucien St. Martin, Marquess of Heartstone."

She wanted to dig a hole and climb in as she recognized she'd just pushed rudeness beyond the earl and onto a marquess.

"Apologies, my lord, for my behavior. I will leave."

"Do not leave on my account," Lucien said, a smile making him even more handsome. "I am just catching up with my friend. Please. Continue, this is far more interesting than I had thought it would be."

"Fuck off, Saint."

Gaze flickering between the two imposing men, she wasn't quite sure what to say. Phillip didn't appear upset with his friend, despite what he said. And the fact he didn't try to check his language before her warmed her. Like it was a bit of acceptance for her to hear this type of banter between him and his friend. Like she was not someone precious or delicate he had to present a certain façade for.

Who is Saint? Perhaps it was because of his name, St. Martin. She didn't have the gumption to ask.

The man smirked and hefted his glass before taking a drink.

Phillip scowled at him before focusing back on Fyre. Looking serious, he reached toward her only to stop and lower his hand.

"Your brother came to me and told me to let you go. He said he would take over the job. I reminded him he had not been able to do it the first time, as he brought you in. After he told me he'd made arrangements with Mr. Caulfield to have all the work you needed, I informed him I would hire you full-time and pay a far more lucrative wage than Caulfield could dream of paying."

Weighing her words, Fyre stole another peek at the man who didn't even pretend to allow them to converse in private. He was right there, listening with unabashed interest.

"Why would you do that?"

"He is selling you to Albie." Gray eyes narrowed. "That is not going to happen. Not while I am here."

"So instead of that, *you* are trying to buy me?"

His brows furrowed. "What? No."

There was no mistaking the snort of laughter from his friend. She refused to look at him. Why piss off two powerful men?

Phillip stepped closer and she retreated the same amount.

"Fyre."

How did men get their voice to resonate so low and vibrate through a woman like that? It did its best to knock her off her focus, the reason she'd come here.

It was not to fall for his charm and sex appeal.

Right, because *that* had already happened.

"You are doing the same thing my brother is. Telling me who I can and cannot work for. How is it selling me off to someone when you are doing the same thing? Just because you are buying does not make the outcome any different. I am well aware of how he struck a deal with Albie. It will not be honored, not by me. He is staying on the schedule on his days. That is all."

The earl fisted his hands, nostrils flaring as he took some deep breaths. "I am *not* buying you. I do *not* own people."

"So you say."

His gray eyes flashed with something she couldn't identify. What she could recognize was she had quite possibly pushed him too far. Phillip stepped toward her, not pausing when she retreated until he was right there. In her space.

Then there was light and room between them. She flushed with embarrassment as it dawned on her who had split them up.

"Perhaps we should sit and discuss this." The man's words were smooth and calm.

The exact opposite of how she felt. With a curtsey, she shook her head.

"I should be going. My apologies for interrupting your day, my lords."

"Fyre, do not move."

She flicked a quick look to where Phillip stood. Lucien remained in front of him, and she couldn't risk staying. The man made her do things and feel things she shouldn't.

Inching back, she gulped when his gray eyes slashed to her. Then the lake-blue ones found her. Nope, didn't help her to breathe any easier. While she didn't have a huge knowledge base on how things were over in England, she did get the concept of these men and their titles.

They could make her life hell.

"I would love to get to know you better, Ms. Fyre. Perhaps you could return for the evening meal and we could talk? You remind me a lot of my wife."

"Thank you for the offer, my lord, but I…"

Lucien grinned and her heart stuttered at that. The man was extremely handsome.

"Perfect. We will see you here at seven. I will escort you home, check out the town, and be back to bring you here. I am sure Phillip has some more paperwork to finish up."

No missing the pointed looks between the two men.

Phillip held her gaze. "Until this evening."

Another curtsey. "My lord."

She walked out of the room and heard the footsteps of the man who was escorting her home. Fyre didn't say anything as the man issued orders like he lived there. Within moments, they were going up the road in an open carriage.

They stopped before her cottage and Lucien jumped out without asking for help, then turned to assist her down.

"I will return in a few hours to escort you to dinner."

"As you wish, my lord."

He bowed over her hand. "Phillip has been my friend since we were boys. He only has your best interests at heart, even if he is going about it this asinine way to show you." Lucien dipped his head and hopped back up. They were off in a flurry of wheels.

"Who was that?"

Elonne appeared at her side, Cara with him, her eyes narrowed in suspicion or jealousy, Fyre wasn't sure.

"The Marquess of Heartstone." Fyre shook her head. "A friend of the earl."

"And what were you doing with him?" The accusation stung, even if it came from Cara.

"He insisted on escorting me home. I am not about to tell a man of his position in society no, Cara. And I am having dinner with him and the earl tonight." She headed for the door, completely unsure of what one should wear to dinner with those two men.

Her brother and sister-in-law followed her, making comments that should have hurt her, but she was far more stressed about tonight.

* * * *

Elonne and Cara had both left and since returned by the time she was to be picked up for the invitation. They were inside her small home, sitting, while Fyre paced. It didn't surprise her that they would try to weasel their way into coming with her.

The rumble of wheels had her swallowing back more unease.

Her brother bolted from the chair when the knock came. Fyre watched from her position as he opened it and found Lucien St. Martin on the other side.

Their meeting and the subsequent dinner could go well, or not even close.

Chapter Seven

"I like her."

Phillip paused in his trek around the study to glance over at where his friend reclined against a chair, appearing as if he hadn't a care in the world. From his fingers hung a glass of scotch. They were enjoying after dinner drinks. A dinner which hadn't gone too badly, considering how much he'd wanted to kill his friend. And Fyre's brother. And her sister in law.

"You like her?"

Lucien chuckled and sat up, claiming a sip before he nodded. "I do. She is feisty, stubborn, has a great sense of humor and I know she will, and is, keeping you on your toes."

"Great sense of humor."

"You, my friend, are sounding like a parrot. Yes. She had me laughing more than once at dinner."

"You were *flirting* with her."

Lucien shrugged and took another drink. "Was I?"

"Sod off."

"Tell me you do not know more about her now than you did prior to this."

That was true, but it didn't resolve his friend from being such a flirt.

"Not that it matters," Phillip groused. "But you also had to bring her brother?"

"That was a strategic move. This meal was because of me. I have no problem inviting a man who is supposed to protect her. Just because you were not allowed to kiss her is not my problem."

Phillip started pacing again. "I have *never* kissed her." Damn it. Just thinking about that pissed him off.

"There is the start of your problem then." Lucien finished his drink and held out his glass.

Phillip filled his friend's tumbler once more. Then he walked back and started once more on his around-the-room path.

"She is not even living with her brother now. She moved." He tunneled his fingers through his hair.

"I know where she lives."

Phillip strode to his friend. "Where?"

"If I tell you, what are you going to do?"

Run over there. Hold her. Kiss her. Get her to understand that there is something between us.

"What difference does it make?"

Lucien set his glass down and leaned back. "Sit down, Phillip."

He recognized his friend's tone and listened. Not that he wanted to. What he really wished to do was beat the information from his friend then go satisfy his need to see his woman.

"What?"

"You need to be careful how you tread here. Tell me you are aware of this."

"Are you telling me you do not think she is good enough for me because she is not royalty like your wife?" The words were growled and dangerous.

"Not even close to what I am saying. This has nothing to do with her upbringing or her family line."

"Then what?" He tossed back the remaining liquid in his crystal. "What am I missing?"

"A lot."

He scowled at his friend. Lucien, however, didn't even flinch under the stare.

"I have known you pretty much our entire lives, Phillip. These are not words I say lightly."

There was a level of seriousness in Lucien's tone that worried him. Phillip sat on his irritation and waited for his friend to continue.

"You know what went on with my wife and me."

He nodded, ashamed he had been part of their issue when finding their happily ever after.

Lucien, as always, knew where his mind had gone. "You are family, Phillip. Ciara loves you like a brother. There is no need for you to continue to hold on to any guilt over that. We have forgiven you, you have to forgive yourself. It has been years."

"Hard for me to just let it go like that. You are my best friend and I did nothing to help you win your woman. I did the opposite. I tried to sabotage it."

"Let it go. This is important."

Phillip tugged on his hair before dropping his head back. "What am I missing?"

"You know how we had you come here to help Trace."

"Of course, that was what prompted me to buy this place. We had to rescue him and his woman."

"An act that was not too long ago. There are still plenty here who have their opinion of where people not with our skin color should be. You cannot be obvious with your intentions if there is no plan to protect her. She would be in danger."

Phillip covered his face with his hands and groaned in frustration and anger.

"I know this. It does not do a damn thing about making me want to stop offering her something safe." And if he thought about it, he wanted her protected. This had become far more than just being obsessed with the woman. He wanted to keep her protected from the harm and evil in the world.

"And *this* is what Ciara has always seen in you, Phillip. She knew there was more to you than the side you enjoyed showing in London."

"I have not been privy to any more discontent between the races. Not since that general was hauled off."

"It is there, make no mistake. If it was not, that man would not be so concerned about his sister."

Phillip sneered. "That *man*, and I use the term loosely, is trying to sell her. She is the one who did my books, he couldn't handle it, but he thinks he has the right to tell me he will be working on them once more while he pawns her off on some lecherous bastard who wants nothing more than to bend her over the nearest table and take her innocence from her."

"I heard you say it all earlier. Does not mean the situation has changed." He smirked. "And I would wager my entire estate you would love to bend her over the table as well."

Fuck yes!

"What the hell am I supposed to do then? I am *trying* to protect her!"

Lucien rose and walked to the window, where he looked out for a charged moment of silence.

"When I woke up in that cabin, I was at a loss to make sense of Ciara. Sure, she had saved me, but she was not anything like the women I associated with. Not even the women I kept."

He pivoted back to Phillip. Waiting for his friend to speak on, Phillip just gestured with his hand when Lucien appeared lost in thought.

"It took a while." Lucien gave a wry grin. "Far longer than it should have, for me to realize that she had no model I could follow. She had not been born in a society that tried to form her in a certain way. She had not been on the streets looking for a handout or a way to improve her station. Ciara had everything she wanted."

Phillip nodded.

"And she was and had everything *I* wanted."

"So I should give Fyre a rose?"

Lucien smiled.

"Best night of my life, my friend. I do not care that I sank to my knees before the woman I love more than anything in this world, before the members of society. All I had to offer her was me and my love."

"I cannot say I am in love, Lucien."

"You do not have to say it. It may not come to you for a while. I see it now, but until you are ready to accept it, what I see is of little consequence. My point is, your way of offering her protection may not be what she wants. Learn about her. Show her you do have the ability to listen and are not just falling back on your title to get what you want."

"How did you get to be so smart?"

Lucien shrugged. "You say this like you are shocked. I have always been the smart one between us."

Striding across the room, Phillip plucked the drink from his friend's hand. "No more for you, as you have obviously over-imbibed."

Rolling his eyes, Lucien just walked to the sideboard and poured himself another. Phillip topped off his drink and settled down in the chair across from his friend.

He'd missed this. Good friends, good times and good drink.

* * * *

Fyre opened her door and froze for a second. She blinked, stepped back inside, closed the barrier. After a deep breath, she tried once more.

She'd not been hallucinating. Parked outside her small cottage was a well-sprung carriage. There wasn't even any need for her to look at the crest emblazoned on the side.

A thin man stood by the door.

"Good morning, Miss Gwen."

"Morning." She gulped and found it within her to be braver than she truly was. "Can I help you with something?"

"I am here to give you a ride out to Hawk's Cove. Lord Edais is expecting you."

"I did not know that I had a meeting with him today." She waved off her statement and shook her head. "I cannot ride with you. Please pass along my thanks to the earl for his offer but I must get to work."

There. Firm yet polite.

Smile firmly affixed to her features, she walked around the horses and set off toward town.

She heard the *clip-clop* of the horses' hooves behind her and she stopped to turn. They stopped as well.

Three more times, she walked then stopped. The result never changed.

"Are you going to follow me to town?" Heat flashed up her neck. She wasn't used to being the focus of people's attention but that was exactly what this man driving the carriage behind her had done to her. Placed her smack in the center of it.

"I am doing as ordered, Miss Gwen."

"And that was to follow me?"

His pale skin flushed as she glared up at him. Reining her temper back under control, she turned so she could face him completely. She didn't have the right to take this out on him. He, much as she did every day, was only following *his* orders.

"I do not suppose that Lord Edais said what this was in regards to?"

He shook his head and she realized he wasn't as old as she'd first estimated him to be. "He did not see fit to tell me."

"I will accept the ride."

She witnessed the relief which poured over him and he hopped down, moving to the door. She shook her head. His brows gathered close and she almost laughed. His expression was tormented.

"I will ride beside you. And you have to take me to my job in town so I can inform them I have been summoned by the earl."

He mulled it over then nodded. Stepping closer, he held out his hand and assisted her up onto the top of the carriage beside where he would be sitting. She made sure her dress didn't have any problems so she wouldn't be flashing skin—she didn't want to get a certain reputation.

Not that me riding around in the earl's coach will help with any of this.

Moments after the driver clambered up beside her, he cut his gaze to her and flashed a smile. One she returned.

"What is your name?"

"Davie, Miss Gwen."

"No need for calling me Miss Gwen. Gwen or Fyre is just fine."

"Fyre?"

He released the brake, snapped the leathers, and the team moved forward. It wasn't long before she settled into the rhythm of riding on the hard seat.

"My brother gave the name to me when we were much younger."

His laugh was contagious and she joined him. Even though townsfolk looked at her with odd expressions as the carriage with the earl's crest moved toward her destination, she didn't mind. As they went, she and Davie chatted back and forth.

He halted the team by the front door of her destination and helped her down.

"I will be right back."

With a bow, he nodded. "Take your time. I will be right here."

She gave a smile of thanks and walked inside. There was a movement behind the curtain separating the front area from the back and she saw her boss, Mr. Shelldor.

"You are almost late."

Biting her tongue, as was common in her interaction with him, she just nodded. "I apologize, sir. I have been summoned out to Hawk's Cove by Lord Edais. His carriage is right out front. Shall I send a message that I cannot come at the moment?"

His head snapped up and she held still, not flinching under his glare, even though she wanted to. Mr. Shelldor was imposing. A large, burly man who seemed to enjoy scowling far more than he did smiling.

Not that it mattered. She wanted the job.

He stomped to the left and stared out the front of the shop. She didn't even look around, knowing that he saw Davie standing out there beside the carriage with the crest on the side.

"Go."

She nodded. "Shall I return after I am done there? Or would you prefer I not come back today?"

He crossed his arms and stared at her. "Come back."

"Very good, sir. I will return as soon as possible."

With a flick of his hand, he turned around and walked into the back, leaving her alone in the store. *That went well.*

Her steps weren't as sure when she made her way back out to the waiting carriage. Davie helped her up with another smile. The horses stepped out smartly and she gripped the edge of her seat as the warm air flowed over her face.

Her belly clenched as he turned them up the drive to the house. She exhaled slowly.

What is it about this man that makes me so...uncertain?

The answer, or rather *answers*, to that were not something she wanted or needed to go into right now.

"Fyre?"

She blinked and glanced down to see Davie standing there, hand out. Waiting. Flushing again, she accepted his help and was soon on the ground.

"I will be here to take you back to town when you are finished."

"Thank you, Davie."

Chin up, she turned her feet toward the steps leading to the door. She knocked and rested her hands in front of her.

The butler, Keating, opened the door and looked at her. She wasn't quite sure what to make of his expression. She hadn't ever been able to read him. Not the slightest bit.

"His lordship is expecting you."

"Thank you, Mr. Keating."

He narrowed his eyes slightly but pivoted on his heel and she took that to mean she was to follow. So she did.

A footman closed the door behind her. As she walked over the spotless floor, her shoes barely making a sound, she marveled over how cool it was in here. Keating paused before a closed door and knocked.

"Enter."

Just a single word and her belly clenched with the need she had decided to call nothing but inappropriate.

With a nod of thanks to Keating, she walked by him and into the room. This time, unlike her previous visit here, she scanned the entire thing, checking to see if they were there alone or if his friend was there with him.

He was.

She gave a low curtsey. "Good morning, Lord Edais." She angled toward his friend. "Lord Heartstone."

"You are a delight to see so early in the day, Miss Gwen. Have you eaten?"

"Saint." It was a warning from Phillip.

The man didn't appear the slightest bit bothered by the threat. He shrugged without shame and crossed his ankles as he continued resting against the sideboard. She couldn't help but notice the amused smile that danced along his lips.

"Just making conversation, as you appear too tongue-tied to say anything."

She placed her attention back on Phillip. He waited for her to look at him.

"You cannot just order me to be here when you wish, Lord Edais."

Her gut clenched as his lips turned up just in the corners, like she'd just issued him a dare and he was looking forward to proving to her exactly how wrong she was.

Chapter Eight

Phillip stood stall and rolled his shoulders, trying his best to get them to loosen up. The day had been cooler than the normal and so many people had been out and about taking advantage of the temperature. Evening had descended upon them and his workers had all called it a day, but he still remained out in one of the fields.

He propped his hands on his hips and turned a full circle, staring at his property. Aches and pains owned his body but for the first time in his life he was proud of what he was accomplishing here. More often than not, he was out working with his men and women in the fields.

Who would have thought him purchasing this place would have awakened something inside him that had him longing to do far more than just drink, gamble, and whore around? He'd changed.

A fact that even Lucien had pointed out while he'd been around for his visit. One, in Phillip's estimation, that had been far too short. He understood though, the man wanted to be with his wife and kids.

They'd spent many of their nights sitting up late in the study, talking about family. Every time they'd discussed how much Lucien enjoyed being a husband and father, all Phillip could do was envision himself in that same situation. With Fyre.

He tipped his head up to get more of the breeze that blew around him, allowing it to dry the sweat plastered to his body. Not that he was ever dry here with so much moisture in the air. But the breeze helped.

Fyre had been religious in coming by on the days she'd agreed to, but he was starting to notice something different in her demeanor. And he wasn't happy with it. She was more reserved and withdrawn.

He quirked his lips as he walked from the field to where his horse stood tied to a branch in the shade. He needed to see her. Technically they didn't have another meeting for a few days.

I miss her.

Plus, he didn't and wouldn't put it past that ass Caulfield to be making himself known to her. Sure, she still worked on his books a few times a week, but he didn't trust the man to stay away from her the days she wasn't going to see him.

Untying his mount, he swung easily into the saddle and, with a touch of his heels, set him on the way back to the stable. As they trotted along, the breeze picked up.

I wonder if she would like to go on a picnic with me?

His lips twitched as he imagined a private stretch of beach with a blanket, food and, of course, his Fyre.

So many things he would love to do with her and to her. Shaking his head, he locked his emotions down the moment he rode up the road to the stable. He passed over the reins with a nod and walked inside.

Keating met him as he got to the top of the steps.

"My lord."

"Keating. Have a bath drawn for me."

"Already waiting in your room, my lord."

He almost smiled. "I am starting to think you actually like me, Keating."

The man stared before giving a small bow and walking away.

Phillip didn't dally in getting cleaned up, for he was hungry. Not that much later, he was accepting a tray of food in his study as he pulled out the books. It had become a nightly habit for him to look them over and make sure he'd not missed anything. Truth be told, he didn't need Fyre to do them anymore. He'd mastered her system and used it with confidence.

But I want her within my reach.

He liked her. Actually liked a woman and hell, she was a woman he'd not even kissed yet. It hadn't stopped the dreams of her that he experienced on a nightly basis, but short of the occasional brush of clothing, he'd somehow managed to keep his hands to himself.

James reported to him faithfully about who went to see her when she was in town. The one thing he had learned was the increase in times that Albie Caulfield made his way to visit her while she was at her other jobs, working.

"I do not understand how this woman can work so much and still appear so soft and put-together."

He'd seen her a few times in town, because yes, he wasn't about to *not* see her on the days she wasn't coming to his house. But he was trying to keep it to a minimum, if that's what it took to protect her.

Honestly, Phillip didn't think that was going to make a bit of difference. Still, he was attempting to be honorable about his actions.

Hard to do when he truly wanted to just walk up to her in the middle of town, yank her hair out of that tight bun she tended to wear it in, let her bonnet flutter away in the street, wrap her hair in his hand and plunder her mouth.

Claim her.

Make it clear that she was his woman. And that everyone else, Albie Caulfield included, should stay the fuck away from her.

He clenched his hand around his fork and had to take several deep breaths before he brought himself back under control. Cutting his gaze to his left, he found a footman standing there, staring off into space.

His house was empty.

He had no one to talk to over a meal. A realization he was no longer okay with. It had been wonderful having Lucien there before, but he wasn't really the person he wanted in the room with him, sharing a meal.

Keating stepped into the room and walked up to him. Fork down, he waited for the man to speak.

"Ms. Gwen is requesting an audience, my lord."

Anticipation licked through him like fire on wood. While wanting nothing more than to pump his fist in the air and yell, he reached for his drink. As he sipped, he tried to figure out why she'd shown up.

But she'd been clear as she avoided him as best she could, that she didn't want to be near him.

A truthful fact, even as it was a painful one.

"Show her in, Keating."

He spent the short time he had left alone in a desperate attempt to get himself back under control.

Something he'd learned he was in short supply of when it came to this woman.

She trailed Keating back into the room and gave him a small curtsey even as she thanked the butler. Then her focus was on him.

Completely.

How it should be.

"Have a seat. May I have them bring you something to eat? Drink?"

She sat away from him and shook her head. "No thank you, my lord. I appreciate you taking the time to see me."

He picked up his fork only to set it right back down. Something was off with her. She fidgeted. One thing he'd never known her to be was fidgety.

"What is the problem?"

"No, problem, my lord. I was just wondering if perhaps…" She shook her head. "Never mind, my lord. I do apologize for the interruption."

"Sit down."

His command came out something far more like a growl than a request, but something had happened to him when she'd begun to move back from the table. And him.

She listened without hesitation, her hands out of sight so he couldn't see if she shook or not.

"Tell me, Fyre, what the blazes is going on. I do not want to hear that you figured it out, that you had made a mistake, nothing like that."

She chewed on the inside of her cheek and gave a small shake of her head.

"It is nothing, my lord."

Phillip pushed back from the table and walked toward her. Fyre held his gaze until he was over halfway to her side, then that brown stare darted away from him, focusing everywhere else in the room.

Dragging the chair right beside her around a bit, so he could see her when he sat, he did so with a groan as her subtle scent washed over him. That did it. She flashed her gaze back to him, concern leeching in.

"Are you all right, my lord?"

Not giving a fuck about where they were or who of his staff may be watching, he reached out and dragged his knuckles down her cheek. God, her skin was so smooth.

"If I say no, will you play doctor with me?"

The silence between them was charged with sexual tension. He hoped he'd not pushed too far too fast.

Fyre leaned infinitesimally closer. "All I know about doctoring is the bloodletting."

His heart skipped more than a few beats. She was teasing him, and doing so with a small smile on her face. This woman continued to amaze him.

"You are a fast learner, you can pick up something else…more…gentle." He tucked some of the loose hair from her bun behind her ear. "Tell me how I can help you, Fyre."

Her retreat from him was complete before she moved. Walls snapped up around her and he mourned the loss of the moment.

"I had wanted to know if we could postpone the session tomorrow."

He sniffed and leaned back in his chair. "What is so important you need to shove me aside?"

She looked generally appalled by his question. Phillip didn't try to assuage her feelings. In his mind, that's exactly what she was doing.

"I was not trying to make you feel…"

He raised one eyebrow, wanting to push. So much. Push his tongue into her mouth. Push her body into his. Push *into* her.

"Maybe if it was an hour later? The same day."

Her distress was genuine, but Phillip knew he wasn't a completely nice guy. Barely nice would be far closer. What he was, was possessive. Especially when it came time to his time with Fyre. With her, he wanted to hoard it all and not share.

"Why?"

"Why what, my lord?"

He stretched out his legs, crowding her in her seat. Trapping her unless she scrambled away and over the table. His lips twitched. He could be very happy with this woman *on* the table.

His staff would have gossip for days.

"Who is so important that you are shoving me aside?" He glared at her. "And do not lie to me."

Fyre closed her eyes and her shoulders slumped. This was supposed to have been easy. Come out here on an unscheduled day and ask him to change their meeting time.

How do I constantly underestimate this man?

"Is it Caulfield?"

She couldn't explain away the anger and jealousy she picked up in his tone. It never failed when Albie came up in the conversation.

"Answer me."

Two words from the Earl of Edais. Two rumbled and dangerous ones.

"Yes."

"No."

Fyre's gaze snapped open at the unmistakable refusal he gave. "What?"

He leaned back and lifted a brow, looking every bit the arrogant member of the peerage he was.

"You asked me a question. I gave you my answer."

"My lord, surely…"

His lips flattened in what she believed to be serious irritation.

"Fyre, I hired you for a job. We sat down and went over the schedule of that job. If you have something else, or someone, who takes precedence over *our* agreement, we *could* end the entire thing."

She blinked back the tears that threatened to spill free. "Why are you being like this?"

He stood and walked away from her. Damn if she didn't want to reach out and grab onto him, holding him tight.

Kissing him.

This wasn't the man she was used to being around. Cold. Clipped.

Albie would change his time. It would cost her, of course. However, he'd sprung this additional paperwork on her, saying he'd 'forgotten' about it until today. It wasn't ideal but perhaps worth whatever deal she would have to make with him to have him accept the time change. But the sad part was, she actually liked the time she spent here, with this man, and didn't wish to give it up. Then again, with this attitude, maybe she had been wrong about him all the way.

"Very well, my lord. I will figure it out. I beg your forgiveness for bothering you with my problems." She slipped from the chair and went to the door.

"Are you going to be here or have you quit?"

Cold, harsh words.

She never looked back at him. "I will find a way to be here." Then she slipped out the door and walked to the front, where a footman opened the exterior door from the cool interior into the hot outdoors.

This was what she'd needed. A reminder that she wasn't even close to being his equal. Not a lesson she would forget. Without looking right or left at the men who milled outside, she walked down the long drive and headed back to town.

Now, *now*, she allowed the tears to slide free. Perhaps Elonne had been right and she should have let him quit that place for her.

She shook her head, still not bothering to dash away the tears on her face. By the time she made it back into town, the tears had mingled with the sweat on her face and weren't an issue.

Fyre attempted to smile at a young boy she passed but couldn't do much more than grimace. Walking into the store she needed to be at, she took a few moments and cleaned herself up, then went to the back and knocked on the door.

She stopped by Mr. Olden's every other week to work on his books. Typically he was out front and just told her to head back. However she'd not seen him and this door was closed.

"Who is it?"

Scrambling sounds reached her and Fyre stepped back. "Gwen, sir."

Silence.

"Come on in."

"Yes, sir." She opened the door a bit and was hit with the smell of sex. Pushing the door fully open, she stepped in.

Mr. Olden was standing behind his chair and sticking out from the other side of the large chair she could see some petticoats. She flushed. No doubt that woman was on her knees and Fyre could only assume as to what was going on.

"Work out front on the books."

She walked to the desk and reached for them. "Very good, sir."

He grabbed her wrist as she began to lift the tomes.

"What did you see here?"

"What I always see, Mr. Olden. You working in your office, waiting for me to do my job so you can get back to yours."

He'd not stopped moving and when he released her, the chair he'd been behind had moved, allowing her to see his pale shaft driving deep into the open, waiting mouth of Mrs. Collier.

By a miracle, her expression never slipped from the fixed one Fyre had put there. She just lifted the books and walked out of the room, closing the door quietly behind her.

For whatever reason, that pushed her to thinking about that act, not with Mr. Olden, heavens no, but with Phillip. She snorted as she pulled up a stool and opened the book.

I have no business thinking of him as Phillip. I have no business thinking of him at all.

Yet, it didn't matter how mad she was at him for his behavior toward her, she still wanted him. Wanted to be on her knees before him. Wanted to have her skin flushed like that, due to time spent with Phillip.

Luckily, Mr. Olden left her alone to do his books her way. He had a bunch of written notes in there for her to address and she did so with expediency. She finished up the job in half the time she had expected it to take.

Carrying the books, she once again knocked and, without looking anywhere but at the desk when she was bade enter back in, she placed them down and left. Fyre was determined not to notice that Mrs. Collier was now bent over the back of the settee, her skirts rucked up around her waist, and that she was being fucked.

Hard.

From the noises she made, Fyre could only assume she was enjoying herself.

"See you in two weeks, Miss Gwen."

"Yes, sir," she replied, shutting the door behind her.

Being done early gave her some time to go see how Albie would make her pay to adjust the time. Her hope had been that Phillip would agree to adjusting, but as he'd refused, she had to broach it with Albie. One of them had to make a change. As she walked over to Albie's business, a heavy weight settled on her chest. She didn't like the position she was about to put herself in.

Not that there was much of a choice.

"Gwen!"

She turned toward the sound of her name and immediately bit back a groan of frustration. Cara.

Her sister-in-law flounced across the street to her, face pinched in displeasure.

"Cara."

"Where is our money?"

The question wasn't loud, and it came out of her mouth like a hiss, but the cold reality of it jarred Fyre.

"What money?"

"The money you gave us before. We need that to survive."

"I gave you money because I was living there, and because of that, I was helping out. Now I do not live there and am no longer eating your food or sleeping under your roof. You do not get my money."

Cara narrowed her eyes and Fyre lifted her chin, waiting. The smack of Cara's palm came without warning, making tears blur Fyre's eyes.

"I never liked you, Gwen. You have grown snobbish ever since you decided to take that job away from your brother, lowering his earnings. He has a family to care for. No matter how often you lie on your back for the earl it doesn't make you a better person even if you are finally out of our house."

So much to address and she didn't want to focus on any of it. Not even a tiny bit. Yet, she did. "What job did I take from him?"

"The one with the earl."

"Is that what he told you? That I *took* that job from him?"

"We know it is true and now my children will be hungry because you wanted to spread your legs for—"

Crack!

Cara gasped and placed her hand on her cheek. Fyre had smacked her across the face.

"Everyone knows it is true. That is why you are there so much of the time."

So many things dangled from the tip of Fyre's tongue, just longing to be freed. She swallowed them back and, ignoring the tears in her eyes for the second time in one day, she turned and continued on her way.

"Are you okay, Fyre?" A boy glanced up at her as she passed, a worried expression on his face, even as he glanced behind her where she assumed Clara still shot daggers at her.

"Sure, James. Fine." She tried to smile at him as she walked along. The boy had been popping up around her more and more lately. Not that she minded, he was a good child.

Albie waited for her and stepped outside into the sun when she approached.

"Are you okay?" He moved closer. "Gwen? Come on inside."

"No, I think I would prefer to stay out in the sun."

She was so cold on the inside. Was that truly what everyone thought of her?

Chapter Nine

Phillip lifted his head to peer at the sun pushing through the thick leaves of the trees he was under. He sat at a table, a tall glass of cold lemonade before him and another in front of the young child who was there with him.

James.

He was currently on his second glass. His entire face had lit up when he'd drunk the first one, so Phillip had seen no harm in letting him enjoy another.

It was nice, actually, sitting there outside. Nothing on his plate at the moment to do. The day, while sunny, had not gotten as hot as previous ones.

Phillip sighed. Fyre was acting different.

He couldn't put his finger on it, but at their last three meetings, she had been off. That was the main reason this child was before him. James had been doing an excellent job keeping him updated on everything. The sad part was, even *he* had mentioned how sad she appeared.

"People are mean to her."

James' blurted statement pulled him back from not-so-appropriate thoughts of the woman they were discussing.

"Who is being mean to her?"

Sure, he'd been a dick, but dammit, he'd been under the impression she would have dumped that fucker Albie to keep him happy.

I seem to be learning a lot about this woman. She does not follow the norms. Then again, she never has, and the moment I learned she was the one who had been doing my books, I should have known she was never going to be what society considers normal.

He didn't care. Phillip loved that side of her. That she wasn't afraid to go after her dreams.

Either way, the thought of others being mean to her pissed him off.

James shrugged, his fingers staying around the glass. "A lot of the people in town."

"Can you give me an example?"

He nodded. "She was called a whore because she still works for you and Mr. Caulfield and is at your places until late."

Fury flew through him.

"Wait, what do you mean *our* places? She meets with Caulfield at night?"

This information gave birth to an ugly jealousy.

James nodded. "The nights she does not come here, she is with him." Another long drink. "I overheard him tell her that it was her payment for asking him to move an appointment time."

I just bet it was.

His stomach clenched. Fuck. This was all his fault. Because he had been an ass and wanted command over all her time.

All I did was make things harder for her.

It explained so much. Why she was cold and pulling away from him, why she arrived on the dot and left immediately after. He clenched a fist and pushed out a low breath between his teeth.

"Thank you for keeping an eye on her, James."

He shrugged. "I like Miss Fyre. She is always nice to me."

Phillip smiled. "She is a nice woman."

"She is, even if her brother is mad at her too."

His insides chilled again. "Why is Elonne mad at her?"

"She argued with Mrs. Cara. I heard it, they were on the street. The woman was mad because she did not get to have the money from Fyre anymore like she did when she lived at the house with them." His mouth twisted with distaste. "It was not pretty and she used some mean words. Mrs. Cara hit her first, then Miss Fyre hit her in the face."

Good girl.

Phillip needed to have a talk with her and today was as good a day as any. She wasn't due to come back out here for two more days, but he wasn't about to wait that long.

"Are you ready? I will give you a ride back into town."

James sucked down the rest of the drink and wiped his hand over his mouth. "I can walk, my lord."

"I have no doubt. But I *am* insisting that you accompany me."

Finally James nodded.

Calling for his carriage to be brought around, Phillip and James made their way slowly to the front. The breeze picked up and he lifted his head into it. Warm air moved along his skin.

When the carriage arrived, the footman held the door and he looked at James. The boy's gaze moved over the opening to the interior before he shook his head.

"I should ride on the back or with the driver."

"No. Inside."

"Yes, my lord."

Phillip followed him in after giving his destination. Then he sat back while James looked around, taking it all in.

"Where should we drop you off?"

"It is fine wherever, my lord. No need to make an extra stop for me."

Letting out a boy hardly seemed like a big deal considering what he was on his way to do right now. In town, he had them let James depart and the boy bounded to the ground with a smile. Then he shot up the street like a flash and was gone.

Phillip took several deep breaths as he waited for them to reach the destination he was looking for — Fyre.

When the door was opened for him, he climbed out and took a look around. Not the best place, but the small cottage he stared at had plenty of potential and it was far better than some of the shacks he'd seen on this island.

He strode to the door and knocked.

There was nothing until he knocked a third time. Fyre swung the door open, her hair down around her shoulders, tempting him like a siren, and yet it was her expression that tore out his heart.

Pain.

Sorrow.

Anger.

"My lord." She tightened her grip on the door. "What are you doing here?"

"We need to talk."

"Give me a moment, my lord." She closed the door and he ground his jaw. A short time later, she opened it and stepped back.

He cursed himself for not bringing a maid along to make this more acceptable in the eyes of many. Gesturing for the footman to come to the door, he left it open as well before following her into her small home.

"If it is all the same to you, my lord, I would prefer you to just tell me not to come back and leave so I can carry on with my day."

Her place was spotless and smelled like baked goods.

"Smells delicious." He gave her a smile, one she didn't return.

"Thank you, and I just made pastry. You are welcome to take one to leave with, if you would like."

He knew, in that moment, whatever small amount of ground he'd made with this woman had not just been lost but crushed and blown away. His fingers moved almost of their own accord, desperate to sink into her hair. To bind her to him. Phillip craved the brush of her lips against his.

Aware that the man standing in the door would just turn his back should he decide to have this woman on her table, he forced himself to remain where he was. *Away* from her.

She didn't rush him, just watched as if she wanted him anywhere but there as she waited for him to get off his chest what he'd come here to say. Fyre had her head bowed, eyes down, and her hands clasped before her.

Not the woman he'd come to know.

"It is not easy for me to apologize."

"Then do not, for I am sure it will be such a strain on you. Good day, my lord."

The snark falling from her mouth sent the blood straight to his cock, making it thicken in its confines.

She is still in there, the woman I want. And she was, he just had to coax her out once more, and this time make sure she didn't go back into hiding.

"Look at me." He commanded her to do this, not wanting to give her another choice.

Her head rose so slowly he was across the room and in her space by the time it had been accomplished. The vulnerability in her brown eyes was a kick to the groin, taking his air and making his knees wobble.

Going against the small bit of sanity in his head, he reached out to touch her, not knowing if he would be able to stop with a single brush.

Fyre stared at the man before her, whose hand currently stroked the side of her cheek. A light brush but one she felt all the way to her core. She didn't have a clue why he was here.

Torn between pulling away and allowing the contact, she stayed, desperate for the tiny crumb he threw her. Behind him she could see the thin silhouette of his footman waiting in the doorway. The open doorway.

"I want you to work for me."

"I do work for you."

She moved back a single step. His eyes narrowed and a muscle clenched in his jaw but he didn't encroach on her again.

"You work in several different places."

Fyre waited. She knew that. What she didn't get, yet, was his reasoning for bringing this up to her.

"This is too much."

"Many of my people work more than one place."

He thought about her words before he exhaled sharply. "*My* people do not."

She struggled not to roll her eyes. *Do his people even work?*

Phillip shifted again and she found before she blinked he was right back in her space, his scent surrounding her. Not that it had left her alone, because it hadn't. Since the moment he'd set foot in her place it had wrapped her up like a blanket, heating her in ways she wasn't sure she was ready to comprehend.

"Do you know why I am telling you this?"

"No, my lord."

"God, what I would not give to hear you call me Phillip." His statement slipped from his mouth so low she nearly missed it. In a louder tone, he said, "Because you are one of mine."

"I am not a possession." The words were hot and rushed as she spat them in his direction.

If she shocked him, he didn't show it. Instead, his lips turned up in a grin that melted her undergarments, making her wet and desperate for his touch between her legs.

"I want to keep you, Fyre. *All* to myself." His gaze smoldered as she shivered from his intense look.

"There are islands around that still allow slavery. Perhaps you should sell your plantation and move to one of those."

He walked around her, touching the nape of her neck in a possessive caress before continuing to look at her small kitchen. Phillip was silent until he came back to stand near her, pushing his presence into her space.

She nearly pulled away so he couldn't feel the scarring on her neck, but couldn't find a way to move out of his intoxicating hold.

"I did not say I wanted to *own* you. I want to *keep* you." He stood in front of her again, demanding her focus. "Naked and in my bed."

Her knees wobbled.

His grin was sinful. "I want to strip your clothes off you and lick you from head to toe. I dream about how you taste and how beautiful you will be as you shatter beneath my touch."

She whimpered.

He touched a curl and tugged on it. She felt the answering pull in her core.

"I lied though. I do want to own part of you. Your heart."

He bent and brushed his mouth over hers, stunning her with the action. By the time she'd recovered, he was already walking out her door with a pastry in each hand. He passed one off to the footman and called out, "Get rid of the other jobs, Fyre. I will cover the difference."

She was alone in her small home, Phillip's scent still strong in her nose. Wobbling, she made her way to the table and sat, trying to piece together what just happened. With a nervous hand, she touched her lips and closed her eyes.

He kissed me.

A kiss similar to the ones Albie had taken, but unlike with him, this one she could still feel. Her body tingled and wanted more.

She nodded. "More."

The question was, did she trust him at his word? Or was this just another power play? She would have to have been blind not to notice the tension between him and Albie. Was she nothing more than a pawn in their squabble?

More importantly, why am I thinking of doing as he said?

Because she was tired. Going from job to job as she'd been doing for the past several years was taking its toll on her. Things were a bit better now that she no longer had to take care of her niece and nephews or that house, but there had been a reason she didn't work in the fields.

She rubbed her chest and the scars on it. Perhaps this arrangement with Lord Edais would help her. If she were brave enough to take the chance.

The man hadn't flinched when he'd brushed the scars along her neck. Fyre shook her head. No, she couldn't allow herself to get wrapped up in some creative fantasy her mind was spinning.

Lost in her thoughts, she was shocked when another loud pounding came to her door. Shaking off her improper musings of one Lord Phillip, she pushed away from the counter and got to the door just before it swung open and Elonne filled the doorway.

His face was set in a mask of anger.

"You are just set on ruining my name and Cara's. How about your niece's and nephews'?"

Stunned by the venom in his tone, she stumbled back. "Elonne? What are you talking about?"

"How you move out and then have men at your place. *White* men."

"Are you referring to Lord Edais?"

"More than one man just stops by and enters your house without a chaperone?"

He moved closer and, for the first time in her life, she didn't feel protected by her brother, but scared of the man who'd always been present and until that moment defended her.

"He had a footman with him, the door was not ever closed and, not that it is any of your concern, but he was barely here for five minutes."

Crack!

He smacked her in the face and a sob burst from her as she clamped a hand over her stinging cheek. Unlike when Cara had done it, her brother had put some real force behind his swing, and it *hurt.*

"You are acting like a whore and you should be ashamed."

Anger surged. Keeping one hand on the warm imprint on her cheek, she stood straight and stared at him. "I am not a child who needs looking after, Elonne. I am a fully grown woman who has her own place. If you would stop listening to the vile lies spit about me by your wife, you would realize I am still the same sister who worked hard while living in your home. The only difference was I gave you money then. Now you see how much your wife is spending and you are mad. I will *not* be your target for that anger."

He scowled and she matched it.

"Do not come back here without an invitation. If I am such an embarrassment, then we can just pretend not to know one another. I have done nothing wrong. I've not done anything to shame the family name, other than do a job that you encouraged me to follow. Get out."

"Gwen—" he began, and she shook her head.

"No. I have nothing more to say to you, Elonne. So you, and whoever your spy is that is giving you all of this information, stay away from me."

"Miss Gwen."

She looked around her brother's wide shoulders to find Marta there.

"Yes, Mrs. Marta?" It was hard for her to put a smile on her face, but she managed to do so.

The woman's eyes flicked from her cheek to her brother and back again.

"I came back for a few more of those delicious pastries we had while Lord Edais stopped by." She smiled and looked at her brother. "Mr. Elonne."

"*You* were here?" Elonne asked, his darker skin growing pale.

"Yes." She walked in like she owned the place. "I am just going to take a few."

Tears burned Fyre's eyes. "As many as you like, Mrs. Marta."

She did and as she headed back to the door she paused, eyes narrowing as she looked at the mark on Fyre's face then to her brother. "You know, I like that Lord Edais comes through here often. It shows to others that he cares about what happens in this small area." She stepped outside. "Do not forget lunch is with myself and Georges today."

"I will be there, Mrs. Marta."

"You did not tell me she was here."

"Goodbye, Elonne."

Rebuffing his attempts to speak to her, she shut the door firmly in his face before going to pour some water on a cloth and press it to her skin, trying to take the sting out. A short time later, Mrs. Marta came back in and took over. Fyre didn't have the energy to argue with someone else.

Chapter Ten

"Yes, yes!"

Phillip watched the woman who rode him with such abandon. She didn't try to hide her want of him. It went as deep as his for her.

Her nails dug into his chest as she took what she wanted from him, unashamed of how her body moved in the moonlight. Sun, moon, he didn't care. She was beautiful, sexy, and all his.

Her breasts moved as she worked her hips, taking him in deep, grinding, then rising up. She had no set rhythm to her actions, she was going off instinct, and it was killing him. He gripped her hips tighter but didn't impede her.

The heavy drapes to his windows were wide open, allowing the moonlight to surround them. She sat still, his cock deep inside her, and opened her eyes to meet and hold his gaze.

"You are not moving, Fyre."

Her smile did something to his insides, made him want to smile back and make her laugh. It was so innocent and full of trust. Humbling.

"I love how you feel in me." A small hip swivel. *"You fill me"* — she bit her lower lip — *"so full."*

"Do you love me?"

She narrowed her eyes and moved her hands down his chest, nails scraping his skin with enough bite to make him want more, but not enough to hurt.

"I love spending time with you."

He shifted his hold and thrust up, making her gasp, her head tipping back, exposing the gentle line of her throat. The scars there didn't take away from her elegance.

"Not what I asked."

"Make me come."

He couldn't stop his smile. This woman, who had been shy, who he'd had to coax to tell him what she wanted him to do, had found herself now and was demanding. He loved it. But then, he loved her as well.

"You want it, take it. Just like you were doing." He skimmed his hands up her sides, swiping his thumbs along her taut nipples before moving his hold back to her hips.

She bent forward, her hair tumbling around them both. *"I want you to do it."* Nose to nose. *"Claim me."*

An order he had no problem following. *"I already have,"* he growled as he flipped them over so she lay beneath him.

Phillip stretched her arms out over her head, wrists grasped in one of his hands as he wrapped a handful of her hair in his other. *"You belong to me, Fyre, and I will kill anyone who touches you in such a manner."* He pulled out until only the head of his cock remained inside her heated core.

"I have no want of another." Her gentle but hungry smile soothed the beast in him. *"Not even when you find your countess will I want another."*

He refused to think about anyone other than her. Driving home with a single direct stroke, he filled her, his mouth there *to capture her gasp. He fucked her, using his tongue in the same demanding way as his cock.*

She wanted to be claimed. He would do that. And more.

Eyes open, Phillip sat straight up in his bed. The darkness of the room told him it was far too early for any sane person to be up. On the other hand, he knew after that dream, he wasn't going to be returning to sleep anytime soon.

He flopped back with a groan and rubbed his eyes. These dreams about Fyre were becoming more and more common. Not to mention harder to forget once he was out of bed.

Yesterday he'd had to step away a few times and stroke himself until he found his release because the thoughts of her wouldn't stop. Everything reminded him of her. This time, right now, he ignored his cock and climbed out of bed.

He had been getting up earlier because when the heat of the day hit, one didn't want to do anything. After washing up quickly with the water in his room, he dressed and headed down to the kitchens.

They were lit and busy as his staff made food. Perhaps sane people were up at this time. He grabbed a little and went out to the stable where he waited as they readied his horse. It wasn't until a bit later that he realized he was on his way to Fyre's, and he forced himself to stop.

That wouldn't do. He could not just show up at her place this time of the morning. Adjusting his course, he went into town and realized only the tavern was open. Nothing more.

He walked in and looked about the place. Still rambunctious, but nothing worse than he'd seen in

England. he recognized a few of the faces there and nodded greetings but didn't stop to speak to anyone. He spied Caulfield off in the corner grinding on one of the females, one hand up her skirts while his other tugged down the top of her dress.

Anger filled him to think of this man daring to even touch Fyre. This was where he should continue to look for his women. Phillip walked out and got back on his horse. Then he went riding. By the time he finished, he'd realized two things. He needed to get more sleep, and he was far worse off than he'd initially imagined.

For he was once again in front of Fyre's place. Morning's light had begun to push away the night, casting a soft glow on all it touched.

He knocked on the door.

Realizing she may not want to open the door without knowing who was on the other side, he knocked again.

"Fyre, it is Phillip. Open the door."

She cracked it open, and the flickering candle inside made her skin glow. Lust slammed him and he gulped. Then he noticed the bruise and his stomach churned with anger.

"Who the fuck hit you?" He stepped toward her.

"My lord, what are you doing here at this hour?"

"Asking you a question. Let me in."

"This is not proper."

"Who. Hit. You?" The question was a low growl.

Her fingers, he noticed, trembled as she gently brushed over the spot. "You need not concern yourself. Please leave."

She wouldn't look him in the eyes and it was killing him.

"Come today, Fyre. Do not make me come after you." He backed away and was riding off before he could think about it because he knew he had been seconds from pushing his way into her place. To hell with the consequences.

* * * *

All day he was antsy, waiting for her to arrive. He worked out in the fields with his men just to have his energy focused on something else. While it had been something he'd done before, even he could admit that today there was an almost possessed air about him as he worked.

He didn't speak to the men beside him, not really, allowing them to do their thing. When the afternoon rolled around, he stopped to get clean. There was a small pool of water he'd discovered while riding that was secluded from others' eyes. That was where he went and stripped down to nothing before jumping in.

It wasn't something he would have enjoyed doing back in England, that was for sure, but here, the water was warm and moved like silk over his skin as he swam. Only once the sweat and grime was gone did he get out and tug his clothing back on. Did he *want* dirty clothing back on? No. However not even he was ready to be riding his horse in nothing.

Mood slightly better now that he'd sweated off his frustrations — most of them at least — then removed the sweat, he nudged his horse back toward home and ran over how little he missed England.

Sure, it would be nice to be able to stop by and see Lucien or Rafe, but the lifestyle, the rules, the matchmaking mamas... He shuddered. *Hard pass.*

Besides, he had his eye on someone here. Rules be damned.

Handing the reins off as he dismounted, he cracked his neck as he walked to the door. Keating opened it with a nod.

"My lord."

"Afternoon, Keating. I'm going to need some food and..." He trailed off as a maid appeared with a footman carrying a tray of food. "You *are* good, Keating, but how did you know I was going to be hungry at this moment?"

"That is for your Ms. Fyre, my lord," he said without batting an eye. "She arrived an hour ago to work on your books. As you told me she was to have all the access needed, she is in your study, looking over your new venture and setting up a new ledger for it."

Heat slammed him, kicking his body's temperature back up to where it had been before he'd taken the brief swim. He was already walking that way before the man finished. "Bring me something to eat as well."

"Of course, my lord."

Were his need to see Fyre not so strong, he would have looked back at Keating, swearing there was a bit of humor in the man's tone. Perhaps the stodgy butler was softening just a bit.

Waiting in the doorway as they finished setting up her food, at his desk even, Phillip didn't speak, just listened to Fyre interact with both the maid and the footman. How polite she was to each of them. The soft cadence of her voice settled something deep inside his chest even though she wasn't looking at or speaking to him directly.

It was the woman. Her presence here. Her effect on him.

He stepped back when they turned and put a finger to his lips. Neither spoke, just walked by him and he took their place, moving farther into the room until he was hit with her scent.

Phillip still hadn't figured out what it was she used in her soap to make her smell so tantalizing, but he would always recognize *her*.

For a moment, he stood there and stared down at her, taking in all of Fyre's nuances. The way her hair was braided and wrapped around her head, how her collar was up, hiding the marks on her neck. The steady strokes she made with the pen as she wrote in a new book, working with care. He knew it was so she didn't mess up. His woman was meticulous in her work and he admired the fuck out of her for it.

"Hello, Fyre."

To her credit, she didn't jump, but he knew he'd shocked her by the way the pen wobbled a tiny bit before she finished her current line. Then she looked up at him and his heart was lost once again.

Fyre didn't understand what it was about this man that did these things to her. Logically she knew it was foolish to even think about allowing a relationship with him. He was a titled English lord and she was a dark-skinned nobody from the islands.

I do his books. That is all.

Yet, it *wasn't*. He'd kissed her. Fleetingly? Yes. Did that make it any less powerful? Not in the slightest.

"Good afternoon, my lord. I will give you back your chair."

"Nonsense. You are in the right place to work. I will sit in a different one after they bring my food. Unless you'd like to sit in my lap as you work."

Her entire body trembled at the suggestion. She grew slick and she shifted on the seat.

Refusing to release his gaze, she gave him a smile. "As much fun as that would be, my lord, I do not believe you would be able to concentrate on your work."

She bit the inside of her cheek as she waited to see how far she'd overstepped. Phillip stared at her before his eyes crinkled at the corners as he smiled.

It wasn't something she saw him do with a lot of people. In fact, only one could she recall. His friend, the Marquess of Heartstone. With that man, he'd been predisposed to smile more. Other than with him, she'd not been able to recall another person that he'd smiled with. Besides her.

"Cheeky. And you are right, Fyre. My concentration would be shit with you on my lap. At least about numbers." A slow blink. "Well, the ones you put in that book. I would have no problem with the ones keeping accounting of how many times I took you. How many times I made you scream my name while being bent over or spread out on this desk."

His gaze darkened, reminding her of the storms that rolled in off the sea. Dark. Dangerous. Potent.

"Your food, my lord."

A muscle flexed in his jaw but he didn't move back. Nor closer. He was a suitable distance away from her, his hands in his pockets. Only then did she notice his clothing was wet. The servants bringing his food were there and gone in moments, leaving as silently as they'd come.

Using the distraction to pull her attention off the lord of this manor, Fyre went back to work, filling in the columns he would be using. She glanced up at the sound of another chair being dragged over. He sat on the same side as she but left distance between them. And food.

In her peripheral vision, she noted the way his strong fingers plucked things up off the main tray and placed them on a smaller plate before he slid it in her direction.

"Eat."

There was a low command in the single word. She mulled that over in her mind as she finished up her current row.

Mainly, why had she considered doing that with just the slightest bit of hesitation? She should know better than to just follow anyone's command. She'd worked hard to be her own person and individual. Hard to do with Elonne as her overprotective brother.

A flash of sorrow pierced her.

Not something I have to think or worry about any longer.

She put the pen back in its spot and stood as she reached for the plate.

"What are you doing?"

Fyre honestly tried not to look him in the eye. But, like everything else in regards to her when it came to this man, she was falling short of her mark. There were things she needed to be and do. Distant. Unfeeling. No fantasy. Massive failure on her part. Rolling her lower lip in her teeth, she blinked before she slid her gaze to his.

"Moving to eat somewhere that is not your desk."

"Why?"

His question was straightforward and, try as she might, she couldn't discover any hidden meaning in his inquiry.

"Because one in my position does not just eat at the desk of an earl."

Phillip was against the side of the desk and in the process of fixing his own plate, but he stopped and pinned both those gray eyes of his on her. Insides clenching at the heat that sliced into his gaze, she fought the urge to shift or lick her lips.

"What exactly does that mean?"

Despite the bubbling heat in his stare, the words were icy.

"I may work at your desk, from time to time, even though I should stop doing that, but I should not be sitting there like the desk is mine when you are in the room. You should be seated here. This is *your* office, after all."

"This is not stopping for a five-course meal, Fyre. This is us eating while we work. You are set up there and while I may be, okay, I *am* an asshole, I am not going to make you move."

"This is not proper." She lifted the plate and edged around the chair, freezing at the low growl that filled the room.

"I will tell you what is not going to be proper, me picking you up and putting you back there. Trust me, Fyre, when I have you in my arms, there are plenty of things I have in mind and *none* of them involve you working on that book or eating the food on that plate. If you are not inclined to learn what those are at this moment, sit in the goddamn chair and eat."

Her instincts screamed for her to run but her muscles were locked and she couldn't move. She lowered herself back to the chair slowly and, without looking at him, she reached for one of the sandwiches he'd placed on the plate for her. Nibbling at it, she kept her eyes forward until she'd swallowed the last bit.

Only then did she adjust herself to look at him. He stared at her, blatant hunger in his gaze, but he didn't move from his seat.

"You are making me crazy, Fyre. You know I would never hurt you, right? And if you tell me no or to back off, I will." He scrubbed a hand over his jaw. "Do you know this?"

"I trust you, Lord Edais. And yes, I know that."

"I want to make sure, because while I am going to give you fair warning, I *am* coming after you. I do not want you to feel like my title makes it so you cannot say no to me."

His tone was low and earnest. He had leaned closer to her, not moving the chair, but still, she felt him closer.

"When the time comes and you trust me enough to take you to bed." A wink. "Or the desk, outside by the water, against a wall, *everywhere*, the minute you say no, that will stop it. I will *never* take advantage of you like that."

Heat surged through her. She wanted that. To be consumed by this man. To have the courage to allow the spark between them to explode into the raging inferno she knew it would be.

Unable to hold his gaze, she put hers back to the desk and picked up the pen once more. Seconds later it was plucked from her hand.

"Eat."

There he went being all growly again and her body reacted. Her nipples tightened, rubbed against the material of her clothing, and she struggled not to slide on the chair. The ache between her legs only grew.

Tipping her head up, she found him scowling down at her.

"Why are you scowling?"

"One tiny sandwich is not enough for you. If you do not want to eat, then perhaps we should talk about the dead man who dared to put his hand on you." He blinked and gave a mocking smile. "I did not forget I saw the mark that someone hit you. Do you want to confirm who it was? I do know, Fyre. I have people all over this island who tell me things, but I want to hear it from you."

She remained mute but shook her head. That wasn't something she wished to get him involved in. It was her mess with her own brother. Not this man's business. How the hell had he found out anyway, and who were his 'people' he had all over this island? *Her* home, not his.

"My lord," Keating interrupted and Fyre yanked her gaze away from him, not wanting to risk the butler seeing her affection for his boss.

She sat back in the chair and took another sandwich even as she picked up the pen again.

Phillip narrowed his gaze but turned to face the butler. The second those intense eyes were off her, she took a deep breath, needing the break. The earl's presence was a lot for her.

The man in question had walked over to speak to the butler and she didn't even attempt to listen. She allowed the world of numbers to pull her back in, calming her nerves and making things right once more. Even as she ate the food on the plate, she worked.

Only after looking up once she had finished did she realize that they were once again the only two in the room. Phillip leaned back in the chair he'd dragged closer and had his ankle resting on his other leg as he watched her unabashedly.

"All finished, my lord." She replaced the pen and almost reached up to see if her hair was still confined. He brought out nervous tendencies in her.

"You love numbers."

She nodded and rose from the chair, setting the plate back on the tray. "I do."

"Good. Now sit back down and explain how you just set up my new venture."

"It is the same as your others, my lord. You told me you understood those."

He shrugged unrepentantly. "This is different."

Suspicion flared. "You are doing this on purpose."

His grin was wicked. "Scared?"

Only that she might not be able to behave. "No, my lord."

He gestured to the chair she had just gotten out of. "Then take your seat. Unless you would like to do this on the settee."

Heat raced through her at the thought of being pressed close to him in a smaller space.

"Here is fine, my lord."

"I cannot *wait* for the day you call me Phillip." His words were low and intimate.

Ignoring the screaming voice in her head that told her this was a mistake, she responded, the brutally honest words sliding free. "I do every night in my dreams."

She'd never known gray could swirl with such passion and heat.

Chapter Eleven

"I do every night in my dreams."

God, he couldn't get her words out of his head. He'd not seen her for longer than a few moments the past few times she'd been out to take care of the books, other issues demanding his attention.

Not that it mattered. The moment he entered his office he could smell her, the incredible scent she wore like a blanket. A smell he was desperate to have on his sheets and all over his skin.

Permanently.

Whenever he walked into his office, it was in pristine condition. Nothing out of place, even the books put back. Again, if not for the knowledge she'd been there or the scent lingering in the air, he wouldn't have known.

At first, he'd thought she had been avoiding him, but he'd realized that it was he who had been otherwise occupied when she'd been here.

He *needed* to see her. And they needed to discuss the fact she was still working all those other jobs.

Did he want to monopolize all her time? Fuck yes. But regardless of his selfish desire, he was one hundred percent impressed with the woman she was and how she made sure to handle her business. She wasn't rolling over and letting anyone take care of her.

Fine, it is not anyone else, but I should be allowed to care for her.

Possessive?

Hell yes.

He walked around his desk, dragging his fingers along the back of the chair she'd been using. Closing his eyes, he envisioned her in there with him. His gut clenched as he envisaged her bent over the books, working to make sure all his numbers were in order.

"My lord."

Phillip rubbed the nape of his neck. "What is it, Keating?"

"You asked us to keep an eye out for someone snooping around. Two of the footmen caught a man in the back, in the stores."

Shoving thoughts of Fyre to the back of his mind, he walked with purpose to where Keating stood by the door. Their gazes met and together they headed to the outbuilding where he stored his harvested items before they were taken to the docks and shipped out.

Davie and Marcus were the two holding the man. Marcus had a pitchfork aimed at him as they stood over him, keeping him on the ground and unable to run.

Phillip didn't recognize the man and walked closer, noting how the intruder paled at the sight of him. The man's tanned skin was pockmarked and he was missing some teeth.

"I did not mean any harm, my lord. Please let me go. You will never see me again."

"You meant no harm? Yet my men find you trying to steal from me? How is that not doing harm?" He crossed his arms. "Who are you and why are you trying to steal from me?"

He blanched and squirmed on the hard, unforgiving floor. Phillip had no sympathy for him.

"My family is hungry."

Phillip didn't blink. He just stared at him.

"The man said he would pay if I did this for him."

"Who said? What man?"

"He will kill me if I give his name. Then he will go after my wife and children."

Waving off his men, Phillip waited until it was just the two of them in there before crouching down by the man. "I do not recognize you from this island. Where were you recruited? And did this man who hired you tell you that I was an earl?"

He hadn't thought it possible for the man to pale further.

"You can have me killed."

"Yes, and I would not lose any sleep over it. I do not tolerate people who steal from me, or try to. So, we will try this again. You will tell me what you know, all of it, and then I will decide if you will be able to see your family again."

"Yes, my lord."

The man got up, slowly, and together they walked outside. Phillip saw Elonne riding up and wondered what he was doing here. He still needed to have words with him for daring to lay a hand on his sister. Right now, Phillip forced himself to remain focused on the problem before him.

It took over an hour to get the information he needed. Then he locked the man up and sent Davie off to confirm the news he'd been given. It would take a while for the man to get there and back. Content that Pavel, the man they'd captured, would not be going anywhere, he made his way back to the main part of the house.

Heading to the kitchen, he smiled at the cook, who fixed him a quick meal. As he finished, Keating found him once more and let him know that Elonne was still waiting for him.

It was after six at night and he hadn't been looking forward to doing any more discussion today, but this man he would see. So he returned to the study and found Elonne standing by the window, staring out.

"You asked to see me, Mr. Parker." He walked behind his desk and watched the man at the window. "How can I be of assistance?" He made his way to the sideboard and poured two drinks. He handed one to Elonne then went to his chair and sat.

"I came here to discuss my sister, my lord." He lifted the drink. "Thank you for this and I appreciate you seeing me. As the man of the family, she is my responsibility."

Leaning back in his chair, Phillip waited for the man to get to the point. The words dangling at the edge of his tongue weren't nice ones.

"I told her to stop working for you and just maintain the other jobs she has. You know this, I know she confronted you." He bounced his broad shoulders. "My sister, she is not listening to me. I was hoping you would be able to tell her she no longer had this job."

"How is this any different than when you were using her to pretend to be doing the work on my books?

Your sister is incredible with numbers and my books have never been in better shape. Every blunt is accounted for and I am not worried that she is attempting to fleece me. And we have already had this discussion and I told you I would not do it."

He placed his drink down on the desk and leaned forward. "To be honest with you, Mr. Parker, I want to hire your sister full time. I want her to only work for me, not everyone else she is working for. You can take over those smaller accounts. My ventures are about to grow and I will need more of her time given she is the best at what she does. I'm accustomed to having nothing but the best and have no plans to change that. So, no, I will *not* tell her she no longer has a job. I mentioned to you before that I was going to take care of her and that still stands. But I will be talking to her about my thoughts on taking care of her, and while I understand you are the man in the family, I am her friend and one of her employers."

Elonne narrowed his eyes slightly.

Phillip rose and walked toward the man, leaving the glass on the desk. "One more thing, and this, in my opinion, is the most important. If I *ever* see another mark on her skin from where you hit her, the next discussion between the two of us will not be even half as civil as this one has been." He lifted an eyebrow. "Are we clear?"

"She told you I hit her?"

"Do you deny hitting a woman that you are easily twice the size and strength of? No, she would not talk about it, but I have eyes and ears all over this island and word reached me." He moved closer. "I cannot stand a man who feels he has a right to hit a woman, and I *will* take him to task. This is your one warning from me."

Elonne gulped but didn't look away. Phillip wanted to give him credit for that. But it wasn't worth it, the fucker never should have dared to lay his hands on a woman, much less his own sister. When he'd found out from Marta what had happened, it had taken Phillip more control than he'd believed he possessed not to go kill him right then and there.

"She is my sister."

"She is a woman who should be protected, not hit. And I am letting you know, she is under *my* protection."

"My sister is not going to be your whore."

"I have far too much respect for her to even continue that discussion. I can get a whore when I want one. I will never look at your sister in such a light. Have a good night, Mr. Parker."

Phillip walked out of the room and, in his peripheral vision, watched as Keating entered to help Elonne on his way.

* * * *

Laughter spilled through the kitchen. Fyre wiped her eyes before tackling the large ball of dough before her. She was hanging out with Georges and Marta in the large bakery belonging to Georges.

The man had broken his arm and she and Marta were helping him so he didn't fall behind. While she could cook and bake, Fyre didn't have his expertise in doing all the breads he did. So the man was giving directions while she did her best to follow them.

The sun had yet to even think about cresting the horizon and she had been at this for two hours already. Every second that passed gave her more and more respect for the baker. At least they had coffee and food to snack on, because this…this was some incredibly serious physical work.

She worked the dough as Georges regaled them with stories of his youth, while Marta formed loaves from the dough she'd already worked to slide into the oven.

Using the mezzaluna Georges had placed beside her, she cut sections off to create more loaves. Her stomach rumbled again. This baking bread smell was making her mouth water.

He moved closer to her, his damaged arm in a sling as he looked over what she was doing.

"You ever want to get into baking, Gwen, you could be a fantastic assistant." A grin. "Perhaps even take over when I am no longer able to work."

"Thank you, but I think I would eat all of this if I started working here. How do you not just eat every bit of it? The smell is incredible."

"It balances out. You work it off."

She nodded. Her arms were already aching and she knew her back was going to be sore as well. But she would see this through because Georges was so nice to her, she wanted to give back.

Feeling as if she'd already put in a full day when the sun finally peeked over the horizon, she moaned as she stretched. She was sore, but in a good way. As soon as Georges opened up his shop, there were people there to purchase the fresh bread.

She and Marta carried bread to people and helped them get their loaves. Marta cleared her throat and Fyre looked up to see Mrs. Callie, the cook's assistant for Hawk's Cove, there in line.

The other woman gave her a smile and a small wave.

"Morning, Miss Gwen."

Unable to not return the smile, she gave a small curtsey. "Mrs. Callie, good morning."

"You work here as well?"

"Helping out Georges as he hurt his arm." She took the sheet the woman handed over and skimmed it fast, making note of how many loaves and what kinds were wanted for the house. "I will be right back."

Fyre didn't take long to fill the order and was placing the bread in Mrs. Callie's basket in short order. With another smile, Mrs. Callie was on her way and Fyre got back to work.

They didn't finish their rush until a little after eight. Having been up since two, she was ready to get in a nap. After ensuring that Georges was good for the rest of the day, she walked home to get changed and head out to do some of her normal things for the day.

At least she only had one person on her schedule for doing books. Unfortunately, it was Albie.

At her home, she cleaned up and was partaking in a small cup of tea when the door opened and her brother walked in. Her heartbeat began to race as the hair lifted on the nape of her neck. Clenching her fingers around the warm cup, she willed them to stop shaking.

Not willing to show him how much his actions scared her, she remained at the table, working hard to make sure to keep her face closed off from all expression. He would pounce like a predator if he knew her weakness.

"Where have you been this morning?" He slammed his hands down on the table.

That got her to flinch.

"You are not my keeper, Elonne. You have no right to barge into *my* home and demand to know where I was." One hand she kept around the mug, the other she hid in her lap, to keep her trembling a secret.

"I was here around six and you were not home." He leaned closer. "Where were you? Were you with that English lord?"

She shook her head and got to her feet. "You have gone too far, Elonne. I appreciate all you have done for me in the past but this is over. Who I am with and what I choose to do is *my* business. You have made it abundantly clear that I am already a disappointment to you and the family because I will not listen to you now that I have moved out. I want you to leave."

"That man is only using you."

"To what end? What *possible* reason could he have to use me?" *The man could have taken what he wanted from me by now and everyone would have looked away because he is a man and an earl.*

"To get at me."

"Again, to what end?" She shook her head at her brother. "We are not exactly in his social circle, Elonne. What good is using me to get to you going to do him?"

He sneered at her, suddenly no longer the brother who had always protected her. And she could say for the first time, she truly feared him. She had no more belief that he would never hurt her. This man was different. He had something hounding him. She wasn't sure if it was the stress of his home life and the lack of money they now had coming in or what. All she knew was at the moment, she was their target. He had changed, and she wasn't confident about the person he'd become.

"Cara told me that you had a high opinion of yourself because I kept you from working in the fields.

Told me you think yourself better." His words poured out in a rush, making her shiver.

Wanting nothing more than to run and hide from this person who only *looked* like her brother, she didn't move. She wasn't sure she even could move from her spot—her legs most likely would not hold her.

His eyes held a maniacal gleam as he stared at her.

"I have to get ready. I am due at Mr. Caulfield's shortly." The words slipped from her mouth without wavering and she was proud for that, at least.

That name seemed to snap his brother out of whatever trance or fixation that had held him. Didn't do a thing to ease her own mind, however.

"You owe me. You owe *us*," he hissed.

Fyre squeezed her eyes shut for a moment before focusing on her brother. Anger pumped through her. This was her brother, the man who had protected her. Sheltered her. Guided her.

But it wasn't. Because her big brother would not be looking at her with such anger and hatred.

She forced herself to move, slowly and cautiously, until she was sure her legs wouldn't buckle beneath her fear. Hands on the table, she stared at the man she used to adore with every fiber of her being.

"No, Elonne. I do not."

His gaze widened before it narrowed on her. "What?"

"I do not owe you or your wife anything."

His face twisted into something ugly and he moved toward her. "I gave you a place to stay. I helped you find work."

"And I gave you and your wife three-quarters of what I earned, plus I cleaned and cooked while looking after your children as your wife shopped. I put back into that household. And I never asked for you to help me. I always wanted to live on my own. When I first mentioned that, you said no and that I wasn't a burden because you are my older brother and your job is to protect me. Yes, when we were younger you protected me. You were with me as I recovered from the accident, but I held those jobs, *all* of them, on my own. Because of my work ethic and how good I am at what I do. I owe you *nothing*."

He moved like lightning, and she was against the wall with his hand around her neck before she knew what had happened.

"I *own* you, sister. And you will provide me with the money I need. You will marry Albie and he will pay me a handsome dowry for you."

She clawed at his hand and wrist, gasping for air. He didn't let go. Spots danced before her eyes and still he wouldn't release her.

"You were a sickly child and I stopped them from killing you after the accident. Now you will pay me back for saving you. One way or another."

His words echoed in her mind as she sank into the dark world of unconsciousness.

Chapter Twelve

James ran toward him as he rode up the street. Phillip slowed his mount and fought to hide his smile at the sight of the boy. His sharp mind and cunning were intriguing to him.

This time, however, James didn't stop. There wasn't even a wave. The boy blew by him, feet churning up the dust as he ran right on past. While his horse snorted, Phillip turned his head to follow where the boy ran, and watched him vanish around the corner.

Not quite sure what happened there, he continued on his original way despite staring after the child. He'd overheard his housekeeper's assistant mention she had seen Fyre this morning helping out Georges because he'd injured his arm, and that alone had been enough for him to leave his home and come into town.

He wanted to see her. And it bothered the hell out of him that he couldn't have her at his place all the time. She lightened up his world. Being the selfish bastard he was, Phillip wanted to keep that around him, all the time.

Stopping his horse at his destination, he swung down and tipped his hat to a few of the women walking along the street. They smiled and blushed but he didn't stop, just walked into the shop he hoped to find Fyre at—Mr. Holmes' Mercantile.

He strode in, boot heels clacking on the wood floor. It didn't take him long to know that the woman he sought was nowhere in the building. Fyre gave off a vibe when she was in a place. Hell, when she was anywhere. And it was one that resonated through him like part of his own beating heart.

That was absent today and he didn't like it.

Mr. Holmes was at the counter. He smiled and nodded. "Good day, my lord. Is there something I can help you find?"

Moving toward the aisle that held the toys he'd gotten before, he shook his head. "No thank you, I was just looking to see if there was anything new for my nephew and nieces. Miss Gwen helped me out last time."

The man *tsked* and muttered something he couldn't make out. "She should be back in a few days."

God, all the questions that perched on the end of his tongue fought to escape. Phillip bit them back. He wasn't about to beg for information. Not from this man. So instead he looked over the shelves quickly and picked up two new items there and took them to the counter.

"These two will work."

"I will charge it to your account, my lord. Would you like me to wrap them?"

"Yes."

He longed to know what was going on. After he finished here, he would track down James and get his answers.

Mr. Holmes wasn't as fast as Fyre, but he was efficient and it didn't take long before Phillip was striding out the door he'd entered not too long ago.

It turned out he didn't have to locate James to learn anything about Fyre, for he spotted her across the street. She had just come out of Caulfield's place and his heart caught.

It wasn't fair. This woman could bring him to his knees with nothing more than a look. But unlike other women, he didn't think she cared about the power she wielded over him. Not in the slightest.

Albie stepped out after her and called her name.

A low rumble of possessiveness rolled from Phillip's chest as he watched her stop and turn back, protectiveness a swift second given how he read her body language. She was scared.

Phillip swung up on his horse and rode across the street. Both people glanced up at him. Albie's expression was dark but smoothed away quickly, Fyre's unreadable.

What wasn't indecipherable? The way she didn't hold their gazes, either one of them, but looked down at the toes of her dusty shoes. The slight tremble to her fingers as she flexed them on the strap of the bag she held.

This wasn't in any way the woman he had verbally sparred with recently at his place. And it bothered him. Who had done this to her? Made her appear…scared and vulnerable. Better question, who was he going to kill?

"Afternoon, my lord," Albie said, shifting slightly to position himself closer to Fyre.

Another move that Phillip wasn't fond of.

"Caulfield." He looked to the woman who had solidified a place in his heart. "Miss Gwen."

A slight curtsey. "Lord Edais."

When she straightened, her collar dipped, and anger lashed at him like a storm-tossed sea when he noticed the marks on her neck.

"We were in the middle of a discussion, my lord. Is there something I can help you with?" Mr. Caulfield's grating tone raked over him and he didn't give a fuck.

I want answers.

"No." Not giving a damn if he ruined the man's day, bastard shouldn't be sniffing around Fyre anyway. "I need a word with Miss Gwen."

Her gaze flicked between the both of them and she licked her lips. "Is it something that can wait, my lord? I should be getting home."

"No." Again, a one-word answer, but he didn't trust himself to try to string together more than that. Not as pissed as he was. He swung down and fisted the reins. "I will walk you to the edge of town." A fleeting glance back to Caulfield. "Caulfield."

They walked in silence until he was confident that Albie couldn't hear them. Sure, there were others who watched, but it didn't matter.

Who the fuck cares?

"What happened?"

"I am sure I do not know what you mean, my lord."

"Do *not* push me on this, Fyre. I will carry you to the doctor right now and have them look you over. Who the fuck put the marks on your neck?" It was a good thing the leathers didn't have feelings because he surely would have wrung them dry or broken them in two had they been stiff.

Her hand fluttered to her neck ever so briefly.

"It is not very gentlemanly to point out the scars on a woman's neck, not even if one is an earl."

Despite the situation, he couldn't help but grin at the primness in her tone. This woman had an uncanny way of soothing the anger within him, using nothing more than a few words and the barest of smiles.

"We both know," he muttered, "I am no gentleman. I work at it for one reason only, Fyre."

She glanced at him, the question blatant in her gaze. He dug the fingers of his hand into his palm to keep from reaching out and cupping her cheek. They'd stopped walking.

"You, Fyre. You are the reason I try. But do not make the mistake of thinking I am a gentleman."

The tiniest smile turned up her lips and his heart cavorted within his chest.

"I think you are far more of one than you want to admit to yourself. But thank you for trying."

He stopped and so did she. "Do you know how badly I want to kiss you right now? How much I long to pick you up and back you into the post there, using it to push us together? I am *no* gentleman."

"Yet you are telling me what you want to do instead of doing it. That, to me, is the mark of a gentleman."

Damn her.

"Would you let me?" Gods, he wanted to move closer to her. "Would you let me kiss you in town? Would you let me do that to you?"

Her fingers danced over her skin once more, enticing him all over again. "I think, my lord, that once again, our discussion is not appropriate. However, I will say this — I believe any woman who is worth your love and affection would jump at the chance to be touched and kissed by you often. Regardless of the place it happened. If you will excuse me, my lord. I need to get home."

She was gone, leaving him alone with his horse in the middle of a town that hadn't quite found its place in the world yet. His body was so hard for her it ached. Ignoring the current state of his cock, he swung up in the saddle and turned his horse back in the direction they'd just walked from.

He wanted nothing more than to follow her, put her on his horse with him and ride out to his lake. That was it.

I will take her on a picnic.

He remembered Lucien and Ciara doing those and enjoying them. Fyre would as well.

I hope.

Finishing up in town, he was still pissed at the reminder that he hadn't learned what had happened to her or who it was that had put the marks on her neck. Fyre was so good at distracting him. Although he had a very good idea who the culprit was.

And it was his responsibility to make sure it would never happen again.

* * * *

Fyre stared at her reflection as she rubbed the cream Marta had given her into the marks still standing out against her darker skin. The woman had been the one to find her and knew who had done it because Fyre had broken down in her arms.

All day she could feel people looking at her, and she'd tried to keep her neck covered as much as possible. Albie had not said a word, but Phillip, he'd known. Somehow that man, the earl who by every single account should be off limits to even her thoughts, *he'd* known.

And had been pissed on her behalf.

But then, that man always looked at her like she mattered. To him. Scowling at herself, she closed down that line of thought. It wasn't one she should be following.

She still shook as she fixed herself something to eat. After she'd eaten, she set about cleaning up and thought about the current state of her life. Something had to give, and if things were any indication, she would end up being the one who had to give all.

I do not want to have to do that.

A firm rapping on the door dragged her from her thoughts. Clutching her scarf tighter around her neck, she went to the door, hesitated and hated herself for it before she pulled it open.

Phillip stood there. Larger than life and everything her mind created for her when she thought about what made her happy, and what kind of man she would like to spend her days with. His expression was hard, unforgiving, but his eyes, they told her a completely different story.

He was concerned for her.

"I was just thinking about you." Fyre blushed as the words slipped free. How she longed to be able to take them back.

One eyebrow rose and the side of his mouth twitched up as his eyes heated.

Determined not to look away from him, she cleared her throat. "Lord Edais, how may I be of assistance?"

He never let go of her gaze, just reached out and dragged the backs of two fingers down the side of her cheek. Her belly erupted into a mess of tumbles.

"I am *always* thinking about you," he whispered.

When he dropped his hand, she felt the loss. Deeper than any she'd felt before. This man had gotten far beneath her skin, all without trying.

"We need to talk."

No more softness in his tone. This was the voice she heard from him at his place, barking orders he didn't believe anyone would dare contradict.

"There is nothing to say if you have come to let me go. Just tell me and be done with it."

She didn't have it in her to curb her tone. Quite frankly, she was done with the men in her life making demands and telling her what she could and could not do. Her outburst clearly surprised him, at least a tiny bit.

His eyebrows went up, both this time, and his lips twitched before he composed his features once more. Two others stepped up beside him and behind them, she noticed a maid.

"I already told you I was not firing you. Stop assuming that is why I am here when I come by. This is about you trying to hide the fact someone attacked you."

It was then she recognized one of the men beside him. The one on the right, he was what passed for the law around the island. Or one of them.

"Twice." Phillip's voice was dagger-sharp.

Her fingers flexed again, her nerves ratcheting up. She didn't typically have any use for the law. They sided with the plantation owners and the larger business owners on the island more often than not.

Were they all corrupt? No. However, enough were to make her suspicious. Plus, she'd grown up with Elonne bad-mouthing them, and that didn't exactly inspire trust from her side.

"I am fine."

"Bullshit," he snapped out before her words could even fade from the air. "You have been attacked twice, no way you are fine."

"May I have a word, my lord?" A deep breath. "In private?"

Liquid steel watched her. "Step away," he commanded without looking away from her. Arms crossed, he didn't say another word until the two men had moved back to the maid who stood there, watching the entire situation. "This is as alone as we can be right now, Fyre. I go inside your house with you and I will be inside your body in seconds, filling you with my cock, making you scream my name as you come apart around me."

She'd not been prepared for the amount of heat that hit her at his blatant honesty.

Licking her lips, she noticed the way his gaze tracked the movement, as well as the low groan that slipped from him.

"Why are you insisting on pushing this?"

The heat vanished, leaving behind the cold man who so many on this island feared.

"Because you were *attacked*. And I know who did it. He lays a hand on you again, family or not, he *will* be answering to me and he will not be pleased with the outcome."

"I cannot have you stepping in to fight my battles."

"I already have." He shoved a hand through his hair. "You are the most obstinate, infuriating woman I have met in my life. I am trying to protect you. Do you know how much I want to make you move into my home, so I know no one can get to you?"

She watched his expression as it morphed into something she could only describe as tortured.

"I did not ask for your protection."

"Of course you did not ask. You are too hardheaded to do so. You are one of my people, Fyre." A jaw clench before he took a deep breath. "You are *mine*." In a louder voice, he continued, "I do what is necessary to protect those who work for me. And if that means I pay to have someone guard you, then that is what I will do. But I will *not* stand for you to have to walk to work after a sorry excuse for a human attacked you. Your choice is go along with this or I will move you to the estate."

Others had begun to gather, including Georges and Marta. Not wanting to be the center of a scene, she sucked in a deep breath.

"You are causing a scene, my lord."

"Oh am I?" He pitched his voice louder. "Good, because I want this to get back to the ones who are cowardly enough to attack a woman. They touch you again, I will *kill* them."

"What are you saying?" she hissed. "You are all but declaring that you are after me."

The immovable man vanished as his features slid into the ones of the man who liked to tease her. His gaze softened and he winked. "If they want to believe that, good for them, but trust me, Fyre, when I make it known that you are the woman I am courting, it will not be because I have to force you to take some protection." He prowled closer. "There will be kissing, and a hell of a lot of it." Phillip's grin made her weak in the knees.

"Everyone can hear you."

His smile grew wider. "I know. Maybe it will get back to that pussy Caulfield and remind him to keep away from you." Phillip stepped back from her and she had to curl her fingers into her palms to keep from reaching for him. "It is going to happen sooner rather than later, Fyre. Fair warning. In the meantime, this is Damon, and he will be watching to make sure no one touches you."

How was it possible for the man to make her feel so much?

The man he'd named Damon stepped forward and nodded. "Ma'am."

"I will send a carriage for you later." Phillip turned to the law officer only to stop and stride quickly back to pause before her. "Unless you'd like to invite me inside and we can continue our discussion there?" That damn infuriating eyebrow went back up.

Fyre knew he was goading her. She couldn't forget his words, even if she'd wanted to. Which she didn't.

"No, my lord. You made your point."

"Pity." Another wink. "Perhaps later then." He walked away without a look back, engaging the lawman as they departed.

Then it was her and Damon along with all the onlookers.

"You will not know I am around, ma'am," he muttered for her ears. "I am just here to keep you safe." He stepped away and she looked at Georges and Marta, whose concern for her overflowed their expressions.

Everything had just gotten so much more complicated.

Chapter Thirteen

Phillip sighed and leaned back in his chair, staring out at the four men before him. Damon and his brothers. They were meeting in a smaller room in the back of the house.

"What do you have to report?"

Damon and his siblings were the men he'd hired to make sure no one went after Fyre again. While he had shown the town Damon, he had been very sure to make sure those in the town didn't know there were four of them to watch her.

When it came to this woman, who did his books and ruled his heart, even if he wasn't ready to admit it to himself aloud, there wasn't any line he wouldn't cross to keep her safe. Even if it meant keeping her safe from herself because she was still holding on to the belief that her brother wouldn't really harm her.

He disagreed.

"Her brother is getting pushier about trying to get closer to her. This hurts her, not seeing him." Phillip opened his mouth but Damon raised a hand and gave a sharp shake of his head. "I know, boss. He doesn't get close. I know the job. I am just reporting as you asked. The sister-in-law is a real gem. She is getting some on the side while Elonne is out working. Not sure who watches the children while she is with any of the five men she sleeps with, but she has her routine."

"And Caulfield?"

The brothers all shared a look. "He is not taking kindly to the fact Damon is with her." This from Kolby as he crossed his arms.

Phillip stared at them, close enough to pass as the same man if one wasn't looking for the differences. He understood why they were so good at their jobs. Well worth what he was paying them. Damon was the spokesman and typically the most outgoing, while Kolby, well, if he were to be completely honest, Phillip didn't want to meet this man if he was pissed off at him. Any of them really.

"Good, I want him unhappy."

"He continually tries to get me to wait out of the room when they are working."

Anger pulsed beneath Phillip's skin like a living entity. "I am sure he does."

The brothers exchanged another look.

"What are you *not* telling me?"

"Miss Gwen is not getting a lot of sleep."

Jealousy rose. "How do you know this?" He focused on Damon.

"Her light is on until the late hours and she is up early."

He groaned and grabbed up his schedule purely for something to do with his hands. For it wasn't like he needed to look at it to know where she was. She was here with him at the moment, setting up to work in his study while he finished up here.

"Okay, thank you." He got to his feet. "Grab some food. She will be done here in about two hours."

All four of them nodded. Damon, Archer, Kolby and Zander. He left them there knowing they would get what they needed and be ready to leave when Fyre was. Right now, he had a woman to see.

A footman was at the door to the study when he reached it and he took the tray from him before walking in. Already, Fyre was working.

Not at his desk this time but at the small desk to the side. She'd begun setting up there, even though his desk had far more space. He walked up behind her and placed the tray down at her left.

"Thank you," she muttered before her body stiffened.

He didn't move back, instead he braced his arms on either side of her, lowering his head to sniff her neck. Brushing his lips along the scarred skin, he reveled in her slight shiver.

"Hello, beautiful."

"Wha…what are you doing, my lord?"

He smiled and kissed her neck. "Making my intentions clear."

"Intentions for what?"

"Mmm. I am sure you can figure that out. Why are you not working at my desk?" He moved to the other side of her neck and provided it with the same attention.

Her gasp pushed lead into his cock, yet he couldn't stop his arrogant smirk when she tipped her head, offering him better access. Not a lot, but hell, he'd take anything.

"This desk is adequate."

"I like you at my desk." He nipped her skin and a low moan rolled from her lips. "I have fantasies of you there. With me." God, he couldn't get over how she smelled. "One of my favorites is when you are sitting on the desk and I am in the chair."

Her breath caught and he tugged on her braid enough to make sure she still listened.

"I slide your dress up, exposing those incredible thighs to my gaze. Push you back and get between your legs."

Her grip on the pen in her hand tightened to the point he could see white in her knuckles. The pulse beneath his lips skittered.

"Then I spread you wide, move aside that cotton hiding your treasure and put my mouth —"

"Lord Edais," she gasped.

He smiled and kissed her cheek. "Oh, so you know that one and how it ends then? I have many others. Would you like to hear them?"

She nodded even as the words from her mouth contradicted that.

He didn't take offense, understanding she was still fighting what was obvious to him. They belonged together. "I am happy to share them if you want to hear. Better yet, I will show them to you."

"We have to work, my lord."

Turning her head so they were eye to eye, he stared at her. Phillip loved the flush to her skin, and it didn't hurt to know it was there because of him. This woman was going to be magnificent when he got to make love to her. He couldn't wait to see how flushed she got.

"One kiss, Fyre."

"Were you not just kissing my neck?"

"I was sampling."

She laughed and tried to stop but he took possession of her mouth, eating her joy. Stiff one second, the next, Fyre melted into him. Alarms went off in his head but he couldn't focus on them because everything he had paid attention to the woman he was kissing.

The subtle shifts she made, getting closer. The way she whimpered when his tongue thrust deep. How she mewled in disappointment when he withdrew. And how she purred when he nipped her lower lip.

Nothing else mattered. He closed his hand around her neck, holding her there as he upped the intensity of the kiss. He slid his left hand around her side and cupped it over one breast.

Her gasp shattered him.

The air in the room shifted and he pulled himself back under control. Tweaking her nipple, he released her breast and flattened one hand on the desktop, his other still around her neck. Another nip to her lower lip and he drew back just enough to see her hazy eyes refocus.

"One taste will never be enough of you, Fyre." He tightened his hold on her neck and loved the flare of passion in her eyes. "We have work to do, or your bodyguard will drag me off you."

"Damon?"

He narrowed his eyes. Another fast kiss and he shook his head. "No other man's name leaves your mouth when we are kissing or doing things."

"That does not even hold any logic—"

He kissed her quiet. "Ever."

"Has anyone told you that you are a very demanding man?"

He smirked and cupped her cheek. "Yes. But with you, I'm *possessive.*"

"How is that fair? You can be possessive, but if I see you with Miss Asherford or whomever, I have to just walk by."

He put them nose to nose, pride thrumming through him. "Are you saying you want to be possessive as well?" Phillip barely breathed as he waited for her response.

"Yes." She swallowed. "I want to be allowed to be possessive as well."

"With?" God, his heart pounded as he waited for words he so desperately longed to hear.

He watched her thick, curved lashes lower, pause, then lift, allowing him to see her eyes again.

"With you."

"Then be fucking possessive." Breathing had become a serious chore. He stood straight and stepped back. "You want me, Fyre. Come get me."

Phillip's words echoed in her ears and her heart. Beyond him, at the door, she saw Damon standing there. She liked the man and had invited him into her place a few times to eat something. She felt bad he had to watch over her.

Damon gave her a small nod and she put her attention back on the man standing out of her reach. Phillip Vallence, Earl of Edais. Allowing her gaze to move over him as she sat in the chair, she took stock.

Lean muscles that had begun to bulk up as he worked on the plantation. His sandy brown hair now hit his shoulders and sometimes he wore it back in a queue, which just made her want to pull the tie free and sink her fingers into it. Then his eyes, those gray orbs that saw so much.

"*Come get me.*"

Was she brave enough to go after what she wanted?
Yes.

Fyre got to her feet and watched as he licked his lips but didn't move. She wanted him to hold her. Wanted his arms around her, his strong, warm hand around her neck, anchoring them together.

One foot in front of the other brought her to stand before him. She tipped her head back to stare up at him. He watched her with unerring honesty, not hiding his emotions. He was waiting for her to make the decision.

With one hand, she reached out, but she hesitated before actually laying her hand on him. What was she doing?

He is an earl.

She read it in his gaze—he wasn't going to eliminate the distance between them. The choice had to be hers.

And in that moment, she made it. Closed the rest of the space between them and placed her hands on his chest. She curled her fingers in the soft material of his shirt before releasing him and sliding her hands higher.

When they got to the collar of his shirt, she grasped again and pulled—down this time, on him and the shirt—as she rose up on her toes. He bent and met her part way.

Her world exploded again as he kissed her. Or she kissed him. Either way, all she knew at that moment was his touch, smell, and presence. Phillip wrapped his arms around her, lifting her off the floor as he moved them backward.

His kiss was ravenous. As was hers.

More.

The single word pumped through her veins, intermingling with the raw need that flowed. She tugged his hair tie free and moaned into his mouth as his silken strands fell over her skin.

"You chose me," he rumbled against her lips. "You are mine, Fyre. Mine." The bump of the wall behind her came as a shock and she gasped. He paused and looked down at her. "I did not think you would come get me."

"How could I not? I have wanted you since I first saw you."

He framed her face with his hands, even the rough skin there, making her feel protected.

"In the shop?"

She shook her head. "That was not the first time, I had seen you many times before."

He gave her a mock frown. "You were spying on me?"

"No, I was avoiding you."

"Why?" His hand graced her neck and gripped again. She breathed more easily.

"I was not supposed to be doing my brother's work. Especially without your permission. So I tried to make sure I was leaving whenever you were there."

"And now?"

Emboldened, she pushed up again and nipped his bottom lip. "Now I have claimed you."

With their foreheads touching, she just stayed that way for a few moments, getting hold of her ragged breathing. Pleased that he appeared to have the same difficulty as she in accomplishing that.

"You have claimed me, Fyre. Of that, there is no doubt. And God, I want you so much my dick hurts. But I will not push you. We have work to do."

She nodded, not wanting to lose his strength. "You have to move, my lord. You have me against the wall."

His chuckle was decadent. "Not how I *want* to have you against the wall." A deep breath. "Behave."

She blinked up at him. "What did I do?"

He squeezed her throat briefly before releasing her. "You are tempting me."

"I would apologize, my lord, but I do not think you would believe me."

"I would not. You are correct."

She let him lead the way back to the desk and she didn't say a word when it was his larger desk he took them to. She sat and he carried her things to her. Fyre glanced at the doorway to find Damon had stepped from the room, but she could see his shadow out there.

"What?"

Phillip sat beside her, making sure their legs touched.

"How much longer will you insist on Damon following me? Him and his brothers?"

"Until you are safe. And how did you know he had brothers?"

"I see a lot more than people think I do."

"I know you do, Fyre." He pushed the plate of food in her direction. "Eat. We have work, then we have to talk about our picnic."

Fuzzy feelings streamed through her. "Picnic?"

"Yes. I want to take you on a picnic."

Oh, how she wanted that too. Her stomach clenched, however, at the thought of her brother stumbling upon them.

Phillip covered her hand with his and gave it a gentle squeeze. "You are safe with me, Fyre." He tipped her head so he could look her in the eye. "Tell me you know this."

"I know."

His smile was sad when he bent closer and gave her a tender kiss. "I cannot wait until you mean that."

Flushing, she pulled back from him and turned her attention to the books she needed to look at. Instantly, she frowned, cocked her head and skimmed over the latest entries once more.

"What is it?"

She tapped the third line down on that page. "From here down, this is not my writing. I did not make these notations."

"What?" His roar shook the space between them.

Fyre didn't flinch. She wasn't scared. At least, not this time.

He shoved away from the desk and went to the door. Meanwhile, Fyre reached over the desk and grabbed another of his books. The same thing—there were discrepancies.

"Well?"

She glanced up at his growl. He stood there with Keating, both men scowling.

"Well what, my lord?"

Thankfully she had enough sense to address him properly when there were others in the room.

"What about the other books?"

"Same thing, my lord. Looks as if the changing began after last week's entries were made."

"Why was there no mention of this when you were here last time?"

"These changes were done since I was here last, my lord. On all the books, the dates they started the changes are around the same time, but if you check each book"—she slid one toward him—"you can see there is a page that was cut out. This is why the writing is close to mine, they had some practice and came in to fill it best they could."

Fyre figured they had to practice on the actual ledger to make sure they could get the right look on the different paper.

"Keating?"

"No one has been in your study, my lord. Not other than you and Miss Gwen."

"So no one has come in to clean?" Phillip lifted an eyebrow.

"Of course they have *cleaned*, my lord."

"Then there have been others in here. I am not saying it was a staff member, but I am saying more people than myself and Miss Gwen have been in here. It was not either of us who cut out a page or tried to copy her handwriting back into the books."

"As you say, my lord."

Fyre bit her tongue when all she wanted to do was yell that she was innocent. It appeared that Phillip was on her side, believing her, but she *was* the outsider when it came to Phillip and his staff.

"Gather the staff, Keating. I want to speak to everyone about this. Come get me the moment they are gathered. I do not care what they are doing."

The butler nodded and slipped out.

Fyre shook her head and started to get up from the chair. She had no desire to sit through this and subject herself to what was coming.

"No, no, love. You are not running. I know you did not do this. But someone is trying to set you up and make me believe you did. Can you tell what they got information wise? I know Elonne had mentioned that people were snooping and that is what I believe this is. Someone trying to find out things about my businesses.

And trying to set you up to make it look as if you are not capable of doing your job."

She wanted to throw up what she'd eaten earlier. Fyre wanted to be anywhere but here. "You think you know who it is."

He grinned at her and dragged his finger along her cheek.

"I think it is your wannabe boyfriend. If I fire you, he has more access to getting what he wants. You." His gray eyes grew tumultuous. "And he has another think coming if he believes his prank is going to drive a wedge between us." He captured her chin and took possession of her mouth. "I am *not* letting you go."

The dance her stomach did was just as intense as it had been the first time, yet she wasn't avoiding it or pretending it didn't exist. Her lips followed him as he started to move away, demanding more. And he gave it to her with a low growl.

She curved her fingers into the papers on the desk, uncovering the courage to take what she wanted, and she knew this was a man she would fight for.

Chapter Fourteen

Phillip was not in a good mood. He still wasn't sure who it was that was trying to steal his information. Sure, he had a thought. Albie Caulfield. But he had no proof.

Yet.

After speaking with his staff, he laid the situation out. If the perpetrator was one of them and they came clean now, he would show clemency. If he found out after he left the room they were a participant, he would do his worst to them *and* their family.

Kolby was in his back office with him, leaning against the wall while Phillip paced. This room had been the one that his friend Trace's woman had been held prisoner in. One of the first things he had done when the ownership had become his was tear out one of the walls and turn it into a room with windows and light.

He couldn't repair what had happened here, but he was able to do his best to be better going forward. He made sure there were no more slaves on his land and that the men and women who worked for him were paid a decent wage. Already the act had put him on the outs with some other plantation owners both on this and the surrounding islands. But he didn't care.

Even before he'd met Fyre, he wouldn't have been able to own a person. A woman he loved and respected, Lucien's wife, looked like those who had been enslaved here, and he never would have been able to look her in the eye again if he'd owned anyone. Let alone himself. Ciara was a special woman and he would never disrespect her.

"What about using a new set of books and setting a trap?" Kolby's low voice wound around him.

He paused by the window that looked out over a large field of tall green grasses. The very field he would cross when it came time to take his woman on their picnic. "If they are smart like we feel they are, they would be suspicious to see just a single page of numbers. Especially if they were just thrown down."

"No, I mean a second copy of the books. Start making another set and when they are ready, you keep the correct set with you and set up the others as a lure."

It would be a lot of work, but Kolby made sense.

"And are you offering up your services to keep an eye out here as well as watching my woman?"

"Yes."

The agreement came with little hesitation.

He narrowed his eyes on Kolby. "You like her."

The man straightened, looking far more dangerous than he had seconds ago, even if he still remained with his hands in his pockets. "I respect her. Just like I respect the claim you two have on each other. But yes,

I do like her and had I met her first, she is a woman I would have gone after."

"How much time have you spent with her?"

The man flashed a grin and Phillip frowned. He was extremely handsome when he smiled, not that Kolby did a lot of that. At least not around him.

"We eat breakfast together."

Possessiveness rolled through him and he clenched his jaw. "I see."

Kolby shook his head. "Your woman is stubborn, Edais. She gave us a demand. We shared breakfast with her or she would set off to make our jobs harder." One shoulder moved in a laconic way. "She is the little sister we never had. None of us is competition for you."

Damn right.

"She knows all of you and can tell you apart."

"Yes. Even the actual twins. She is never wrong about which is Zander and which is Archer."

"Would you be able to do this during a house party?"

"Watch over the books?"

"I am thinking I have been here a while and I should throw a party. Have people stay over, do things like we did in England. Activities, food, drinking. If the one doing this comes or thinks this would be the opportune time to make a move because of all the people, that will be their mistake."

"In a month or so? We could get a few things set up in your study to be able to keep an eye out."

"Yes, this is going to work. I am going to go track down my woman for our picnic and tell her she is staying for the week of activities as well. But first, we have to copy the books over so whoever is doing this does not become suspicious."

Kolby nodded. "I will update my brothers." Without another word, the man vanished.

Alone in the room, Phillip turned another full circle and walked out. Fyre was in his study and he headed straight there. The moment he spied her, head bent over her work, his heart eased in his chest. The ache there faded and his entire body relaxed.

For a moment, he just waited in the doorway, observing her.

"Ready for the picnic?"

She jumped, put the pen down and looked over at him. "You scared me."

"The proper response is 'Yes, Phillip, I am ready for you to take me away from here and have your wicked way with me.' Or at least, that is the answer I am looking for."

Her gaze sparkled. "Yes, my lord. I am ready for a picnic."

He walked toward her. "Not quite what I said, but thankfully, I hear what I want."

Her smile grew. "Of that I have no doubt."

"Can you ride?"

"I can."

Heat slammed him at the thought of her riding him, hair free and the sun making her skin glow as they enjoyed each other outside. His cock grew hard.

"You are a temptress." He held out his hand. "Come."

It didn't take them long to get horses and be on their way. Phillip didn't go fast, allowing the horses to pick their own speed. Although he had multitudes of questions, he didn't voice them. Just watched Fyre as she took in the beauty of the island.

When the cove came into view, her sharp breath told him all he needed to know. She'd not been there before and she loved it.

They dismounted and tied the horses in the shade. He spread out the blanket and unpacked the food as she walked along the nearly white sands of the cove's beach.

"When did you find this?"

He got up to join her and slipped his arm around her waist as they ambled along. "About a month after I arrived here. I come here when I want to be alone."

"Is that a warning? Are you planning to kill me?"

"With pleasure? Yes." He kissed her, moaning as her taste settled into him once again.

She sank against his body, trusting him to hold her up. Arms tight around her, he had to wrench himself back. "We need to eat."

With her kiss-swollen lips, unfocused eyes, and the way her breath escaped in small, fast pants, he almost forgot all of his plans and took her there on the sand.

"Food."

The cook had fixed them sandwiches and he ate three to her one. After they were done, he turned and put his head in her lap, smiling when she immediately sank her fingers into his hair. Stroking. Petting.

"I have a proposition for you."

She *hmmed* and looked down at him. "What is that?"

"I have a plan to catch the ones doing this to the books, but I am going to need your help to get it ready in time." A shrug. "Actually, Kolby suggested it. Will you help me?"

"Whatever you need."

He picked up her hand and pressed his lips to her palm. "You do not even know what it will be."

"Are you planning on taking advantage of me?"

"Yes."

His admission came fast and without any hesitation. Phillip watched her. She was addicting. To every sense, and some he hadn't been aware of having.

She paused for a moment. Even the touch of her fingers halted, much to his dismay. Without taking his eyes off her, he moved his head into her fingers, providing a silent command to keep petting him.

She listened and started again. Finally she pursed her lips and tipped her head toward him. Her expression, however, hadn't changed.

Hell, he was even finding the furrow between her brows adorable.

"I am not sure I should believe you."

He took her other hand in his and laced their fingers. Bringing their hands to his mouth, he nibbled on the tips of her fingers.

"Believe me." He drew one tip between his lips and swirled his tongue around it. Her grip in his hair tightened and his cock hardened at the sexy mewl that slid free.

"You would not warn someone before taking advantage of them." Her voice was no longer crisp and clear, but faint with passion.

He loved it.

Another slow swipe of his tongue. "For most people you are correct. I would not."

She tugged, trying to free her finger from his mouth. He denied that request.

Her lips twitched. "Most people?"

It was his turn to grin. "You caught me. Only you, Fyre. To hell with anyone else."

"What are you talking about then?"

"I plan on taking *every* advantage I can with you." He kissed each finger. "Kisses. Stolen caresses. I want you so aroused you cannot think straight."

Phillip turned so he lay on his side as opposed to his back, facing the water before them. He knew his willpower wouldn't be strong enough were he facing her core. The desire to taste her was nearly all-consuming.

Fyre had her legs bent to the side, but he settled his hand on her thigh, moving toward her knee.

"What about what you need help with?" Her voice, thready, almost broke the lock of restraint he struggled to retain his iron grip on.

He skimmed his hand down over her knee and back up, wishing he could feel skin. And he told her so.

The responding bite of her nails to his scalp reminded him he wasn't alone in his increasing desire.

"You should not say such things, my lord."

Fuck it. He squeezed her calf before pushing up so they were face to face.

"Would you rather I *show* you what I want to do to you, Fyre?"

She bit her lower lip even as she readjusted her fistful of his hair.

God damn he wanted to suck on that lip for her. "Yes."

His cock nearly exploded.

Had she really just admitted that aloud? Considering the deep, shuddering breath Phillip just took, she believed she had.

Phillip's gray eyes glowed with a hunger she had never seen before. Such raw, stark hunger.

For her.

All for her.

Phillip didn't back off. Part of her had thought he was just teasing, pushing her to see how far he could get. But a line had been crossed and he wasn't playing.

Neither was she.

He pressed her back into the thick blanket beneath them, the silken strands of his hair sliding forward as she released him to place her hands beside her. Phillip was large and warm over her even as he slid an arm around her, guiding her down.

His arms settled on either side of her and the hand that had been on her back now rested on the nape of her neck, his callused fingers wreaking havoc on her senses. His weight was upon her and she instinctively widened her legs, creating more of a cradle for him to settle into.

For the first time in her life, a man wanted her, not for anything other than desire. Eyes locked on her, he dipped his head and placed light, teasing kisses along her cheek, nose and chin. Avoiding her mouth.

She squirmed beneath him. "My lord."

"Phillip, Fyre. Damn you, call me Phillip."

"Kiss me."

"I am. Give me what I want and I will give you what you want."

He was hard against her and she grew wetter. She'd not been with a man but she knew about it, she had seen people doing it and heard others. Until Phillip it hadn't been of interest to her.

She rocked against him with a needy whimper. The low growl that she got in return let her know he wasn't as strong about resisting her as he was pretending to be. She gasped as his hand settled upon her thigh, *under* her skirts. His grip was firm and sure.

Phillip lifted her leg up higher on his waist, allowing their lower bodies to align better. This time when the move came, he was the one rocking into her.

"Christ, Fyre. You are going to be the death of me." His lips continued to nibble along her skin like she was a delicacy. His favorite.

Emboldened and wanting this freedom, now, with *this* man, she stopped gripping his shoulders and sank her fingers back into his hair. The move arched her back, pushing her chest deeper into him.

"Phillip."

Her admission of his name wasn't loud, but by the way his eyes darkened further, she knew he'd heard her just fine. His mouth covered hers and he gave her the kiss she so desperately wanted from him. Heated. Passionate. Tongues tangling and their cores grinding against each other.

She rocked harder against him, seeking something just out of her reach. The low rumbles that fell from him encouraged her. Phillip stopped kissing her and put them nose to nose, his grip on her thigh flexing as he moved her higher before letting go and putting his arms on either side of her head.

"Take it, beautiful. Take what you need from me."

She didn't understand. The ache only grew. Fyre shifted again and Phillip's jaw clenched as he moved against her.

Yes! That.

"Phillip..." Her voice had risen and his name fell from her lips as she sought an octave one level higher.

"Do you trust me?"

She yanked on his hair. "Yes."

His hand was between them, not under her skirts like it had been upon her leg, but over them. He cupped her, replacing the hardness she'd been rubbing against. Her whimper of disappointment was short-lived as he began moving his hand.

Pleasure spiked through her and she wouldn't have been able to stop her hips from grinding back if she'd had to. He pulled the reaction from her, tapping into some intrinsically instinctive action. Her moans poured from her, breathing coming faster, more jaggedly.

Phillip pressed hard against her and she splintered, crying out his name in a sharp, short cry of raw pleasure. Shock at how good that felt kept her off balance.

The man wrapped her tight as she came down from the shuddering high he'd given her and laid them down on the blanket, one of his thick legs between hers. She was encased by him and she had no wish to be anywhere else.

"You are going to kill me, Fyre. I cannot wait to do this without our clothes on and using my mouth and my cock to make you shudder like you just did."

She melted into him, her own pleasure not fading but rising.

"You," she whispered, the feel of his hardness unable to be ignored. "You would have me do something back?"

His fingers tangled in her hair, making her realize he'd gotten it out of her bun to fall around her shoulders.

"Not today, beautiful. This was for you. I need you to trust me with your body and I am not having our first time out here. It will be inside." A deep kiss. "Where I can take my time learning every curve you have." And another. "Have your taste on my tongue before I share yours with you."

He nuzzled her throat and she whimpered, melting into him, and another wave of pleasure overtook her at his honest words.

"I do trust you."

"I know, but I want it *all* from you, Fyre. I will not lie about this. Nor will I rush what we have just because my cock wants to be inside that tight, hot pussy of yours."

She flushed, grateful he couldn't see her face. His words should embarrass her, make her shocked and possibly offended, but it wasn't even close. They aroused her.

"What now then?"

He chuckled, pulling back to look her in the eyes.

"Round two?" He lifted an eyebrow. "Or, I could tell you what my plan is and you can see if you are still willing to help."

There was a thread of vulnerability in that statement. Fyre held Phillip's assessing gaze without blinking.

The Earl of Edais was a lot more than what he allowed most people to see. And she had fallen for both sides. The cold, seemingly uncaring man who snapped orders and the one who was with her now. The one who put her wants and desires above his own. The man who would forgo his own release because he didn't want to rush her into anything.

Lifting up, she brushed her lips to his. "I already told you, my lord. I will help you. Tell me what you need."

The heat in his eyes nearly scared her. Possessive, proprietary, and all-consuming.

"A few things."

On a deeper level than she'd known possible, joy lit her from the inside. How could this man, an *earl*, be so hesitant to ask for help from her? What did she have?

"You have them."

His chuckle warmed her throughout as he tucked her close. "What if I wanted you to be naked in town?"

"Then I would say I had misunderstood the looks you give me and how possessive you are when you think of someone like Mr. Caulfield looking at me, and that as I was wrong, you are okay with him seeing me completely naked."

A low growl rolled from him and he nipped her neck. "Never."

"That is how I know."

"You sound smug."

"And you should tell me what it is you need."

"When did you get so bossy?"

"A few minutes ago."

He kissed her again, until she lost track of time. When he pulled back, his face was a mask of smugness.

"Much better." He brushed the back of his hand along her cheek. "It has to do with you making a duplicate copy of my books."

She blinked and waited, expression blank.

"I need them soon. I know it is a lot of work and I will pay you extra for the additional hours you will be spending, but I would need them before the end of the week."

Running it over in her mind, she knew it would mean a lot of late nights. But she could and would get it done. For him.

"What else?"

He looked as if he'd expected her to ask about the first thing and was a bit shocked she didn't have more questions about it.

"I will be having a house party in two weeks and I want you there."

"That is not a question."

He narrowed his eyes. "Will you please attend the party?"

"Why me?"

"Besides the fact I want you in my house?"

"Yes. Will I be there to work?"

"No, you will be there as a guest."

Her shock took a bit to fade and she lay there in his arms as he explained his plan.

Chapter Fifteen

Phillip stood at the window of his study and stared out over the grounds he could see. The day was wet. The storm raging through had been over the island for the past two days, almost like it had been moving and decided to stop for a spell.

He had sent out the invitations and had given the books to Fyre to take home. She had been a bit unsure about that, but he trusted that with Damon and his brothers watching out for her, she and the books would be safe. Not necessarily true, but it was the only thing he was able to tell himself to keep from hovering over her like he wanted to.

The downside to all of this was her telling him she would not be able to come to Hawk's Cove and get the books done. So he was not seeing her all week. And that pissed him off. He wanted her where he could watch her. And do other things to and with her. Even though the week was nearly up, he was close to going out of his mind.

Sure, Damon and his brothers were great, but what could he say, he was possessive of the woman who was his but didn't know it yet.

His nights and days were spent dreaming of how she'd come apart in his arms, and that hadn't even been with his fingers inside her. God, she would kill him when they were actually allowed to touch intimately. Without clothing.

He continually flashed to their picnic, where she'd shattered beneath his touch. Her gasp, the arch of her back as she'd come against his hand, the way her eyes had become nearly luminous with her desire and passion.

His body ached for hers. He readjusted himself and continued staring out the pane of glass that had not gotten any warmer throughout the day.

"My lord, you have a visitor."

He had no desire to see anyone if it wasn't Fyre and he knew that wouldn't be the case. Covering up his yawn was harder than he'd thought it would be. But he did, turned, then waved at Keating to bring this person in.

It wasn't who he had expected. He had figured that her brother, Elonne, would be showing up but it wasn't him. It was Albie Caulfield.

The man swaggered in like he was more powerful than everyone believed. Hell, perhaps more than *he* believed, but Phillip wasn't impressed. At all.

Did it help that this man was after the woman he wanted? Nope, just made his disdain worse.

"Mr. Caulfield. Must be something important to get you out on a day like today. To what do I owe the honor?"

Silence stretched as Albie removed his hat and walked to a chair before the desk. Phillip sat after he did, not offering him a drink or anything of the sort. Didn't matter to him that the man was wet from his ride here.

"I have come to return your invitation and to speak to you about another matter." He cleared his throat. "A bit more delicate."

God, he wanted to punch him in his face.

"And where is the invitation?"

"I gave it to your butler. Accepted of course."

"Of course," Phillip replied dryly. "And this other matter?"

He licked his thin lips and shifted on the chair. "It is about Miss Gwen." A bit more shifting. "Have you seen her this week?"

Annoyance unfurled in his gut, stretching its tendrils to hit as much of him as it could. Then grew.

"I hardly think you are in a position to ask who I have seen this week. But to answer your impertinent question, no, I have not."

Anger and something else flashed across Albie's face. "She has said she is unable to add more of her time for me. I did not think you had seen her."

Phillip wanted to lean forward, reach over the desk and throttle this man. He did neither. Going against his body's demand, he leaned back in his chair and steepled his fingers like he was bored. In truth, it was the only way he could keep from leaving Albie Caulfield a bloody pulp.

"Just because I do not see her, does not mean she has not shown to do her work. Mr. Caulfield, your obsession with my employee has passed the line of being a nuisance."

Caulfield narrowed his eyes. "She worked for me first."

Phillip waved away that claim. "She is too kindhearted to tell people no, unlike myself. I know that you and her brother are trying to trap her into working only for you. Kind of like you are buying her. She has told both of you no and yet you persist." Now he leaned forward, resting his hands and forearms on the desktop. "She is *my* employee and always has a place here, so when she comes to you and tells you she is no longer doing your books, you will take that and be a gentleman, bowing out of her life."

"You think her brother will approve you getting a hold of her? We all know what members of the peerage think of women and how little respect you have for them."

"This coming from a man who I see with his hands up the skirts of a whore at a pub, all the while professing to care about another?" Phillip shook his head. "My personal relationship with anyone is not your fucking business and you would do well to remember that. And do not forget that yes, I am a member of peerage, and *my* reach is far greater than *yours*."

"Are you threatening me?"

An indolent shrug. "A threat would be for someone who was a worthy opponent. That, Mr. Caulfield, was simply a statement of fact." He got to his feet. "Now, if you will excuse me and see yourself out. I have more things to do for this party to be ready."

Albie also stood. "You are not rescinding your invitation?" Shock and a slight hint of worried suspicion tinged his question.

"No reason to. You, as a businessman and fellow plantation owner, are still welcome to attend. The more delicate matter between us is done. I have told you where I stand on it."

"What if she agrees to my courting her? Will you back off?"

Anger grew wings and flew. "No."

The man blinked a few times, like he hadn't expected that word to leave Phillip's mouth.

"It would be her decision."

"Her decision was made long before I set foot onto this island or you would have married her already." He gestured to the door. "Good day, Mr. Caulfield."

Once he'd departed, Phillip went to the sideboard and poured himself a drink, downed it then poured himself another.

The insufferable ass. Until Fyre told him no in his own personal pursuit of her, he would allow no other a chance. He rubbed the heel of his palm over his aching cock. Day or night, all he had to do was think about her and he was hard.

Finishing his second drink, he glanced out the window once more at the storm raging and was glad that he had given his people the day off so they could be inside and dry.

Glass down, he strode to the door and went to find the woman who was making his party happen. His housekeeper.

This woman had been a godsend to him and was essential in keeping his house running at optimal efficiency. Even Keating didn't challenge her.

She was in her small office and got up from her desk when he knocked on the doorframe.

"Mrs. Alison."

"My lord. How may I be of service?"

Grinning as he walked in, he waved her back to her seat then took one for himself. "I am here to talk about the house party and see what else you need from me." He stretched his legs out. "More staff? What?"

"Everything is fine, my lord."

He leaned forward. "You sure? I am happy to get you more if you need it. I do not want you quitting on me in the middle of this, Mrs. Alison, or your husband to come after me because I am stressing you out."

She flushed, her tanned skin unable to hide the red racing up her cheeks.

"You should not say such things, my lord."

Phillip slumped back in his chair, hand over his chest. "Crushed. All the beautiful women are taken."

She waggled a finger at him. "I see plenty of women who would love to be the mistress of this house for you, and not just for the party."

With a wink, he sat forward. "None of them are you, Mrs. Alison."

He was thrilled she was teasing him back. It had taken him a while to get his people to trust him. To understand he wasn't like the man who had been here before, when Trace had been presumed dead. That wasn't him and that would *never* be him.

But again, trust was a delicate being and he had to earn it. Phillip didn't mind putting in the work. This was *his* place and these were *his* people.

"I have more things to work on once you approve the menu."

He leaned back, shaking his head. "I trust you, Mrs. Alison. You make the menu and approve it. I will also want to do another party this Christmas, but for the staff. All of them. Not a house party, but a celebration for a good year of work."

She paused and put down her pen as she looked at him.

"What is it?" he asked after a few moments.

"If our stations were not so different, my lord, I would kiss you for that."

Eyebrows waggling, he bounded up from his chair and bent down to her, tapping his cheek. "I never turn down a kiss from a beautiful woman. Lay one on me."

* * * *

The knocking startled her, but Fyre had become quite efficient at making sure the earl's books remained out of sight when someone came to the door. Hiding them, she hurried to let whoever was there in. The rain still came down in sheets, blowing in all directions and making her so glad that the small cottage she rented was sound and kept her safe and dry.

The door opened before she could get there and in stumbled her brother, sister-in-law and her nephews and niece. Soaked to the bone.

Swarmed by the children, she didn't mind how wet they were as she had missed them so much. Hugging them, she kissed each of the young ones while she handed out towels as they told her how much she had been missed.

Composing her features, she handed cloths to her brother and his wife. "What are you doing here?"

Elonne didn't meet her gaze and she was hurt yet okay with it. She hadn't forgiven him for his behavior. Not that she was good with Cara either, but she adored her nephews and niece.

"Can we not stop by and see their aunt?" Cara's tone grated on her nerves.

"Of course," she assured the children. "*They* are always welcome in my place."

The adults picked up on her tone. Elonne glowered in her direction but still wouldn't hold her stare. Cara just glared.

"You need to watch them."

Eyebrows up, she waited for her sister-in-law to elaborate on the statement. No one said anything further.

So she prompted, "Why?"

"There is a thing we have to attend tonight but they are too young."

"Have they eaten?"

"No, it is too early. You will feed them."

Fyre narrowed her eyes at Cara, knowing full well the woman was lying through her teeth. It was past the time they should have eaten.

"And are you back for them tonight or do I get them until morning?"

"Morning."

She grinned at the kids, who watched her with uncertain expressions. "Wonderful. We will make a grand time out of it. You two have fun." Just like that, she dismissed them.

It broke her heart how the children weren't sad to see their parents go, but she thrived on how they hugged her.

"Now, let me see, it has been a while since I have seen you. I hope I have not forgotten your names."

They all looked at her, lips pursed as she tapped a finger against her chin.

"Aunt Fyre, surely you remember me. I'm Carlo."

She gripped his chin and angled his head to the side. "Are you sure? I thought you were Elonne II."

He giggled and wrapped his arms around her. "I missed you."

"Missed you too. All of you, you also, Isabella. We need to get dry and after, we will get some food in our bellies."

* * * *

Two hours later, the trio of children were fed and drowsy as the rain continued to pound the windows. As they began to doze, she moved them to her bed and tucked them in, heart aching over their absence from her life.

After she was positive they were out cold, she pulled the two books she was currently working on back to the table. She didn't want to have all of them in the open now in case they woke, she could easily move these to where she was hiding them as opposed to trying to make six books vanish quickly.

She worked diligently until the candle was low in the holder and her eyes burned. Shaking out her hand and the cramping that had started, she closed the books and put them away.

Then she headed for bed and climbed in with the kids, who moved and shifted for her before draping all over her. She woke the same way and the rain still pounded down.

While they continued to sleep she fixed a special breakfast to share with them. They all ate together, sharing stories and memories that made her heart ache. The children helped her clean up—she never let them skip that part, wanting them to grow up knowing how to keep a tidy house.

She kept a sharp eye on the hour .

Where are Elonne and Cara?

She couldn't leave the children alone. Not here. They were notoriously nosy and she didn't want them finding the books by accident. Even if they weren't here in her place, she was nervous about leaving them, given what Phillip had told her of the plan.

Just thinking about him had her lips curling up with pleasurable memories.

"Why are you smiling, Aunt Fyre?"

"Happy to see the three of you," she said without missing a beat. "I miss you all so much."

Opening her arms, she hugged them all.

It was time for her to head to work and they still hadn't arrived to pick up the kids.

Elonne II watched her and cocked his head to the side. "You have to leave." It was a statement.

"I do, yes."

"And we are in the way."

She shook her head right away. "You are children, precious, and never in the way."

"Not what Mom and Dad say."

She froze. Closed her eyes and counted to get control of her emotions. Then she looked at him again.

"Are you underfoot when she says this? Or are they speaking in general?"

Part of her knew it was wrong to pry through the children but she also had no doubt that her sister-in-law would lie through her teeth.

He glanced over at his siblings and shrugged. She got it, he didn't want to speak in front of them.

"Carlo and Bella, can you check the bedroom please and make sure you did not leave anything?"

They dashed off and she focused on her oldest nephew. "What is it you are not telling me?"

"They fight. All the time. I think Mama is sleeping with other men and Papa is always angry."

"I will speak with him. Right now, I have to get to work. I will take you to Mrs. Marta and see if she cannot keep an eye on you three. But you have to be good for her."

"We cannot come with you?"

"No." She softened her refusal with a small smile and shake of her head. "Mr. Larson will not be happy if I have children running around his store while I work."

More and more the thought of taking Phillip up on his offer of only working for him crossed her mind. She was exhausted, and was getting nervous about who else was watching her.

Elonne II's face fell. She cupped his cheeks and kissed his forehead.

"I wish you could."

"What about if you work at Lord Edais'? Would we be okay there?"

"I would have to ask him first. But I am not going there today."

"Could we come with you when you go?"

Suspicion raised its head inside her. Ensuring it didn't show on her face, she shrugged.

"I do not know, sweetie."

"What about for the party?" Carlo posed the question as he and his sister walked out of the back room.

"What party?"

"The one that earl invited all of us to. A house party," Bella said, clapping her hands excitedly.

Her smile didn't slip even though pain lanced her. "I have not gotten an invitation to that, so I do not know what you are talking about." Sure, he had mentioned it, but no invitation had arrived for her and she wasn't going to alert them that he'd told her but didn't send her one. That would lead to nothing but more questions from these three. And to be honest, she was putting all her free time into getting the second set of books completed in time for the party.

Except she did know. He had told her she was doing all these extra hours to get the books ready for this party. She hadn't known, however, that he had invited her brother and his family but not her.

The door flew open and she spun around, putting the kids behind her. Elonne stood there, face angry.

"We have to go."

She glared at him but didn't say a word, just kissed each of the kids and walked with them to the door.

He sent them on the way out the door and stared at her. She didn't back down from his glare. A brief flash of shame filled his expression, but it lasted about as long as a heartbeat.

"You are welcome," she snapped when he began to close the door.

"For what?"

"Watching your kids with no warning it would be needed. And for keeping them even though I will be late to work now."

"They will be here again tonight."

"No."

He blinked and froze. Damn if that fear didn't start to creep back into her.

"No?"

"I no longer live with you, Elonne. I said I would help if I could. I cannot. I have late work tonight with both Mr. Caulfield and Lord Edais. I cannot have the children here. It will be late when I get home. I will not have time to care for them. You and Cara watch them or pay someone else to do it." She shooed him out the door and closed it after her. "I have to get to work."

Waving to the kids as she walked briskly away, she wondered if they would be there when she got home that night.

Chapter Sixteen

He was becoming a stalker.

No other way to state it. Phillip accepted he had officially begun stalking the woman who occupied all his focus.

Gwen "Fyre" Parker.

Which made the *was becoming* a *had become*.

These days without seeing her at his place had become hell. To alleviate that, he had gone into town and hung around just to catch a glimpse of her. She was a drug to his system and it craved more.

So much more.

He walked back into his house in a foul mood, having seen her walk into Mr. Caulfield's business. His one consolation was that she still wouldn't go out to Caulfield's home to do the books like she would for him.

Still didn't set him at ease. Not even with the fact that Damon and his brothers were there to protect her.

Moody, he worked, ate, and sat slumped behind his desk as the day began to end when Keating knocked on the door.

"What?" He frowned at his butler. "Did I not say I wanted to be left alone?"

"Miss Gwen is here to see you, my lord. She was hoping you had a moment."

Fire licked his blood and his cock jumped to attention. "Send her in."

God, he hoped he sounded like an earl and not a boy about to get his first woman. He would bet his entire estate that Keating smirked knowingly before he nodded and backed out of the room.

Moments later she was in the room. He stayed seated, aware his hardness would be visible if he stood.

"Miss Gwen."

"Thank you, Keating," she said with a smile. "I appreciate you seeing me without any notice, my lord." A small curtsey.

His butler was gone and seeing the door close behind him was all the prompting Phillip needed. He was up from his seat and striding over the floor to where she stood, holding a bag by her side.

The fact she was wet from the rain that still hadn't let up didn't deter him in the slightest. Phillip reached her and wrapped his arms around her, drawing her flush to him as he conquered her mouth.

The first swipe of his tongue along her lips and she parted them with a cock-swelling moan.

One hand drifting to the curve of her ass, he sank the other into the hair at the nape of her neck, beneath the bun that had come undone slightly. A wriggle of his hand and it was down, sending her damp hair cascading around his hand as it tumbled.

A thump as her bag hit the floor, then her arms were around him as well, anchoring them tight. Pressing her full breasts into him. She matched him stroke for stroke and he growled as her taste was reintroduced to his system.

Turning them, he backed her to the desk and lifted her to sit on the edge while he pushed his way between her legs, digging his erection into her softness. Her whimpers were going to kill him.

"Fuck, Fyre. What I want to do to you." His words were growled along her lips as he held her gaze, smirking at how hazy her eyes were with pleasure. "Hi."

Her full lips curled up. "Hello."

Another fleeting kiss. "Phillip. For fuck's sake, call me Phillip."

"Hello" — a pause — "Phillip."

"I love the sound of my name rolling off your lips, Fyre." He flexed his hips and captured her resulting moan in his mouth again.

"I did not come here for this," she panted when he allowed her up for air.

"What did you come through the rain for?"

He skimmed his hands up and down her sides, swiping his thumbs along the outsides of her breasts as they passed.

"Books," she gasped, her body arching closer to his.

"Books?"

He slid a hand beneath her dress and smoothed it up the outside of her leg.

"Oh!" She shifted on the desk. "You should not be doing that."

"What books, Fyre?" He wasn't going to let her think much about the reasons this shouldn't happen between them.

"Yours. I...I finished the copies."

"So fast?"

"I did not want to keep them longer than necessary."

"You could have brought them to the party." God, the top of her thigh was so fucking smooth, he wanted to taste her skin here. "I cannot wait until you let me lick you from head to toe."

She trembled in his arms and he inched his hand along her thigh to the inside.

"I am not coming to the party."

"You are."

"I did not receive an invitation."

That was jealousy and hurt in her tone. He stopped his hand scant millimeters from her core and lifted his head to hold her gaze.

"I will have them write one for you, Fyre. I thought you knew how much I wanted you there when I asked you on the picnic. You know, as I touched you through your skirts."

Her hands gripped him tighter. "You are under them now."

He grinned. "Yes, yes I sure as hell am." He dragged a finger along her outer lips, eyes focused on her expression.

Phillip shifted his left hand to resettle it against the nape of her neck. He continued to tease between her legs. Light touches on lips that grew wetter as he continued the strokes.

Holding her gaze, he watched myriad emotions dance over her features.

"I thought you only said the words."

He frowned.

"And what, I only said it to get your assistance to fix the books?"

She shrugged.

Phillip dragged his finger between her pussy lips. "I want you at the party." He circled her clit. Hot, slick and hell on his control.

He focused his eyes on her face, noting every nuance. "Make no mistake about it." Another brush of his fingers. "That is the reason I am throwing the damn thing. Why I invited people I do not really want to know."

She opened her mouth but he kissed her to keep her silent.

"Let me finish." A plea? Most likely.

Phillip pushed one finger into her wet heat, his cock throbbing and uncomfortable.

"Fuck, you are tight, baby." Her legs fell open, allowing him even more access, and it took everything he had to not take more advantage.

"I invited your family, other business owners, even Mr. Caulfield. One reason. I want *you* under *my* roof." Finding out the one screwing with him and her about his books had suddenly become secondary.

Fyre whimpered, pressing closer. His finger dipped deeper and he was so ready to experience her channel around his dick.

"And if that is what it takes to accomplish that, then so be it."

Lowering his mouth to the spot where her neck and shoulder met, he inhaled. Her scent was unlike anyone else's, and he would always recognize it.

Another whimper left her.

"I promise, baby, I will take you there, but I want to make sure you understand I want you to come. I have a room I think you will like."

"I understand." She moved against him. "Phillip, please."

His name.

Her lips.

Pure fucking heaven.

Pumping his finger slowly within her, he smiled into her skin.

"You aching for me like I do you?"

"Yes."

A single response, breathy and needy. He had to know.

"Since our picnic, have you touched yourself like this?"

Her hips rocked faster.

He pulled back to take a look at her face.

Dark skin flushed with need.

"Baby?" Thumb on her clit, he continued the slow pump.

"Yes."

He heaved a sharp breath. "God, I want to watch you do that."

She grasped his wrist, grip hard and tight. "Phillip!"

"Tell me yes."

He didn't know why he was dragging this out, he wanted her to shatter for him, allowing him to feel it this time.

She put her gaze on him and swiped her tongue over her lower lip.

"Only if you let me watch you, too." He jerked at her words, his fingers thrusting and pushing her over the edge.

Because of her words and how perfect her pussy felt rippling around his finger, he came in his breeches.

Hard.

* * * *

The warm pan of bread wobbled in her hand as the knock on her door startled her.

"Coming." Setting it on the counter, she placed the towel over one shoulder and went to the door.

Her brother, Cara and the kids stood there. It had been a few days since they were there last and she'd not expected to see them until the party at Hawk's Cove.

"Aunt Fyre!" The unanimous cry from her favorite trio in the world had her smiling.

She hugged them, then stepped back to let them all into her place.

"This is a surprise." The grin the children had pulled from her faded as she faced her brother and his wife. Her brother had a hard time meeting her gaze. She waited.

"We need some money."

Four words blurted out from her brother that were both a surprise and yet not.

"How much?"

Her response shocked them, and she knew this when they shared a "You are not going to ask why? Or how it happened?" look.

"I would assume it has to do with the fact you still spend money like you have three-quarters of my pay to use." A pointed look. "You do not." Fyre didn't even try to hide her irritation.

"You owe us." Cara's tone rubbed her wrong and she didn't even look back at her.

Elonne shushed his wife. "Things are tight."

"Maybe Cara should get a job."

He frowned. "I provide for my wife and family."

Refusing to back down, Fyre crossed her arms. "Yet here you stand before your sister asking her for money."

"We housed you."

"Yes, Elonne, you did. Do not pretend it was all because you loved me. I had to work and hand over most of my money. Plus cook and clean as I took care of your children. I was a housekeeper who had to give my money away. Your money problems are just that, yours. They are not mine. This is a one-time thing."

"Who do you think you are, talking to me like this?"

Tears burned her eyes. "Your sister. Not a servant and not a *slave*."

"We took you in." Cara's voice grated against her hypersensitive feelings.

"And I paid for it." She looked at her brother. "Tell me how much and to whom."

The price he gave made her legs weak, and not in a good way like when Phillip did.

"Just give him the money." Cara crossed her arms.

"No, because he would give it to you."

"I am his wife."

She ignored Cara. "Elonne, leave the amount and to whom by the door when you leave. I will not do this again." Wiping her hands off on her towel, she sighed. "You can always pick up more work with Mr. Caulfield."

His gaze sharpened. "What did you do?"

"I no longer work for him."

Elonne growled and stepped closer. "I told you to work for him."

"You also told me to stay away from him because he wanted me for something else." An indignant sniff.

"Just because you want me to marry him to help you makes no difference. I will not marry him."

"I am the man of the family—"

"Then tend to *your* family and stop having to come to the disappointment of the family for help."

"Aunt Fyre."

Ashamed she had let her emotions get the better of her with the kids in earshot, she smiled and turned to Carlo.

"Yes?"

"Does this mean you will not be at Lord Edais' party?"

"I will be there. My note came yesterday." She made sure to give each child affectionate touches as she went back to her kitchen. "Have a great day and please close the door on your way out."

She remained facing the oven as what had been her only family left. Refusing to let the tears fall, she got back to enjoying her day off.

After a light lunch the rain picked up once more. Settling down in her chair, she began to work on her sewing.

* * * *

There were no visits to see Phillip until the following week. Her disappointment was huge when he wasn't there but out on his property, and she found it was a struggle to keep her emotions under control.

Despite having more accounts of Phillip's to keep track of with his newest ventures, the work did not take her that long. Immediately after she finished, Fyre gathered her things to leave Hawk's Cove to head home.

Keating appeared as she closed the door to the office behind her.

"Miss Gwen."

"Have a nice evening, Keating."

"He would want you to stay."

"And that is hard for you to say."

He gave a small frown, to which she gave a very unwomanly snort.

"Worry not. You can tell Lord Edais you offered as he instructed, but I declined."

She walked away, not bothering to look back. Thunder rumbled as the rain picked up. Only allowing herself one sigh, she stepped out on the porch then down the steps into the deluge.

* * * *

Before Fyre was even halfway home a carriage came up from behind her. One horse, wet and decidedly unhappy, pulled the covered ride. Fyre couldn't get any farther off the road without being in the ditch and the water it was collecting. She had no desire to be in there. There had been times in the past she had been run off the road by someone on horseback or driving a coach. She really hoped this wasn't going to be one of those times.

This one stopped. Well, slowed enough to keep pace with her.

Nerves kicked up for an entirely new reason. She kept her narrowed gaze on the road ahead of her.

"Miss Gwen."

She wiped off the water that streamed down her face and squinted up at the man in the lantern's flickering light.

Archer.

"Why are you out here?" She pitched her voice over the wind and rain.

"Taking you home." He shook his head to — she assumed — stop her instinctive refusal. "I will put you in here if I must, Miss Gwen."

Taking him at his word, she scrambled up as fast and as best she could, her wet skirts, combined with the mud on them, not making it easy. She landed on the seat beside him with a grunt.

That was not ladylike.

Archer didn't comment on it and, as soon as she had regained her seat, he snapped the wet leathers and got them moving again.

Exhaustion set in and her teeth began chattering, even though it wasn't all that cold. As if he knew, he asked the horse for a bit more speed, even while making sure to keep them as safe as he could.

She could barely keep her eyes open by the time he stopped before her house.

"Thank you, Archer."

"I like you, Miss Gwen. I would hate for you to get sick or injured. Get some sleep but make sure you dry off first and have some tea."

She paused in disembarking from the coach. "Tea?"

"My mother was an herbalist. She always gave us tea on nights when we were out in the elements."

"Sounds like she was a smart woman."

"Never let us forget it either. Go on. I will wait until I see a light on inside."

She hurried off, knowing he wasn't lying and not wanting him out in the bad weather longer than he had to be. Where he and his brothers were staying while they kept an eye on her, she didn't know.

Once inside, she swiftly lit a candle and opened the door once more to make sure he could see. The flame flickered and bent in the howling winds, making her trip out there short. Heaving a sigh once she shut the door again, she made short work of stripping off her soaked clothing and drying off before sliding on warm, clean clothing.

She heeded his advice and took the time to fix herself a cup of tea. Seated in her chair, she enjoyed the heated brew while she relaxed and did a bit of sewing as well, determined to finish the quilt she was working on.

Spreading it out on the back of her small couch, she ran her critical eye over it, thinking of the other colors to add in order to make it worthy of the person it was going to be given to.

Chapter Seventeen

Phillip walked down the steps to greet the guests who had arrived. The day was beautiful and people had been arriving all day. Not the woman he was waiting for with bated breath, but others. Smile firmly in place, he finished navigating the final few steps to meet Mr. Caulfield.

The man looked at him, expression still a bit unsure and suspicious.

"Afternoon, Mr. Caulfield. I am glad you were able to make it."

They shook hands then Phillip pushed his deep into his pockets as he watched his guest.

"I appreciate the invitation. Must say, I was surprised that it came."

Phillip shrugged like it didn't make one bit of difference to him. "I thought it a good idea to meet the other business owners and plantation owners in the area." He gestured with a hand. "All of that will be mentioned at the evening meal. Get settled in and, if you would like, there will be drinks in two hours in my library. I have some other guests to greet."

With a nod, Phillip walked off, feeling incredibly smug that he hadn't actually punched the bastard in the face. It burned to know that man would be under the same roof as his Fyre. The only thing making it bearable was that the woman in question would be under *his* roof and not somewhere else.

Especially with that asshole around.

He stepped outside and moved around the terrace, looking out over his fields. The sound of children laughing gave him a moment's pause before he walked to the end of the porch and stared in that direction.

Fyre's nephews and niece were out running in the open space, laughing and making up games. There was a ball, but it had been left behind and they were engaged in what looked to be a rousing game of tag.

He leaned against the corner pillar and watched them enjoy being outside. Eventually they coaxed Mr. Tennemin's children into the game as well. Mr. Tennemin was a plantation owner from a nearby island. One of the farthest ones away.

And he is here before Fyre.

Deep in his gut, Phillip would admit, he was scared Fyre would not come to the party. He squashed that because she had told him she would be there and his woman did not lie to him.

"My lord."

"Keating." He didn't turn away from the playing children. In a way, they reminded him of Lucien's and Rafe's children, playing as they did.

"Everyone has arrived with the exception of Miss Gwen." The man cleared his throat. "I was thinking I could send a footman with a carriage to see if she needed a ride."

That got him to turn. He smiled at his butler, who stood there as if he were carved from stone. "You do care about her, Keating. This proves it."

The man sniffed. "She is late and we have a schedule, my lord. That is all."

Wiping the grin from his face, he nodded. "Of course, my mistake I am sure." He pushed his hands into his pockets again. "Send a carriage."

"Very good, my lord."

Understanding hit him. "You already sent one, Keating, and this is your way of telling me I should have sent one sooner."

"Far be it from me to argue with you, my lord." The man walked away, leaving him alone with his need to laugh.

He could admit that he felt much better knowing a carriage was on the way to bring her here. He didn't want to think about the fact her brother had arrived without her.

* * * *

She still had not arrived by the time they had the evening meal, and Phillip had become beyond worried. At the head of the table, he looked out at those gathered. People of all skin colors and backgrounds who had one thing in common now. They owned businesses. His initial guess of ten people had nearly doubled. Even with the women who had married the businessmen away from the table, there were still females there.

He knew his staff would be run ragged and for that reason, he would be offering them a bonus.

"I want to thank you all for coming. I only have one goal to come from this week of getting to know the others who own businesses in the area and on surrounding islands. I want to look into coming to one another for supplies instead of paying some of the larger companies that charge more. If we are able to help one another out we can not only increase our own profits but also make a stamp on the world by showing our products to be superior."

Mr. Tennemin leaned forward. "Then the rumor you were looking to buy us out is not true?"

"Buy you out? Mr. Tennemin, I have enough work right now, thank you. I want us to form almost a coalition. That would mean we look out for one another. If we see something we know could help a fellow owner, we let them know. If we are moving a small or even a partial shipment, reach out and see if another has something ready to ship in order to help share the cost, instead of paying for a full load when we are not using all the space."

Phillip set down his fork and took a drink from his glass. "If you look around, you will see that everyone around the table has one main thing they are known for. Sure, some of us have secondary items as well, but obviously there is *one* thing that works the best for us, because that is what we move mostly. I have been looking at the numbers and it hurts to see how much money is just tossed away because we are too proud, or arrogant, or whatever reason for not being willing to work together."

There were some murmurs but no one argued outright.

"I am not sitting up here saying you have to do this or I will kick you out of the events that are happening this week. I only ask that you think about it. I have some time set aside for us to discuss it, otherwise there will be a slew of other activities going on. I will say this, though." He paused while everyone looked up the table to him. "I will *not* work with people who still use slaves and refuse to pay their workers a salary. So if that is your belief then please, feel free to get up and leave right now."

The room was quiet until Mr. Caulfield spoke almost cautiously, like he expected to be tossed out for speaking. "I notice not all of the people on the island are here. Is this something we are trying to keep from them?"

"Not at all. I will be reaching out to the others. But I wanted to start smaller to see if this was something that could get going. Then once it is set, we bring in more."

He looked around the room at them all, noticing how most nodded at him. Even Elonne seemed like he was on board.

"And the women?"

Phillip glanced over to Mrs. Chari and gave her a smile. "You are a business owner. I want you here." He pushed his plate to the side, giving the footman who picked it up a slight nod. "Waiting for things to arrive from England and other places can be unpredictable. And expensive. When we order something and it gets here, there are times that the price has nearly doubled."

Everyone nodded in agreement about that. The problem was this was something that was happening more and more often, so the people of the island weren't able to get all the items they had requested without spending nearly double what they had expected to spend.

This was his home and these were becoming his people. He wanted to protect them. And himself.

"How would it work?" Mr. Larson posed the question.

"I do not see anything changing other than we go to one another first. Like if I need building materials, I go to Mr. Oler and see what he can provide for me instead of putting in a huge order to England and waiting for months to get the items at a higher rate because of the distance."

Mr. Caulfield nodded. "And if I had a crop ready to ship out and had the passage booked, but because I am a smaller plantation and won't take up all the cargo space I see if, say, Mr. Tennemin had a shipment ready to go and then we split the cost of the ship."

Phillip leaned back in his chair with a grunt. He may not like the man but Caulfield was getting the point of this. "Exactly. Needs will still be met, but we will no longer be working against one another. Mr. Caulfield and Mr. Tennemin do not sell the same thing. Again, they are not, nor should they consider they are, working against each other."

Small murmurs of discussion broke out as those gathered talked about and mulled over what he had proposed. Pushing away from the table, Phillip gave them all a nod.

"That is the main reason for us gathering here, but it is also to get to know one another better. There will be drinks served in the sitting room in about an hour. I have a few things to attend to but I will see you there."

He walked out and immediately found Keating's sharp gaze. The man gave him a slight negative head shake and his gut dropped.

Where was she?

* * * *

Fyre wrung her hands together as the footman pulled down her two pieces of luggage and placed them on the ground. It was late. Too late for her to be arriving at the earl's estate for a party. Darkness had already settled across the island.

Davie paused beside her as the carriage rolled away. "Miss Gwen?"

"It is late. I should not have come."

"Nonsense. He has been worried about you. Your room is ready."

Two other footmen came down and picked up her bags, leading the way to the door. She followed, paced by Davie. Unease was a tumultuous storm in her gut. She tried desperately not to think about Davie's proclamation that Phillip had been worried about her.

I have to stop all this fancy in my head. He is an earl, and not for the likes of me.

Keating's was the first face she saw when she stepped through the door. His cool gaze brushed over her before he inclined his head.

"Miss Gwen."

"Mr. Keating. I apologize for my late arrival."

"You are a guest, Miss Gwen. Your apology is not necessary."

She forced a smile to her face. "Either way, it means you and more of your staff have to go out of your way to accommodate me and I do apologize."

A maid arrived and Keating gestured to the stairs. "Please show Miss Gwen to her room."

"Right this way, miss."

Her smile to Davie was not the least bit faked. "Thank you, Davie."

His cheeks flushed. "It was my pleasure, Miss Gwen."

She lifted her skirt and hurried up to the second floor after the maid. The young woman didn't speak, just walked to a door off to the left and opened it. Peering inside, Fyre noted her bags had already been taken up.

"Would you like me to put away your things, miss?"

Fyre didn't realize that the maid was asking her, for a moment. She blinked and shook her head. "No, thank you. I will do it in the morning. I think I have kept enough people in the house awake. Thank you."

"Abbie, miss. If you need anything just pull the cord and I will come right away."

"Thank you, Abbie. I will be fine tonight. Could you make sure I am up by six please?"

"Of course."

Fyre knew she should wake by then but wasn't positive her body wouldn't protest the early wakeup. She did not want to be the last one to anything.

After assuring Abbie that she would be fine getting ready for sleep on her own, she got the girl on her way. Washing up, she swiftly changed and crawled between the crisp sheets of the bed. Never had she been on anything so soft.

Getting up in the morning would be difficult for sure.

Eyes closing, she drifted off into a dream world that she didn't want to retreat from.

* * * *

As she'd requested, Abbie was there to wake her in the morning.

Crawling with reluctance from the comfort of the bed, Fyre yawned and stretched.

"Would you like a bath, miss? I can have one brought up."

"It sounds divine. Thank you, Abbie. What about others? Are they up yet?"

She shook her head. "No, miss. Only you and the staff are up right now."

"Thank you."

"I will have it here right away."

True to her word, Abbie had a steaming bath waiting for her within a short time. Once she was alone, she stripped and sank with a moan into the heated water.

Oh, this is heaven.

"Those moans, baby. You are killing me."

She turned with a gasp that morphed into a low groan as Phillip's mouth captured hers, his tongue dipping with familiarity between her lips.

"What are you doing here?"

His hot gaze moved over her as if she weren't beneath the water, hidden from his view.

"I missed you and you got in late. Everything okay?"

"My lord—"

"Phillip." He dragged his hand over her cheek and down her throat.

Nipples tight and the throbbing between her legs picking up its pace, she swallowed back her whimper.

"This is improper."

"Want me to leave?" His lips followed the path his hand had just taken, nipping and laving her skin, leaving her more flushed than she had been.

"No."

"You are such a fucking temptation sitting here. God, I know you are naked and I want to plunge my hand below the water and feel you come apart around me again." His lips were at her ear. "I relive that moment every night when I jerk myself off to the memory of how you bowed your back and cried my name."

Head against the edge of the tub she was in, she watched his face. The raw need there was a thing of beauty.

He pulled back a tiny bit but she felt it. Everywhere.

"Why were you so late?"

"I had to help Mrs. Marta with a few things. I did not think it would matter when I arrived."

"I was worried." He unpinned her hair from where she'd gathered it on her head. He thrust his fingers into the strands and she didn't care about the ends landing in the water.

"I am fine."

He huffed. "I am allowed to worry about my woman." She widened her eyes at his statement and he shook his head. "Are you going to argue with me?" He captured her chin. "Because if you are, we really need to have another discussion."

"You need a woman befitting your station."

"I am looking at her. Right now." He slid his hand under the water and in her periphery, she watched him grip the edge so hard his knuckles paled beneath his tan. His shirt sleeve instantly soaked, molding to the powerful muscles in his arm.

He locked his gaze on hers, refusing to release her. Beneath the water, he skimmed his hand up her thigh and wedged it between her legs. She widened her thighs for him without him saying a word, and gasped as one finger dipped into her heat.

"Oh, Phillip."

The moan tumbled from her lips without thought or care to who may hear it. His lips were there the next second, covering the cry that slid free as he pushed another finger inside her, his wrist pumping with leisurely strokes.

Like it wasn't scandalous for him to be in her room as she sat in a bath. Like no one would say anything if they were discovered with his fingers deep in her pussy, kissing her like he owned her, heart, body, and soul.

Even though he did.

"Fuck, baby. The way you moan my name makes me want to claim you in a way that will make you never want another man."

She had already crossed that threshold.

Pulling his mouth from hers, he kept their foreheads touching. "Tell me you know this, Fyre. You are my woman and I am going to claim you. For all fucking time."

"It is—"

He thrust his fingers deep and her protest gave way to the gasp of pleasure that poured from her.

"Mine," he growled, curving his fingers just so to hit that spot in her that tumbled her over the ledge and into blissful oblivion.

Knock knock.

"Fyre. Open up. It is Elonne."

Panic flared but Phillip didn't even remove his fingers from her slit. No, the infuriating man continued to pump them, waylaying her thoughts.

"One moment, Elonne. I am just getting out of the bath."

"Hurry." His snapped response earned a growl from the man who touched her body with such reverence and hunger.

"You have to stop," she whispered. "And hide."

"Stand up then."

Her eyes grew round. "You are here."

His smile made her toes curl. "I am, and if you do not want Elonne to see us like this, you should probably stand up and get in a robe."

"Phillip, please."

"Fine," he groused, thrusting deep once more before pulling his hand from between her legs. He didn't leave but held the robe for her to step into.

After Phillip planted another mind-blanking kiss on her, she tied the robe's sash and went to the door, opening it to find her brother there and the man who had turned her weak gone from the room behind her.

"We have to talk." Elonne tried to walk into the room.

Fyre countered, "I am not dressed, Elonne. Brother or not, you can do me the courtesy of waiting until I put on my clothing."

He scowled. "You really were bathing?"

She rolled her eyes and swung the door open for him to see the tub. "Yes. Now give me a moment to dress." She closed the door on him and turned back around, hoping that the earl would be there again. He was not.

Chapter Eighteen

Phillip leaned against a tree and watched the women and children enjoying a game of croquet. So much so a few of the husbands had begun venturing over to join in. This was the third day of the party.

He had his staff keeping an eye and an ear out for anything that would be considered discontent among those there. He had made his stance clear and he would not hesitate to toss someone if they were rude to another because of race.

"Good afternoon, Lord Edais."

He glanced to his left and hid his irritation, which never failed to surface the moment he spied Miss Asherford crossing the ground to his side.

Offering her a little bow, he returned, "Miss Asherford."

Her light blue dress was one of the finest here but honestly, it wasn't the dress he cared about. The one he was keeping an eye out for was lavender, and covered the body of a woman he could not stop thinking about.

Last night, after the evening meal, she had joined those gathered in the room and had gone over numbers. A few of those there had been offended at first when they'd discovered she had been there to talk that very thing she was so good at. Until the people she worked for had spoken up on her behalf. Phillip's chest had swelled with pride as he'd watched a roomful of business-minded people, men mostly, who were set in their ways, listen to the woman he would have by his side. Even Caulfield and her brother Elonne had not been able to speak against her.

"Are you not participating in the games?"

She offered him her hand and he took it, assisting her in the final few steps to his side. Then he released her immediately.

"I do not think I am cut out for this game," she said, fingers glancing over her chest.

"Some of the others are inside playing cards. Perhaps that is more your speed."

"Oh, I misspoke. I am not too old to play this, just feel like there are other things I could be doing to work up a sweat. If you catch my meaning."

He'd caught it since he'd met her.

Holding her gaze, he tipped his hat before pushing away from the tree. "I fear you are looking in the wrong place for that. I am not interested, Miss Asherford." He began walking off. "Enjoy your afternoon."

Elonne was out there with his children. He and Mr. Tennemin were talking as the children had abandoned croquet and made up games with their own rules. The adults continued to play with them. He didn't see Cara, but he did see Albie Caulfield.

And Fyre.

They were walking together toward the group, but where they had come from, he wasn't sure. Jealousy ran hot and swift through him.

Caulfield lifted his head and locked gazes with him seconds before he laughed aloud. Others glanced at them, and Phillip had to swallow the growl that threatened to erupt.

"Are you going to play, Lord Edais?"

He glanced down to see one of Mr. Tennemin's sons standing there.

"Is there room for me?"

"Of course," the boy said with a smile. "Lord Edais is playing and he is on my team. We have to play one the adults know."

He struggled to hide his smirk. "How about you, Mr. Caulfield? Fancy a game?" Phillip pitched his voice to carry over those gathered, conversing. Looked like they were back to playing the game where you hit the ball through the wires with the mallets.

He watched as Fyre encouraged the man to play. Feeling obligated to extend the invitation to her, even though he wanted her far from Caulfield, he did. "And you, Miss Parker?"

"No thank you, my lord. I learned at a young age that this game and I are not friends. I am sure my brother could tell you how many times I tended to hit him with the ball instead of sending it where it should be going. I will content myself to watch."

She was invited to sit beside Mr. Tennemin's wife, and once she had settled on the blanket, he made sure not to stare at her like he hungered for her more than food.

Caulfield was on the other team and the game got rowdy and loud. The children and adults alike had a grand time from all appearances.

His heart approved because he got to hear Fyre laughing and cheering on the children. For a few moments he got to witness her and her brother interact in a way he'd not seen before. And as fast as it had come on, it vanished the moment Cara made her way out to the field. Her children pulled into themselves and weren't as joyous. An unfortunate change and one the other children picked up on. Eventually, the game finished with lackluster enjoyment. Even Elonne carried himself in a different manner when Cara was around.

He didn't like the change. The only one who outwardly was the same was Fyre. Not that there was any way to mistake the dislike between the two women, but she didn't cower from her sister-in-law or appear frightened by her.

* * * *

By the time the sun had begun to lower itself to the horizon, all of his guests had come out to get in on the games. He'd had to set up another course as well. It had taken a bit for the children to accept it was okay for them to play with Cara out there, but it did him good to see them loosen up once more.

Even Mrs. Tennemin got up for a few whacks with the mallet. Only Fyre didn't play. Neither he nor the children could entice her. It sat wrong with him, for he could see her desire to be included. The servants came out to clean up and to carry in the blankets and dirty dishes from the numerous finger foods that had been brought out. Everyone had begun to head inside for the evening meal.

"You have a visitor, my lord." Keating stepped into view when he reached the door.

"Very good, Keating. Do not hold the meal on my account."

"He is in your study."

Phillip scowled as he watched Caulfield walk in, escorting Fyre. The man needed to get the news. That woman was off limits.

"Party not going well?" Damon's question had him pausing as he walked into the study.

"It is going much better than I expected. Why do you ask?"

"You look like you sucked on lemons. If the party is okay then it must be that Mr. Caulfield is around your woman."

He managed a grunt.

Damon laughed before he sobered.

"You saw something." Phillip rubbed the back of his neck.

"Someone is testing the door. No one got in this time, but the person *is* here."

The need for vengeance burned Phillip's blood. If it was Caulfield, that would make everything better. Because then he would have a legit reason to keep that bastard away from Fyre.

"What time?"

"A few minutes before two-thirty."

Too many people had been elsewhere at that time for him to start making a definite allegation. There were some people for sure that he could eliminate.

"Round-the-clock watching?"

Damon nodded and cracked his neck. "Are you still wanting one of us on Miss Gwen while she is here?"

"No, focus on the books. I am confident they will be the draw right now."

"Sure thing, boss."

"You four have all you need?"

"Yes. We are fine. I should go."

"Keep me updated."

"Of course."

Phillip headed to the dining room, slowing as he neared. The sounds of conversation and utensils hitting plates reached him. Stealing a look about the room before he walked in, his gaze immediately landed on Fyre.

She was toward the other end of the table from where he would be. And Caulfield was beside her.

I do not approve.

Miss Asherford was up by him. He barely contained his groan.

He walked in and conversation halted. He gestured for them to continue.

"My apologies." Phillip took his seat.

Within moments he had food before him and was engaged in conversation with Mrs. Tennemin. Miss Asherford was trying to contribute but it was little more than giggles and flirtatious comments.

The third time he had to move her hand from where it had moved up on his thigh, he noticed that Fyre watched him.

Shit!

Even with the formal dining table length between them, he could see the walls going up. Frustration welled within him. He didn't know how else to make her understand and realize she was the *only* woman for him.

Not true, there was one way, but he didn't think she was ready for him to make his interest in her public. Lucien's words echoed through him. For the first time in his life, he struggled to do the right thing for *her*, not what would get him the result he wanted the fastest way possible.

He watched her curl into herself as the meal dragged on. Nothing so much outwardly, for she didn't turn away discussion, but he could *feel* her retreat.

And it fucking killed him to know he was the cause. Earlier this day, she'd fallen apart for him in the bath as she'd come around his fingers, her pussy hot and gripping him like he could hardly wait for it to do to his cock. Now, by the night, she had been hurt. Again, because of him and that she had been accurate that the other woman was much more accepted to touch him in public.

One of the footmen approached him and handed him a note. He opened it and frowned.

"Everything okay, my lord?"

"Fine," he answered Miss Asherford without much of a glance. The urge for him to holler down the table to demand Fyre look at him was strong. The moment dinner had finished he made his way to her side and waited with impatience for her to look up at him.

"Miss Parker, I know this is time away from work, but I would have you look at something if you would not mind."

She got to her feet immediately with a nod. "Of course, my lord."

"You know where my office is. I will be there in a moment." As she walked to the door, he looked at the rest of them and said, "Again, my apologies. Some work has come up. We will return momentarily. Please, adjourn to the parlor and enjoy the drinks and games."

Without giving them a chance to respond, he strode off after her to the office. Closing the door behind him, he didn't even pause, just walked up behind her, turned her then claimed her mouth with his own.

Fyre's mind shorted out. There were a lot of things that she wanted to say and should have said to this man who constantly tossed her world upside down. None of that mattered, not the second his lips touched hers.

All she thought about was the pleasure that owned her body. She whimpered and pushed up on her toes, desperate to get closer to him. To touch him as he'd done to her.

He pulled back and rested his forehead against hers, breathing just as hard as she was. At least that was something they shared.

"I am so sorry, Fyre."

She blinked, not understanding. "For what are you apologizing?"

"Miss Asherford. I know you were watching us tonight. I do not want her."

"What you do is your business, my lord." She didn't want to think any more about that woman touching this man. It pissed her off and made her want to hurt someone.

Namely, Miss Asherford.

"Really?"

The single word was low and drawn out. With a sniff, she nodded and stepped back.

"If there is no work for me to do, I should be getting back, my lord."

A growl rumbled through the air and stunned her into freezing. Hesitant to meet his gaze, when she did, she was met by a furious pair of gray eyes.

"I will not allow you to put a wall back up between us, Fyre. If that means hauling you into my arms in front of everyone and kissing you like I long to do, then so be it. Or you can just give me a few fucking moments with the woman who owns me completely before I have to go back out to a group of people and pretend my heart does not beat wildly out of control when I look at you. Or that I don't want to rip Caulfield's arms off and beat him to death with them for touching you."

"Miss Asherford is a much better choice for you."

The growl grew louder and his jaw flexed as he continually clenched it.

"Keep pushing me, Fyre. Keep pushing and see what happens."

She backed off, sensing how close to the edge he seemed to truly be positioned.

Fyre paused for a moment, then walked back close to him and reached up, settling her hand along his cheek. He shut his eyes and pressed into her touch. Taking the moment, she skimmed her stare down his body and noticed the hardness contained in his breeches.

Her decision was made. Good or bad. Smart or stupid. It didn't matter any longer. While she was permitted to have this man, she was going to take every advantage allowed and indulge.

Just so I have memories of our time when it is all over.

She slid her hand down to his chest and placed her other there before smoothing them along the hard planes. Phillip opened his eyes but she didn't hold his questioning look, instead, she watched her hands as they moved.

"One day," she muttered. "One day I want to do this without clothing on so I can feel the heat of your skin, smell you."

"Whatever you want, baby."

Another glance down to the thickness there and she almost reached for it but didn't. Moving her attention back up to his darkened gray eyes, she patted his chest.

"Books." She had to remain focused, it wouldn't do for her to head back out there looking rumpled.

His groan was only partially playful.

"You are going to kill me, Fyre."

He gestured for her to lead the way and she did, aware of his large presence behind her the entire trek to the desk. Without asking, she took the chair and tried to ignore how his masculine scent pushed straight through her and set up an incredible throb between her legs.

Phillip went to where he kept his books and pulled one down and carried it to her.

"Can you make a new entry in here for me?"

Reaching for the pen, she nodded. "Of course. What for?" A thought occurred to her. "Did someone break in?"

He skimmed the backs of his fingers down the side of her face with a soft smile. "They are trying. But I want to put something in here that will make them become foolish and follow up with a bad decision."

She harrumphed. "I would think that trying to steal from an earl would be foolish enough."

He laughed as he sat on the edge of the desk. "Not everyone is properly scared of my title."

"Everyone on this island is scared of you and your title."

Phillip snorted. "Not everyone."

He showed her the paper he wanted her to copy from. She frowned but didn't question him.

"Name one who is not." She didn't look at him as she wrote.

"Easy. Gwen Parker."

Her lips twitched as she put down the amount and finished up the line. "Just this set? Or did you want this in your other set as well?"

"Just this one. No way I sell people for real, Fyre. Please tell me you believe that."

She placed the pen back in the inkwell and turned in the chair to better face the man who had taken a seat on the edge of the desk. Lower lip caught in her teeth, she nodded even as she reached for him.

The second her fingers closed over his cock, he groaned and captured her wrist.

"Fyre."

There was an ache in her she couldn't explain away. But his immediate halting shoved insecurity all over her and she froze, gaze shooting away from his.

"No, baby. Look at me, please."

It took her a moment to swallow her embarrassment and do as he asked. The hunger in his gaze floored her.

"I cannot wait to feel your mouth around my cock, believe me, I dream about it. But that shit will not be happening here. I want you where I can take my time, where we *both* can explore. And that time is not now."

"Okay." She bit her lower lip again and he growled.

"Stop that." He swooped in and captured that same lip, sucking it into his mouth and nipping it before he ended the kiss. "You have no idea how much that turns me on. This is *my* lip to bite."

He eased off the desk and moved a respectable distance away. Seconds later there were three sharp knocks on the door.

"Come." Phillip sounded like he always did, in control.

The door opened and she realized had he not stopped her, her mouth could have been on his shaft at that very moment. Her mouth watered with the knowledge that it was something she desperately wanted.

Keeping her eyes on the book, she looked over the entries and finally lifted her head to see Keating there. But it was those behind him who seemed far more interested in what was going on in the room. Not just her brother, but also Caulfield.

Thankfully, she still looked as put-together as when she had entered this room. Not by choice, but the earl seemed to have a much better sense of preservation than she did. And she was grateful for that.

The glare Caulfield shot her let her know he was still livid that she had dropped him as a client. It hadn't just been him, but he had taken it that way.

"Thank you, Miss Parker," Phillip said, even as he walked to the door with Keating. "Lock up behind you, please."

"Of course, my lord. I will not be much longer."

"Good, join us when you finish here."

The door closed on those staring in and she released a sigh of relief. All she waited for was the ink to dry, then she closed the book and returned it to its spot. After making sure Phillip's desk was spotless, she walked to the door and stepped out before turning back and locking it behind her.

Mr. Caulfield met her just outside the entrance to the parlor.

"Might I have a word, Miss Parker?"

She didn't want to be alone with him but it would be rude to walk away. "Of course. Perhaps you could escort me to the drinks?"

That way he could say whatever was on his mind but her aversion to being alone with this man would be assuaged because they would be in a room with others.

"I was hoping to do so in private."

"We are in private right now, Mr. Caulfield."

His thin lips flattened more.

Keating walked into view, two footmen behind him, Davie one of them.

"Everything okay, Mr. Caulfield? Miss Parker?"

She had never thought she would be grateful to see Keating.

"Yes, Mr. Keating, thank you. Mr. Caulfield was just escorting me to the parlor." She swallowed back her aversion and slipped her arm through his to keep him from lashing out at the servants.

Phillip's gaze lasered onto the way their bodies touched the moment they entered the room. But he held his tongue and continued his conversation with those around him.

"We need to talk about you still working for the earl. Your brother promised you to me and I will not let him out of that."

Her stomach plummeted at his words and it was a struggle to keep the panic from showing as she mingled the rest of the evening. Especially when all she wanted to do was crawl into the soft bed waiting for her.

Chapter Nineteen

Phillip stood in the shadows and watched her get ready for bed. He didn't give a damn that he was being a voyeur as this was the woman he planned on marrying, which would give him that right for the rest of their lives.

She rubbed some sort of cream on her neck, over the scars there, and the one on her chest. Then she worked it into her legs and the rest of her body. His cock was painfully hard as he watched her stand there, wearing nothing more than a shift, one leg braced on the stool as she smoothed the cream down the toned muscles. Then she switched and killed him all over again doing it to the other leg.

After she had finished that, she took a seat once more and brushed out her hair before braiding it and allowing the thick rope to hang over the side with the scarring on her neck.

"Are you expecting to meet someone later?" He stepped into view. "Is that what this entire sexy process is for?"

She didn't jump, just met his gaze in the mirror. "This is my nightly routine, my lord. Perhaps I should be wondering why you are in my room yet again."

He prowled over the floor to stand behind her. "You know why I am here, Fyre." Bending at the waist, he sniffed her, and his body reacted. Somehow hardening even more.

How the hell does she smell so good? What was that she put on?

The only sign of her nervousness was the tremble of her fingers as she finished tying the ribbon at the end of her hair.

"I have had this dream since I met you, so I am not sure this is not just another of those."

His heart thumped in his chest.

"How do I prove that I am not a dream, but flesh and blood?"

She spun around on the seat, facing him directly. "Touch me."

"That is not going to be a problem. But surely there is something else, because I refuse to think my dreamself is stupid enough not to touch you every fucking chance I get."

Her smile weakened his knees.

"Make me yours, Phillip."

His control snapped and he hauled her up into his arms, slamming his mouth over hers like a possessed man. Which he was, in a sense. She had bewitched him from the word go.

Her moan poured into him and he slid his hands around to cup her ass, encouraging her to jump up, and she listened, wrapping her legs around his waist. His cock nestled perfectly against her core had them both humming in pleasure.

He carried her to the bed and sank to his knees as he laid her back on the narrow bed. Part of him wanted to take her through the hidden passageway to his bed, where there was far more room, but here they would be forced closer and he loved that idea.

"I want you naked." Phillip had been dreaming about that since he'd met her, and the tease of seeing her in the bath hadn't helped. Only made his craving worse for her.

Phillip removed her arms from around him and stared down at her. The trust in her gaze floored him.

"Yes," she whispered. "You naked is a great idea."

"You first." He reached for the buttons on her shift but she shook her head.

"Same time."

He stole another kiss before nodding and backing up enough to rip his shirt off over his head. Her gasp had him smirking. However, when she stood beside the bed and rolled her shoulders, allowing her shift to slide down her magnificent body to the floor, the smirk went with it.

"Christ," he moaned. "You are fucking perfect."

"I have scars."

He admired her hourglass figure, toned legs and arms, high breasts with dark chocolate nipples that were already hard points, and the black hair between her legs that glistened with the proof of her desire.

"They do *not* take away from your beauty, Fyre."

She lifted her chin and gestured at him. "You are wearing more clothing."

He had his pajama bottoms on. "Baby, I need to keep these on so I do not lose control."

Fyre shook her head. "You said clothes off."

"I meant yours."

Her lower lip poked out. "I want to see you."

He picked up on her insecurity and prayed to any god who was listening that he wouldn't embarrass himself. Hell, this woman had already made him come in his pants just from her moans alone. If she touched him now, it would be all over.

With a sigh, he pushed down his pajama pants and watched her expression. Her shyness vanished and the hunger that took over was ravenous. God, his cock hardened further.

"Bed." His command came out all growly and demanding.

Damn it, he only had so much control, and the way she was looking at him seriously eroded it.

She listened, perching on the edge of the bed, her eyes never leaving his cock. Phillip wrapped a hand around his length and gave himself a few pumps.

Fyre moaned and swayed toward him, licking her lips, and damn if he didn't nearly lose it again.

He had said something about going slow and taking his time with her, but right now, he wasn't sure he could uphold that decision.

"Lie back."

Again, no hesitation on her part.

"One leg, foot on the floor. Your other, flat on the bed."

She hesitated and he stroked himself a few more times. "You want this, baby. I know it and you will get it. God, I promise, you'll get it, but I need you to listen to me. I am barely holding on to my control and I have to make sure you are ready for me."

"I am ready." Even as her protest escaped, she did as he'd asked, and it was his turn to groan again.

Her pussy was open to him and he could see the pink past the darker lips. She glistened and her clit teased him as it peeked out from its hood. He walked closer and sank to his knees, her heady scent flooding his nose.

"You smell fucking perfect and I cannot wait to taste you." He kissed the inside of her thigh, loving her tremble.

"Phillip."

He wasn't going to tease much—he couldn't hold off that long.

Bending closer, he ran a finger over the slit and flicked her nub, making her hips bounce up. He released his aching cock and placed a hand along her belly, anchoring her down.

Then he settled his mouth on her.

Seconds later, her fingers speared his hair and she pulled even as she ground against him, legs clamping around his head, hard. Her essence spilled into him as he thrust his tongue deep inside her, craving it all. When he pulled her clit into his mouth, he pushed in two fingers and scissored them, needing her prepared to take his shaft.

She came again, coating his fingers. He eagerly licked her cream off and rose over her as his fingers sank back between her legs.

"I could eat you all damn day, baby." He took possession of her mouth and shared her taste with her. "I love how you taste."

Sweat covered her and she breathed hard. "Please," she begged. "I want you inside me."

He removed his fingers and smeared her cream on his cock before fisting it and lining the head up to her opening. Nudging forward, he put the head in, eyes locked on her face for any sign of discomfort.

She shifted restlessly beneath him, legs around his waist, trying unsuccessfully to pull him in.

"I am." He pushed a bit deeper and she sucked in a sharp breath, causing him to pause.

"I will not break, Phillip. Take me."

She dug her fingers into his forearms as she lifted her hips again in invitation. He couldn't hold off any longer and thrust forward with one surge, sinking fully inside her tight pussy.

"So fucking tight." He opened his eyes, sweat gathering on his forehead. "Are you okay?"

Her eyes were unfocused and it took a moment for her to be there with him. She skimmed her short nails along the back of his neck and nodded.

"Never better. Move."

* * * *

Fyre smiled as she watched everyone around her. Despite her misgivings of coming to this week-long event at the plantation, she was having a good time. Though she knew that Elonne was doing his best to see if something was going on with her and Phillip.

There was, but he never saw.

Phillip was never anything but proper toward her in the groups. Even if she was in one of the meetings he had with the business owners, his professionalism showed through.

He was a different man in the wee hours of the morning, when he snuck into her room and either made love to her there or took her back to his bed where, as he claimed, there was more room for him to play with her.

And play he did.

Sore in ways she hadn't understood a person could be, sometimes it was hard to keep the wince from her face as she moved. And she was in good shape, just, the man was insatiable. And she'd discovered she suffered from the same affliction of being insatiable. There was no way for her to get enough of him and what he did to her.

"I see you are having a good time."

Lifting her head to the speaker, she gave a slight nod to Miss Asherford. "I am, thank you for noticing. Are you?"

The woman lowered herself gracefully to Fyre's side and spent some time artfully arranging her skirts. The venom in her gaze was unmistakable when she looked back at Fyre.

"The earl will be mine, darkie. You would do well to remember your place."

"I did not realize I was a threat to you securing the earl. I work for the man and he has always struck me as more than capable of making his own decisions."

Many people thought because she was of darker skin and a female that she didn't listen and wouldn't stick up for herself. Those people would be wrong. While it may have taken a bit longer when it came to defending herself against her brother, she still was no pushover.

"When I land him, you will be let go, unless I keep you as a slave." Her sneer grew icy, sending a chill through Fyre despite the heat of the day. "You remember how it was when we could have slaves and the man here did, right? There is a movement for that to come back. The earl will get on board, and he will see his idea of paying those less than us is foolish when we can force the labor."

Compelling her fingers not to clench, Fyre turned her gaze to the impressive house and dread curdled in her stomach as she thought of all the pleasure she had found inside those walls, completely ignoring the pain of those before her who had been held there against their will and gone through hell.

"You say 'we' like you have actually worked a day in your life, Miss Asherford. We both know you have not. You rely on your father to care for you and keep you dressed in such a manner. A true daughter would help their father, not be a burden."

Fyre got to her feet, unable to stay. "And do not think your movement would succeed without a fight. People on this island, *my* people, will not sit back and allow others to own us like cattle once more." A slight curtsey. "Enjoy your day."

Fyre headed back to the house, emotions a twisted mess.

As always, Keating was right there when she stepped through the large doors to the home. This time she didn't see the beauty, but the ugliness that had come from the plantation being here.

"Miss Gwen," he said with a nod.

"Not today, Keating. I cannot pretend with you right now." Her chest burned and she rubbed it as the room shifted to the right. "Please just leave me alone."

He didn't. The tall man supported her until everything stopped spinning.

"Miss Gwen? Are you all right?"

"Yes, of course. I just need to get home." Darkness swarmed and that was all she remembered.

* * * *

She wasn't sure what had happened but she woke a bit later in her room with Abbie there, sitting on the bed with her, a damp cloth to her head.

"What is going on, Miss Abbie?"

The girl gave her a smile, one that overflowed with concern. "You fainted in the entryway. Mr. Keating had some of the footmen bring you here. He told Lord Edais and Lord Edais sent for a doctor." She dipped the rag, wrung it out once more and settled it back upon Fyre's forehead. "The doctor said you were just exhausted and needed some rest. So, I am keeping an eye on you while you do that."

Abbie smiled as she poured some water into a glass and helped Fyre take a few sips, then she laid her back and adjusted the rag.

"Thank you."

The rag vanished once more. "For what?"

"Staying with me."

The young woman squeezed her hand before she got back to the task of keeping her head cool. Fyre dropped off to sleep once more and when she woke, it was to find the earl in there whispering with Abbie.

She closed her eyes when he looked in her direction. She didn't want him to know she was awake. Not much later, the door closed and she snuck a peek. Abbie was the only one there.

"I have to head home."

Abbie spun toward her. "You are awake. The earl will be so pleased. He has been worried."

She couldn't think about that right now. Sitting, she rubbed the nape of her neck. "Will you help me?"

"You wish to leave *now*? It is night!"

"I think it best. I cannot participate in anything, and I am just a burden on the staff here."

"Lord Edais will not be happy if you leave without telling him."

She smiled. "I work for him too, Abbie. He is not really ever happy."

The woman giggled, and Fyre hoped that meant Abbie would be assisting her. She lacked the energy to walk home.

"I cannot get the earl's carriage, but I will ask Davie if he will take you home in the wagon."

"Thank you."

Her return smile was full of worry but she slipped from the room. Fyre got up and dressed. Her chest still ached, but nothing like before. Perhaps she *had* done too much. With the addition of the sex at night, it was likely she had just pushed too hard. She had given in to the children and played croquet a few times but, as she'd admitted before, she was dangerous on the field and had soon conceded.

It didn't take her long to pack her bags and she was waiting on the bed when Abbie returned. Disappointment swept her features as she took in the scene before her.

"Can he help me?"

Abbie nodded. Lips flattening, she took a breath and stepped forward to take the bags. "Follow me. He will meet us outside."

Fyre rose. "Us? Abbie, you should stay here." They left the room and she did as Abbie said—followed.

"I am going with. If we are found out, we were simply out trying to find some time alone."

"I am putting you in danger."

"You want to go home, we will get you home." Abbie looked around before sneaking off to the left.

Fyre followed.

True to Abbie's word, Davie was there with an older pony attached to a wagon. He took the bags and tossed them in the back, then helped Abbie climb up there before assisting Fyre to sit in the seat beside him.

"Thank you, Davie."

"You wanted to get home."

He snapped the reins and, with the creak of the wagon, they got moving. He didn't light the lantern until they'd left the plantation.

She rode in silence as Davie and Abbie bantered back and forth. It was fun listening to them. When he rolled up before her place, he was ready to assist her down before she could move.

They helped her in and Abbie lit a few candles as Davie set her bags down before her room.

"Thank you both," she said.

Abbie squeezed her hand. "Feel better." Then she slipped outside, leaving her alone with Davie.

"He will not be happy about this, Miss Gwen."

She didn't even pretend to not know who he spoke about. Fyre shrugged. "He has a house full of guests. I doubt he will even notice."

"We both know, Miss Gwen, that Lord Edais notices everything when it comes to you." He shook his head. "I will not lie for you. When he asks me what happened I will tell him, but I will not seek him out to tell."

"I would never expect you to risk your own position more than you have. Thank you, Davie."

He flushed and tugged on his hat. "I should go. Good night, Miss Gwen."

The click of the door reminded her she was now just how she pretended to be. Alone.

Yet this time alone meant no Phillip as well. And she didn't like that.

Chapter Twenty

Phillip had two more days of *this*. Now he remembered why he hadn't done these parties often in England. It was exhausting. And he couldn't believe how needy guests could be. Except one.

Fyre.

She did her best not to create any more work. He had spoken to Abbie, asking her if she needed anything more for Miss Parker, but all the maid had done was shake her head and tell her that other than a bath, she did not ask for anything.

He sank behind his desk with a groan.

"Party woes?"

Without looking, he sent a gesture to Kolby that was not remotely polite. The man chuckled.

"You have news?"

"I do. But I have to say first, a heads-up about your woman leaving last night would have been nice. We are going to be a man down here because we are covering her once more. I took that upon myself because you said she was safe while here, but as she left..."

It took a moment for the news to sink in. Hands spread on his desk, he shook his head and took several deep breaths. "She left? When the fuck did this happen?"

Kolby eyed him like one did a dangerous animal — with extreme caution. "Last night. Davie and Abbie took her in a wagon. Archer followed and watched over her last night. Zander took the position early this morning."

She never said a word.

Phillip wanted to roar for his horse and ride to her side, demanding an explanation. He stayed right there and forced his jaw to unlock.

"What about the books?"

"In regards to those, we found the woman responsible for trying to get in."

He blinked. "Woman?"

"We let her get the information because we were not sure if you wanted to have her followed to see who she is meeting to give this to."

"Who the fuck is stealing my information?"

"Mrs. Parker."

"Fyre's sister-in-law?"

Kolby nodded. "I do not know if she is working alone here, but she picked the lock like a professional and knew exactly where to go for your books. There was no changing of the lines this time, but she did seem interested in that latest entry."

His gut churned. That was the line he'd had Fyre add about selling people.

"She take a copy?"

The man nodded, tunneling his fingers through his dark, unbound hair. "Yes. She was in and out in moments." He shifted his weight on his feet. "I do not know where she went after that, I could not see her once she left the room. Damon was on her and he will be here shortly. With Archer sleeping after keeping an eye on Fyre at her place we did not want to leave the room unguarded."

"Thank you," Phillip said, getting to his feet. "Tell Damon to meet me here when he can. Get the sleep you need. I know you have been watching this room all the time."

Kolby canted his head to the side. "Not *all* the time, my lord."

"When were you not?"

"When you and Miss Gwen were in here the other day, utilizing the desk for something *other* than writing."

Shit. He'd forgotten about them the second she had touched his cock. His skin heated at the thought of her bent over his large desk as he fucked her from behind.

"Do not mention that to her."

The man grinned and held up his hands. "I did not see a thing."

"Keep it that way."

Kolby left, and about twenty minutes later Damon arrived. After talking with him about Cara and where she had gone after being in his office, he knew one thing for certain. Cara was not working alone. But it didn't sound like her husband was in on it.

He hoped he wouldn't have to take both parents from the kids, but if that was what had to happen, so be it.

So right now his question was, who had Cara met after breaking into his office? If Damon hadn't seen anyone leaving, chances were it was a staff member who knew the passageways to move through to get unseen from place to place.

While he hoped none of his people were involved, he was not looking past that. He pushed those thoughts away while he made his way down to share breakfast with his guests.

As they talked, laughed, and tried to one-up one another in tales, he thought about Fyre. He couldn't help but look over to Elonne and Cara throughout the meal. She didn't seem to give a damn one way or the other, but Elonne was watching him with a suspicious look. As was Caulfield.

* * * *

Later in the early afternoon, Phillip had some boats set up for them to take a spin around the lake on his property, while there would be snacks along the shore.

"Where is my sister, my lord?"

He took his focus from Cara, who sat with another wife, and settled it on Elonne. "Afternoon, Mr. Parker."

"My sister?"

"I was informed this morning that your sister had decided to return home. My guess is that is where she is."

"What did you do to her?"

"Watch your tone, Mr. Parker. I do not like people assuming I did anything. I have not seen your sister since I checked on her after she fainted in the entryway." He glared at Elonne. "Why did you not check on her?"

"I did not know."

Phillip faced Elonne and glared down at him, unimpressed with this man now. "When we first met, I admired how you protected your sister, took care of your family. Not anymore. You have dared to lay a hand on her and have made her cry. Let me tell you something, Elonne Parker. Your sister is a fucking treasure and you should be thankful you have her in your life."

"She is my sister."

Phillip lifted an eyebrow. "I believe I just stated that. But while she is your sister, she is going to be *my* wife. And unlike you, I promise you I will protect my own. From whatever the danger, even if it comes from within her own family."

"You cannot marry her. She is promised to Mr. Caulfield."

Phillip snorted as he tried to control the raging fury the mere thought of that man touching Fyre created within him. "That man will die if he lays a hand on her. And you would do well to stop trying to sell her. I know when a man is in financial hardship, just like I know you expected *your sister* to take care of your issue. She paid off a large debt of yours. I put the money back in her account and paid off the rest of your IOUs, but if you get in trouble again, no one will save you."

Elonne's eyes widened. "Why would you do that?"

"I told you, your sister is going to be my wife, and I will do whatever is necessary to protect her."

Elonne held his tongue for a moment and Phillip waited, sure he would be coming with something else. He wasn't wrong.

"You cannot marry her. I will not allow it."

"Mr. Parker, it is past time you realize your sister is a grown woman with her own thoughts and desires. You cannot tell her anything."

"I do not know how things are in England, my lord—"

Was there a bit of a sneer on 'my lord'? Phillip believed there was.

"I am sure you have a point to make." His tone was cold and sharp.

"Here, on *this* island, family is everything. And Fyre will put family first, no matter how much money you dangle in front of her. My sister will never take your side over mine."

Gah, it bothered the fuck out of him to think Elonne may be right about that. But Phillip hadn't exactly inherited anything meek or cautious from his father.

Biting off his proprietary words when others joined them, all he could do was smile at Elonne. The prick grinned right back, clearly sure of his position.

Phillip shook his head. No, she wouldn't turn her back on him and what they could have together. He had nothing to fear.

Did he?

* * * *

Her own bed wasn't as comfortable as the one she'd enjoyed at the party. And it was lonely without her earl in it with her. She sighed heavily as she shifted to her side and snuggled down deeper beneath the blankets she didn't truly need on a night like this.

Phillip had put out so much heat with his own body that she had been on a different level of warmth lying beside him. Now, alone, she shivered. Not that it was cold, but *she* was.

I am a mess.

After tossing and turning for a few more moments, she swung her feet over the edge and walked to the kitchen. Realizing she didn't want anything that was in there, she huffed in frustration and went back to her bedroom.

"Missing something?"

She screamed and jumped at least a foot. He was there when she came down, strong arms wrapping around her, his scent filling her, bringing comfort and arousal all in the same breath.

"Phillip." His name fell on a gasp from her lips.

He tunneled his fingers into her hair, tipped her head back and kissed her.

There was no holding back. When his tongue swiped along the seam of her mouth, she opened immediately, needing him back inside her. His growl of approval reverberated through her.

She chased his mouth when he pulled away, even though she couldn't see him.

"You left me. Without a *fucking* word."

His grip flexed in her hair, but there was no fear in her. As tight as his hold was on her, it didn't hurt, and his fingertips massaged her scalp lightly even though he had no give on her hair.

"Why are you here?"

The rumble leaving his chest grew louder. "Are you sure that is the question you want to go with? Not telling me why you ran from my party without a word, sneaking away in the dead of night?"

"I was going to come back in the morning for the last day." She'd realized her mistake the moment she'd gotten home and all day she'd been miserable.

He kissed her again, nibbling on her lower lip. "You never should have left."

Phillip trailed his lips down along her chin to her neck. Shivering where he licked and laved, she tightened her grip on his shoulders, trusting him to keep her upright.

"I am sorry, I know I said I would be there to help you."

"I do not give a damn about that. I care about you and me. Us." A shuddering breath. "I cannot protect you if you are not letting me know what is going on."

Fyre paused for a moment, pushing away the desire licking her veins and focusing on his words. And the tone.

"You were scared for me."

"Yes." His admission came with no hesitation.

She moved her touch from his shoulders to his face, touching the features she had memorized and could visualize even with no light. The gray eyes, hawklike nose, thin lips that delivered such passionate kisses. Lean features that more often than not scowled.

Until he looks at me.

There was this expression he got when he watched her. Kind of a longing, loving one. She couldn't quite name it, but she never saw anyone else receive a look like that.

"Why were you scared for me?" He didn't say anything, just held her tighter. She pulled back, scoring her fingers along his neck. "Tell me what is going on."

Phillip lifted her and carried her to the bed. It didn't take long and soon they were both lying there, Fyre once again warm in a way only this man could make her. Body draped on top of his, she snuggled close as he held her loosely against him, hands stroking along her back. Her legs were inside his, bracketed, and there was no way to ignore his hardness as it pressed into her while she lay upon him.

"Cara." Phillip kept his voice low.

Seeking inside his shirt, Fyre closed her eyes in the darkness of the room, allowing her hands to skim along his heated skin until she pushed them behind his back, holding him as he held her.

"What about her?" It was sad, really, that she wasn't shocked to hear her sister-in-law's name from his lips. That woman had always been someone Fyre didn't trust.

"She was seen picking the lock to my office and going in to get information from the books."

"I would not be surprised. Especially if whoever she is working with or for were offering her money. Who did she give it to?"

"We have not seen her alone with any male other than Elonne."

"Why have you not been checking out the women there? We are just as capable of being vindictive and conniving as are men."

He nipped the shell of her ear. "Hard for me to follow a woman around without appearing suspicious, baby."

"And I was not there to help you." She sank into him. "I am sorry, my lord."

"You should be. But not for that. You should be sorry because you had me scared and worried." His hands moved down to her ass and squeezed.

"I needed space."

Phillip thrust his hips up, pushing that erection into her more. "How much space? And starting when?"

Fyre sat and lifted her nightgown so it was out of the way. His fingers had already freed himself from his breeches. It didn't take much at all for her to rise a bit more, curl her fingers around his thickness and guide him home into her as she sank back down.

"Not that much and later. Much later." She rocked on him, biting her lower lip as he filled her.

Nerve endings alive and sparking, she took a moment to gather her breath. He gripped her hips, holding her in place.

"Fuck, you feel perfect on my cock, baby."

Letting go of the bunched material, she leaned forward, bracing her hands on his chest. "Move," she demanded.

His chuckle vibrated beneath her palms. "No. Take it from me. Ride me."

She closed her eyes in frustration and need. "I do not know how, I have never..."

He released one hip and sank his fingers in her hair, guiding her down to him. A brush of his lips. "There is nothing you can do wrong here, baby. Try something. If you do not like it, try something else. Show *me* what *you* like. Teach me how to pleasure you how you want, in the ways you enjoy."

Face hot, she sat back, knowing if there had been light she would not be able to do this. She was comfortable with him, yes, but taking the initiative like this? It was something she would have had to build up to, if he could see her. But as it was dark, she could pretend this was nothing more than another fantasy.

With Phillip.

"What if I do not know how I like it other than what you have shown me?"

He ran his hands up her side, thumbs swiping along her taut nipples before settling once more upon her hips.

"That is what we are learning now. I am happy with whatever you do to me, baby. My dick is inside your wet, tight pussy. No place I would rather be, so take your time if you want."

She didn't want. Fyre moved her hips and the groan that left his mouth was heaven to her ears. She wanted him to whimper and cry for her as she did him. Lips curling up in what she was sure was a vixen smile, she started rotating her hips, seeing what she liked the most. And how much she could torture the man beneath her before he snapped.

Chapter Twenty-One

Rubbing the back of his neck, Phillip stared out the window. He was no closer to finding out who Cara worked for, or with, than he had been while the party had been going on at his home, and that had been a month ago. Though he had been in communication with a few of the business owners who had been there.

This cultivating relationships thing was fucking difficult. And it didn't help that all he wanted to do was be with Fyre.

Naked.

All day long.

He pinched the bridge of his nose and exhaled sharply. Dreaming about her and the way she responded to his touch wasn't doing a damn thing except making him aroused once more.

Not true, it also made him far more irritated, because it was just reminding him of something he could not have.

Keating knocked and entered with his usual blank expression. "A visitor to see you, my lord."

"Who is it, Keating?"

"A Mr. Tennemin."

He sat up straight. "Send him in."

"Of course, my lord."

In the four weeks since the party, he had only communicated with this man by missive thus far.

Mr. Tennemin walked in with the same arrogance and swagger he'd had at the party. Phillip stood and offered his hand.

"Good to see you again, Mr. Tennemin."

They shook and after each had a drink, they took their seats.

"To what do I owe the pleasure?"

"Your dark—"

Phillip growled as his hand tightened around his glass, and the man cleared his throat even though he didn't look the slightest bit remorseful for the word that had been tumbling from his mouth.

"The woman who keeps your books, Miss Parker, was it? I would like to speak with her."

Phillip hadn't known he had such restraint. Edgy as his pulse kicked up, he tried to slow his rapid breaths. Tunnel vision owned him and he could only see his fist driving directly into Tennemin's smug face. Leaning toward the man with a deliberate motion, he prayed he wouldn't kill him right now.

"Why did you come to me instead of going to speak to her directly?"

"I know she is in your employ but I figured you were taking advantage and sleeping with her. I did not wish to be seen as poaching on your property."

One drink would not be enough. He set his glass on the desktop to merely keep from chucking it at this man's head.

"A few things to get straight, Mr. Tennemin. Miss Parker is a grown woman capable of making her own decisions. She is a fucking genius when it comes to numbers. I do *not* take advantage of people who work for me in such a fashion. I will, however, protect that woman with everything I have. She is mine because she is *my* woman, *not* because of the color of her skin, or that she works for me, and you would do well to remember that."

"*Your* woman?"

"*Mine*." He leaned closer to the desk, hands flat on the smooth surface. "Do you have a problem with the woman who will one day be my wife? For something as asinine as her skin color? Because if you *do*, we can forget all we talked about while you were here previously and I will give you one fucking second to walk out that door before I *toss* you out."

"I cannot say I approve —"

"Then get the fuck out of my house and do not bother to sully my step again."

Mr. Tennemin held up a hand. "But," he plowed on as if he had not just been threatened, "I have never met another man who was willing to buck what people have deemed to be the right way. I liked her, my lord. She knows what she is talking about and I would like the chance to see if she can help me with my books as well. I no longer have slaves. I did for a while, but that has passed. Much like you here, my people get a wage. I am just worried that if we go forward and you marry…her…there would be repercussions. Businesswise."

Phillip shrugged with the cool arrogance he had been born into. "I am a *fucking earl*. I have contacts almost everywhere and where I do not, my friends do. Here, England. Scotland and Ireland. Africa. India. I have places that will purchase my wares. Those who do not want to do business with me, I will set out to crush, it is that simple."

Mr. Tennemin nodded and finished his drink in one swallow. "Okay. Can you direct me to Miss Parker?"

"I will take you. She is at another job right now."

Yeah, he knew her fucking schedule. At least she no longer worked for Caulfield. Didn't mean he trusted the bastard to stop trying his shit.

They were on horseback not too much later, riding to town. Mr. Tennemin asked some questions about the lands surrounding Phillip's property and he answered a few, not telling him he was in the process of buying up more land for his own ventures.

Slowing when they entered the town, he watched the man beside him as they rode up the street. Tennemin tipped his hat to the women, regardless of their color, and responded to greetings. Still slightly on edge about his beliefs, Phillip realized at some point he was going to have to trust someone to get this collaboration moving more how he wanted it to go.

Not that he didn't love England, but the time to wait for things was flat-out asinine and they could do better. Should, for the livelihood of those who lived on these islands. If that meant he had to spearhead the motion, he would do it.

Whatever it took to make Fyre's life easier.

For a while he had toyed with the idea of asking her back to England with him, but he had realized he loved it here. The entire island's vibe was different than what England gave him, plus, he wasn't faced with all his exes and the foolish and selfish mistakes he had made in the past.

James came running up—from where, Phillip didn't know, but one minute he wasn't there, the next, he was.

"My lord." His dark gaze dashed to Mr. Tennemin. "Sir."

"I am looking for Miss Gwen."

While James' eyes sparkled at the news, the smile never came. "She is with Mr. Caulfield, sir, in his store."

Flipping him a coin, Phillip nodded at him and they rode off. Fury rose. She had no reason to be in his shop as she no longer worked for him.

"Spies in the town?"

"Always good to know what is going on and where my people are."

"Maybe I will try that."

"Something I learned in England, Mr. Tennemin, is that the working class knows the news far faster than the upper ever do. Their network is incredible, and one would be foolish not to take advantage of people in their employ to get the news they are after."

Tennemin grunted. "Are you planning to head back to England?"

"No. This is my home."

Another grunt was his response. They halted their horses and swung down before tying them up. Together they walked up the step and into the store.

Phillip knew where she had sat when she worked here, and his eyes cut there without fail. Phillip hated seeing her in here. It didn't help to know that Caulfield hovered over her.

This time was different. She was not seated, nor was she working. She and Mr. Caulfield were having a discussion, one that Phillip didn't think was all that friendly.

"I told you," she snapped, "I do not work for you anymore. If this is what you had to discuss with me, we could have addressed this outside, no need to come in here."

"Your brother said —"

"Excuse me," Mr. Tennemin interrupted.

Phillip was grateful, because all he wanted to do was wring the bastard's neck.

Both glanced at them and stepped back from each other. Phillip made himself stay put as Mr. Tennemin walked to them.

"Mr. Tennemin," Albie said, a smile turning up his lips. "To what do I owe the pleasure?"

"I was actually seeking out Miss Parker. I had some more questions for her after the talk she gave us at the party. I was unable to get a chance to talk to her while we were there. But I can come back if I am interrupting."

Caulfield nodded. "That would be great because we —"

"Just finished," Fyre said. "I am free to talk now, Mr. Tennemin."

Phillip shot the man a look before nodding once to Fyre and Mr. Tennemin, then he walked out. Their discussion was not his business, and he was not going to impose himself on the conversation. No matter how much he longed to.

He went to Mr. Olden's sweet shop and looked around, needing to keep his mind occupied. No one was out front when he entered and he picked up a few things and took them to the counter. Still no one to assist him.

Irritation growing, he went to the door by the back and knocked once before opening it.

Shocked would be putting it mildly and yet, perhaps not. Mr. Olden was fucking Mrs. Collier on his desk, his tie in her mouth and her hands secured behind her back. The older woman was without a stitch of clothing on and her pale skin flushed when she saw him there.

She struggled for a few moments but was unable to get away from Mr. Olden or his plunging dick.

Phillip looked at the man and said, as if he wasn't fucking a married woman before him, "I picked out some items and am leaving a list on the counter. Add it to my account."

"Very good, my lord. Would there be anything else you would like?"

From the way Olden's gaze moved between him and the female he currently fucked, Phillip knew the offer was about the woman on the desk and he shook his head.

"Just the candy. Good day." He backed out and sighed heavily once the door was closed.

Leaving the list as he'd promised, he put the items in a small bag and went to the door. Fyre and Mr. Tennemin were not in sight. Phillip secured the package on his horse and saw a familiar figure step into view, give him a nod, and vanish.

It didn't take him too long to get in an alley between shops and step out of sight to wait. Archer appeared.

"You have something?"

"Whatever you are starting, there are some who are not happy at all. You need to have protection."

"Keep it on Fyre. I can handle myself." He leaned against the wall. "Specifics? Names?"

"Nothing concrete yet, but we are listening. Just…watch your back."

"Understood."

* * * *

Fyre watched Mr. Tennemin walk away as she mulled over his words. Work for him? She had recently gotten rid of a few smaller accounts because she was getting burned out. Mr. Tennemin had a much larger one. Not quite like Phillip's, but far more than some of the smaller stores.

Part of it felt like a betrayal, shucking off the smaller accounts to land larger ones. This was her island, she should put them first, right?

Why should I do that? Most of them have no use for me other than my skill with numbers.

"We were not finished talking."

Albie Caulfield was not a man who gave up easily. She realized this now.

"Mr. Caulfield, we were. I have said my piece. I am sorry you and my brother have created some deal that I did not agree to, nor *will* I agree to."

He got in her face, dark blue eyes hard with anger. "You owe me."

She drew back like he'd hit her. "I owe you? For what?"

"You were supposed to be mine, Gwen. I was going to have you, then the damn earl shows up and you shove me aside."

"We were barely friends, Mr. Caulfield. You gave me a job but wanted me within reach for extra activities while I worked on your books. And let us not pretend that was not the real reason you agreed to give me the work. You did not think I could do the numbers, but you wanted a woman near."

"You always insisted on meeting at the shop."

"I am not a stupid woman."

"No, you are not. But you do reach above your station. The earl only keeps you on because you are spreading your legs for him."

A flash of unease hit her. She buried it, not having time to think about it right now, nor did she want to give him the satisfaction of knowing he'd got to her with those words.

"Are you calling me a whore, Mr. Caulfield? Is that why I was the one who let the extra work go? Because all of the men wanting to sleep with me was too much? Or my brother told me to so I could keep myself for you? Why would you want a woman who only keeps a job because she spreads her legs?"

"Darkie women have high sexual needs. They cannot be expected to act like white women, with decorum."

Forcing down her rage, she clenched and relaxed her fist. "We are done here. Leave me alone and do not speak with me again."

She walked out into the street, eyes burning with angry tears just waiting to fall.

He grabbed her arm, tightly and painfully, before spinning her back around to him. In that second she understood she shouldn't have turned her back on him.

Fyre gasped at the radiating pain shooting up from her wrist.

"You do not walk away from me." Spittle flew from his mouth at his words, some landing on her. "He promised you to me and damn it, I will have a taste of what you are giving free to the fucking earl!"

Mr. Caulfield yanked her closer, lowering his face to hers. She smacked at him, trying to get away, but he was too strong. His breath, heavily minted, fanned over her and she fought not to gag.

"You *are* going to be mine."

She was ripped free and when Mr. Caulfield hit the ground, Fyre hit as well, landing on the same wrist he had grabbed and twisted. More pain radiated up and she bit back her cry.

Phillip stood between her and Mr. Caulfield. His hands were fists at his sides and he advanced on the man sprawled out on the ground. A stream of words rushed from him but she couldn't focus. Not on anything.

James was there to help her up and she kept her eyes downcast as she tried to brush off her skirt, but the pain in her wrist pulled a cry from her lips. Phillip whirled back to her.

His expression was angry. His eyes concerned as he watched her.

In turn, she observed him, and he appeared to be working through something. He glared back over his shoulder then took the two steps that with his stride put him directly in front of her. He was gentle with her as he picked up her injured arm.

His fingers danced along but barely touched her wrist. "Are you okay?"

She nodded.

Phillip cupped her face and made her look at him. "Fyre," he murmured. "I need to hear the words." His thumb swept along her lower lip as he stared.

"This is improper, my lord."

He clenched his jaw. "I do not give a fuck. In fact, I want everyone to know."

"Know what?" How was she supposed to think when his touch played havoc on her senses? "And I will be fine. My wrist is hurt."

"I am taking you to the doctor to get it looked at."

"Not necessary."

"Oh, trust me, it is very much a necessity. You do not let me do this and I will carry you there."

"Why?"

Phillip released his hold on her injured wrist. She held it and sighed. Fyre lost her breath when he cupped the other side of her face with that same hand. He tipped up her head and when their eyes locked, he blinked.

For an instant, she could see the worry in his.

"Because you were hurt. You fell and you cried out. Do you have any fucking idea what that did to me?"

"My lord, people are watching."

"Good."

Not what she expected him to say.

"I cannot do this anymore, Fyre." There was no modulating his tone now and she knew his words were carrying to everyone listening. And there were more gathering as the moments went on. "No longer will I hide my feelings for you. I cannot, *will* not, do that. Everyone needs to know that you are *my woman* and I will do *whatever* is necessary to keep *you* safe."

Phillip kissed her.

Chapter Twenty-Two

Phillip probably should not have done that. He did not have regrets over kissing her in public, but he probably should have given her some warning. Fyre lived up to her name. When she raged, she raged.

And he fully expected to get the brunt of her wrath.

Fyre touched her lips with shaky fingertips, blinked almost as if having to nudge herself out of the shock of his action, and lifted her gaze to his once more. He hated that her hand still shook as she lowered it to her side.

Everything in him demanded that he gather her close and not let her walk away. To make her stay and face the portal to chaotic hell he had pushed them into. But he only held firm, refusing to release her gaze.

"What have you done?"

Her question was so low he nearly missed it.

"Claimed my woman."

When she stepped back from him it took every bit of his resolve not to pursue her and draw her back close to his chest.

Where she fucking belongs. With me. By me. Touching me.

The voice in his head was so loud with its assuredness, he nearly winced from the force of the thoughts. No matter how true they were.

"Your woman."

Fyre didn't make it a question. To him, it sounded as if she were mulling it over, not sure she agreed.

People were gathering. He didn't give a fuck about them. His concern was Fyre. And he didn't take his eyes off her.

Comments were flying back and forth, people who he had heard speak highly of her, whispering about him having kissed a dark-skinned woman on the street. In the middle of town. Phillip growled low in his chest. Apparently their support of her only went so far.

She heard him, her eyes widening a tiny bit more. And he decided fuck it. Moving into her he curved his fingers around her upper arms, bringing her back that small amount that she'd retreated from him.

"You do not know what you have done."

"Wrong," he countered. "I know *exactly* what I did, Fyre. Every second since I saw that fucker touching you, I've known what I was doing. I can tell you how many steps that I took to cross from where I was to here. How if you had not cried out, I would not have stopped hitting that excuse for a man. And, how fucking much I want to kiss you again."

"I will be an outcast."

"No." His words were firm and unyielding. "You will be my countess."

Her eyes flew up to his, wide and uncertain. "You should not say things like that, my lord."

Beneath the reprimand, he could hear the longing.

"You are exactly right, I should not say them. I should ask you first."

"Not what I meant."

"You know me, Fyre. I am an earl who lives by his own rules no matter the consequences." In his peripheral vision, he noticed her brother watching from the fringes as well. "Tell me, will you be my countess?"

She tried to look away but he captured her chin and held her still, locking onto her eyes once again.

"We are in the middle of town."

"I know, and once you answer me, we will be heading to the doctor to get your wrist looked at."

"I brought him over, thought he could be of some use here."

They both looked to see Mr. Tennemin walking over the dirt street with the town's doctor keeping stride with him.

"Thank you," Phillip said, gratitude filling him.

He looked back to the woman whose soft skin still rested between his fingers. "Fyre?"

She bit her lower lip and he *tsked*, before using his thumb to roll it from her white teeth.

"Yes."

Her response was soft but sure. His heart nearly burst from his chest. Moving his hand from her chin, he slid it back to cup her nape, pushing his fingers into her hair before he kissed her again. This time he lingered over the kiss, nibbling along her lower lip and swiping his tongue along the seam.

When she opened beneath his perusal, he groaned as he pushed in to tangle with her tongue. Struggling to remain decent in public, he ended the kiss and rested his head against hers, breathing just as hard as she was.

"We need to let the doctor look at your wrist."

He remained at her side while the doctor escorted her off of the street. Scanning the faces there, he held the ones who showed signs of disgust or anger with a glare, but smiled, slightly, at the ones who looked genuinely happy for them. Probably more for Fyre than him, but people tended to like her more between the two of them.

As the doctor wrapped her left wrist, Phillip stood there, spinning his signet ring as he watched this other man touch her. Yes, it was in a purely professional manner, but it didn't make him like it any more.

Skimming the crowd, he spied James and beckoned him forward. The boy came and looked up at him.

"Can you do something for me? Head to Mr. Larson's shop and get me a silver chain. Tell him to put it on my account."

"Yes, my lord." He turned and dashed off, bare feet sending up plumes of dust as he ran.

The moment the man finished tending to Fyre, Phillip stepped in closer, tucking her against his larger body. Tremors pulsed through her and it ate at him to think she was worried about how bad things were going to be.

"Thank you, Doc."

"Of course, my lord. Honored to be able to help."

They shook hands, then he put his attention back on the woman he would love and protect for the rest of their lives.

He nudged her chin up so their eyes could meet. "Head up, baby."

Despite the uncertainty he saw swimming in her eyes, she listened to him. Pride filled him.

"I do not think you know what you are doing, my lord."

A true smile kicked up one half of his mouth. "I know *exactly* what I am doing, Fyre. I told you that. Exactly."

"You are going to regret this one day, when you decide you truly want to marry."

There was a definite challenge in her tone. The part of him that loved bantering with this woman and seeing the sassy side that would argue right back with him, the side he usually only got to see when they were alone, perked up.

Dipping his head closer to hers, he dragged his gaze over her smooth face and barely resisted the temptation to kiss her one more time.

"Why is that?" Phillip touched the pad of his thumb to the corner of her lush mouth.

"I will not let you go."

Six words that were drenched in possessiveness and determination.

"I plan on holding you to that for the rest of our lives, baby." He gave in to his need and tasted her lips once more. A short kiss that left him, and her, breathless.

"My lord." James came back over, clutching a wrapped package.

"Thank you, James." He took the small box and flipped the boy another coin. Arm still around Fyre, he repositioned the box between them. "Take the lid off."

She did, and he grunted with satisfaction at the chain that lay there. It would be strong enough for what he needed. Brushing his lips over the top of her head, he shifted and reached into the box, withdrawing the chain.

"What are you doing, my lord?"

"Giving you my ring." He pulled off his silver signet ring with its gray stone and slid it on the chain as he stepped around to her back. Reaching around her, he placed the heavy ring at her neck and moved the chain to her nape so he could hook it. "Feel okay?"

She didn't speak while she lifted the ring in her hand and looked at it. He found himself holding his breath. Then she tipped her head back and his heart caught in his throat. Phillip was fully captivated by her brown eyes sparkling in the sun.

"I am never giving this back," she murmured, nibbling on her lower lip.

"Not even when I give you a wedding ring you can wear on your finger?"

A soft smile filled her face. "Nope, not even then. This is mine."

Leaning close, he kissed her again, not giving a damn about the people around them.

He spoke low, keeping the words between them. "Like I am, Fyre. *Only* yours. *Always* yours."

* * * *

Her life had changed in so many ways since Phillip had made his public claim on her earlier in the week. Actually, she was close to having survived a full week after his announcement. Fyre still lived in the small cottage she rented and still worked for the few people she did. Phillip was not on board with that, he wanted her in his house and protected.

She wasn't ready to give everything up.

"Fyre?"

She blinked and looked over to find that very man lounging in the doorway to his office. Her heart skipped a few beats as she watched him.

"My lord." She began to rise from her seat but he waved her back as he strolled into the room, kicking the door closed behind him without slowing.

"I do not get any time with you, Fyre. I am not a fan of this arrangement." His gray eyes remained pinned to her as he crossed the floor to where she sat in his chair.

Her heart kicked in her chest and she curved her fingers around the arms of his seat.

"We have the same amount of time as we had, my lord."

He narrowed his eyes. "Are you laughing at me?"

She had to bite the inside of her cheek to keep from laughing aloud at the mock affront in his tone. Summoning her most serious tone, she shook her head and replied, "Of course not, my lord. That would be ill-mannered of me to do so."

Phillip bracketed her, one hand on the back of her chair and the other on his desk, and lowered his face to hers.

"Seems like you are."

She shook her head again, then popped close to kiss him and sat back. "Never, my lord."

"Not good enough," he rumbled, bringing her close once more and pressing their lips together.

She had to agree. Kissing this man was incredible. He flicked his tongue along her lips and she opened beneath him, welcoming him in. Wetness slicked her as she shifted on the seat, needing more. Unable to get enough.

Growling low in her throat when he pulled away, she found his gaze on her, lit with happiness.

"We have to talk."

The somber tone to his words churned her gut.

He tapped the end of her nose. "Nothing about us, baby. The *other* thing."

"Let me put the books away."

She did and he just sat on the desk and watched her. The amount of hunger in his gaze threw her, but he didn't make a move other than to stand when she walked toward him. Unease filled her.

Fyre wasn't confident in her ability to keep a man like Phillip satisfied. He had far more experience than she did, and even though his ring hung around her neck, losing him was still a viable fear for her.

For her to see him move away when he used to pull her close didn't ease any of her fears.

"I have a carriage ready, thought we would take a ride since it is so nice outside."

"If you wish."

He clenched his jaw and nodded. "I wish."

Outside, Phillip helped her into the seat of the open carriage then popped up beside her. With a snap of the reins they were off. No footmen, no maids, just him and her.

Fyre tipped her face up to the sun and smiled as the warmth beat down upon her skin. She loved it here.

"What are you thinking about?"

She didn't open her eyes, just continued with her head back, embracing the heat. "How much I love this place."

"Would you ever consider moving?"

That got her to look at him. He moved his gaze from the road to her and back again.

"Moving where?"

"Nowhere specific, just would you consider ever leaving the island?"

"I have not given it any thought, but I suppose so. Going to other places is intriguing to me. I think I would like to experience snow. I heard about that once and to be able to look around at a land covered in pristine white" — she shrugged and gave him a small smile — "that would be an experience I think I would like."

"Snow is cold."

She nodded. "I heard that too." Angling toward him more, she fixed her gaze on his profile. "Do you like the snow?"

"No."

His answer was so fast, she blinked.

"Why not?"

"Cold. The damn cold that never goes away. No matter how many fires you have burning or the heated bricks in the bed at night, there is just always a bone-chilling cold that never leaves me." He cracked his neck. "Lucien's wife, Ciara, grew up with snow. She lived in the mountains and during winter she had a lot of it. Ask her if it is fun."

"Surely there are fun parts to snow?"

"Stuffing it down Lucien's back and hitting him in the face with a snowball, yes."

She laughed and loved the smile he sent her.

"You two must have caused a lot of trouble for your mothers."

"Our governesses, yes. Our mothers had nothing to do with raising us."

She flattened her lips. "And is that how you see your children being raised?"

His hands tightened on the reins and she thought perhaps that wasn't a proper question for her to ask. Phillip stopped them and set the brake before looking at her. And it wasn't just him turning his head, he faced her on the seat, expression serious.

"Are you needing to tell me something, Fyre?"

His thumbs stroked her skin as his warm hands made her feel safe and protected.

"About what?"

Phillip didn't speak for a moment, just gazed at her like he was searching for something. Something she didn't have, and Fyre was not sure she liked that.

"If you are looking to make fun of me, my lord, just take me home."

"Baby, I am not making fun of you." He curved his hand around to cup the nape of her neck. "I just forget how honest you are and that you do not play games."

She didn't know how to respond to that, so she just sat there quietly. Waiting for him to make it clearer what this thing was she had missed.

He moved his fingers along her skin and she trembled from his touch, wanting more of it. Everywhere. But she didn't move, just waited.

"Are you carrying my baby, Fyre?"

She heard his question. The words made sense and yet, they did not. "Why would you ask me that? We are not married."

"Baby, you asked me about how I thought about something in regards to children being raised. We have not been safe during sex. I have not been pulling out of you."

It clicked, all of it, and she flushed.

"No, my lord. I am not carrying your child."

"Not yet." His eyes burned with a fire that should have worried her. Instead all it did was make her wish she was carrying his child already.

Chapter Twenty-Three

Phillip stared at Fyre seated on the blanket with him. They had spent the past hour discussing how they had not been able to get Cara and whomever she was working with. He was frustrated, but he wanted more than just Cara. He wanted the person she was dealing with and the mastermind behind this entire thing, the person or people trying to bring him down and ruin the reputation he had built in Hawk's Cove.

Fyre sat at an angle from him, her lower lip caught in her teeth, as was common when she was deep in thought.

"Are you still thinking it is a man she is meeting?"

"My gut says yes but you keep insinuating it may be a woman. Why?"

"Cara has always been about money. Part of why she let me live there so long was because she got most of the money I earned, and that was basically her pin money."

"Still does not explain why you think she is working with another woman."

"You know how this island used to have slaves."

His gut tensed but he nodded.

"One of the daughters of an owner and Cara were…together." She shifted on the blanket, obviously uncomfortable with the direction of the conversation. "Even after slavery was banned from the island, she still got together with the woman. Even after she married my brother. Believe me, she will turn her eyes from the problems of others so long as she is cared for, be it coming from a man or a woman."

"Shit."

"She does not know I saw them one day in a barn, but I did." She wouldn't meet his gaze. "I know it was not the first time that she cheated on my brother. Men and women alike."

Phillip scrubbed a hand down his face. "And you have *seen her* with both men and women?"

"Yes." She still wouldn't meet his gaze.

"Fyre. Look at me."

It took a while before she would.

"What are you not telling me?"

"I am just ashamed. I did not tell my brother because I did not want to ruin his marriage."

"And he may not have believed you anyway and all you would have done was shove a wedge in your relationship."

She nodded.

"Cara made her own decisions, baby. Even now she is making her own. It is obvious her concerns are about her and not the rest of her family. Do not feel guilty about that." He tugged on the hem of her skirt. "Her time will come to answer for her betrayal."

"It is not right. Her children are incredible but all she does is hurt them."

Another tug on the soft green material of her dress. "Those children have you in their life. They will always be loved and know it."

"I was thinking, maybe we could follow her and Elonne one night when they go out, see if she meets anyone else. If it was a woman, Elonne wouldn't be suspicious, I don't believe."

He narrowed his eyes. "We?"

"Not me, because I would offer to watch the children."

Phillip drew her closer to him, setting her legs over his, lifting her skirts up more. "If you offered to do that, would she be suspicious?"

"Maybe." Her breath hitched as he stroked her skin. "But I can say I missed them and she would know that was true. I do miss them."

"Do you want to watch them at my estate?"

"No, that she wouldn't allow. And I do not think it proper."

He grinned, thumbs skimming the insides of her knees. "I want you in my bed, Fyre."

Her brown eyes grew darker. "I want it too."

"But?"

"A week after you making your claim in the middle of the street seems rushed."

"Not for me."

Frustration welled up within him and he tried to contain it. When she winced, he knew he had failed.

The sorrow in her expression nearly killed him. "Why are you hesitant?"

Fyre shook her head. "We should focus on catching Cara."

"Baby, look at me." He waited until she did. "*You* are what is important. The money will work itself out. I am—*we* are—aware someone is trying to undermine me and what I am trying to do here. You are more important to me than that."

"Money is important."

He nodded. "It is, but you do not get to believe because *it* is, *you* are not."

"I always worry about money. Someone in my position has to."

Her statement pissed him off on two levels. One, because he knew she spoke the truth, which made the truth of what her brother had done even more heinous in his reality. And two, because she didn't have faith he would be there to provide for her.

"I do not know what it was like for you before, Fyre. I can assume, but I did not live it. All I can do is promise you that is a concern for you no longer." He forced his anger back down, but it wouldn't stay put and surged up again. "I swear to you, it is not something you have to worry about going forward."

"I do not mean to upset you, my lord."

Swallowing his anger, he gave her a smile. He dragged his hands along her legs, loving the way she melted and her eyes heated with a passionate desire he swore no other man would see.

"Frustrated is not the same as upset, Fyre. I want a kiss."

She blinked, then smiled as she leaned forward to touch her lips to his.

Phillip moaned and tightened his grip on her, his cock pressed hard to his breeches. Pushing his tongue deep into her mouth, he allowed all of the angry, negative thoughts to go where they should. Away.

They had focused enough on everyone else by now. It was time for them.

He pulled back slightly, grinning when he heard her mewl of disappointment. Coaxing her to come with, to follow his mouth, she was soon on his lap, straddling him and cupping his cock between her legs. Her wet heat was easy to feel.

Yet it wasn't enough.

Hands up under her skirts, her core rocking on him as their tongues dueled, was not fucking enough for him. He craved more.

She shifted on him and he growled low in his throat when her small, strong hand snuck between them to grasp him.

"Fyre."

"Show me," she whispered against his lips.

God, to keep her touch on him, he would show her whatever she asked.

"What?" he rasped the single word question. "What do you want me to show you?"

She squeezed his length and gave short strokes. "How to please you."

Phillip closed his eyes before he could garner the strength not to just push her back and slide into her slickness. She was waiting for him, eyes wide and luminous, when he finally opened his again.

"You do, Fyre. I swear to you, every time you touch me, you please me."

Her smile grew wider and he knew she had allowed the earlier talk to fade as well. She inched back and he bit off his rumble of discontent as she moved away from his touch.

Fyre didn't leave his lap, no, she only moved enough so he could free himself. Or she could, which she did. Her skirts were still ruched up around her waist and he could see her pussy, the soft hairs there glistening with proof of her arousal.

He braced a hand behind himself to keep from falling to the blanket beneath them and losing whatever view she was about to present him with. Like fuck he was going to miss this. His cock sprang up, hard and swollen, the head an angry red and leaking.

"You asked me before, if I touched myself."

His heart thundered.

"Show me how to touch you." Fyre's words were low but there was not a shred of uncertainty in them.

How the hell had he gotten so lucky? Fyre was shy about many things, but this? Out here, in the middle of the day, she asked him to jerk off so she could learn what he wanted? Luckiest fucking guy in the world.

Readjusting his left hand behind him to better support himself, he took his right and curved it around his dick. Bemoaning the loss of her touch, he took solace in the fact that she was mesmerized by his grip on himself. Flicking his gaze down to her hands, he watched her fist the material of her skirt tight. But she didn't cover herself again.

He approved.

"It varies, how I like it. Sometimes hard and sometimes gentle. It would be easier for me to show you with your hand here, baby. I could tell you then."

Up and down he worked his fist, twisting slightly with each tug.

She didn't answer, and he looked back up at her face and saw the stark hunger there she was not able to hide. Her hips were miming small thrusts, as if she were recalling him driving into her, over and over.

Her legs were on either side of his and he knew she was on a solid foundation, so he jerked his chin at her. "Touch yourself."

Fyre held her skirt tighter as she snapped her gaze to his.

"Touch yourself for me, baby." Her tongue peeked out before vanishing. "Show me as I show you. One hand, use the other to hold your skirt up higher, so I can see all of you," he coaxed.

She obeyed, and the moment her index finger slipped through her pussy lips, he very nearly lost control again. This woman, a woman of a station he never would have looked at over in England, had come into his life and set it on its end. He had already come in his breeches like an untried youth at one fucking touch from her. And now here she was, barely touching herself, and he was ready to do it again.

Fyre shifted on his legs, widening her own a bit. He stared at the hunger on her face for a moment before returning his gaze to where her finger slid and circled her clit. He tightened his grip, determined that she would be coming first.

"Show me what pleases you. What you do in the night when you think of me."

She sank her teeth into her plump lower lip even as she moaned his name.

Fuck, he wasn't going to survive this.

Fyre wasn't entirely sure what had happened to make her so brave and shameless this sunny afternoon. But, straddling Phillip's legs, she was showing him how she pleasured herself. Sort of. His name slipped out, but she was trying to keep it contained.

Her nub was stiff and sent shockwaves through her each time she touched it. She wasn't able to pull her gaze from his cock. *Beautiful.* She wanted to put her mouth on it. Thinking of being on her knees before him while he thrust it deep made her pussy clench. Without thinking, she pushed her finger in completely and moaned.

Phillip jerked, reminding her she wasn't alone with her fantasy. He was right here before her, his thick length so close she could touch it. She *had* touched it before she'd gotten shy and asked him to show her. Truth was, she wanted to explore. Him.

One finger turned to two as she pumped her wrist. She kept time with Phillip's strokes. His eyes were locked on where her fingers dipped inside her, while she couldn't stop watching the pearly drops that oozed from his cock. She licked her lips and used her thumb on her clit.

It was too much and she stiffened, back arching as she shattered around her fingers, Phillip's name falling from her lips once more.

"Fuck, that is beautiful."

Heat sliced up her cheeks but she didn't look away from his hungry gaze.

"Tell me what you want, Fyre." His tone was thready and she knew he was on the edge.

She pulled her fingers from her slit and he opened his mouth. Without hesitation, she slipped them in and moaned as he sucked her flavor from them.

"I want to taste you."

His gray eyes darkened to nearly black. "Fyre..." It was a low rumble of thunder coming from his mouth.

She readjusted so she was between his legs instead of hers being over his. Her skirts were haphazardly down but not completely. She licked her lips and nodded. "I want to be here, on my knees, tasting you."

He gulped. "Come taste."

He didn't have to ask her twice. She scooted forward, bent, and took his broad head in her mouth, tongue swiping up the liquid already there.

"Fuck me!"

His cry spurred her on. She sucked, lapped, and ran her tongue along the head before skimming it around the crown. Putting her hand on his shaft, she nearly purred when he covered her hand with his own, showing her what she wanted to know, how he liked it.

When her hand moved down, she took more of him in than she comfortably could. She choked, backed off and tried again. It took her a moment, but she got a rhythm down she could do. No way was she taking all of him in.

Yet.

His hand dropped away and she paused, thinking she had done something wrong. He had fallen back, hands fisted in the blanket they lay on, her name leaving his mouth in a chanting rhythm. *He's enjoying this*. Hiding her smile, she closed her eyes and began bobbing again.

Not much later, he threaded a hand into her hair, fingertips scraping the back of her head. How and when her hair had been taken out of her bun she wasn't sure, but she didn't care.

He pushed her down as his hips thrust up and she relaxed her throat the second time around, trusting him. Wanting to please him as he always did her. His taste and smell only heightened her own arousal and her pussy throbbed, wanting relief. She squeezed her legs together and focused on Phillip.

Time vanished for her and she had lost herself in the pure pleasure of sucking him when he tugged on her hair. Opening her eyes, she found him looking down at her, sweat beading on his forehead and the tendons in his neck highly visible.

"Baby," he gritted out. "I am about to shoot my load."

This time she didn't hide her smile, just watched him and hummed her okay around his shaft.

"Gonna fucking kill me," he muttered.

His grip tightened even more and she let him set the pace, didn't try to stop him from thrusting deep until he hit the back of her throat, making her eyes water. His grunt was her only warning before thick streams of his release hit her tongue and throat.

Swallowing it, she eagerly lapped along his length and looked up to find him watching her again, more hunger in his gaze. She blinked and found herself on her back, skirts shoved around her waist as he hooked one of her legs high on his side and pushed into her.

"Yes," she moaned, arching to take him in deeper.

Phillip slid into her with one stroke. It wasn't fast, just a long continuous push. And she was full. Of him. How she loved to be.

And she told him so.

* * * *

"Why would you do this?"

Fyre held Cara's gaze without flinching. It had been a few days since she and Phillip had discussed the plan of following her sister-in-law while she watched the kids, but she had been busy. As had he.

"Because I miss my nephews and niece. Thought we could have a night together and the two of you could do something without the kids underfoot."

"Are you keeping them here? Or going to your *fiancé's* house?"

No denying the venom in that last question.

"Staying here. I live here. Why would I take them over there?"

Cara glared at her. "Because you are constantly trying to show everyone on the island that you are better than they are."

Moving her gaze from the hateful woman in front of her, Fyre shrugged as she looked at her brother, who only briefly met her gaze. "Then do not let them stay with me. I was asking to see them because I miss them. But I am not going to stand here and listen to your rudeness."

She spun on her heel and made it five steps before her niece cried out for her. "Aunt Fyre!" Hardening her heart, because she couldn't take them if they weren't allowed to be with her, she turned with a smile fixed on her face.

"Hi, sweetie." She opened her arms, hugging the girl when she got to her.

"Are we coming to see you?" Such hope lined her words.

"That is up to your parents. I do not know." She chucked her under the chin, determined not to let her smile fade. "If so, I will see you later. Right now, I have to go help Georges make some bread."

Isabella hugged her again. Hard. "Miss you." Her two words were barely audible but they reverberated through Fyre.

I have so focused on my own happiness I have neglected three of the most important people in the world to me.

She vowed to do better.

She kissed Isabella on the head. "Miss you too, Bella. I have to go." She turned and walked away before she begged them to let them stay with her. Something like that Cara would be suspicious of for sure.

The afternoon was full of hard work as she helped Georges, and her body ached as she walked home. The road was full of people and they waved at her, calling out greetings, whereas before she would have been ignored for the most part.

Everything had been different since Phillip had made his claim. When the people thinned out, a man on horseback came into view and she went to the side to let them go by. As the rider got closer, she realized it was Albie Caulfield.

He stopped before her, leaning over his horse's neck to look down at her.

She gave him a nod as she had always done and said, "Good afternoon, Mr. Caulfield."

"I would have treated you right, Gwen." His words were slightly slurred. "You should not have shunned me, or made me a laughingstock. I have a plantation and my own business. No one here is as rich as your damn earl, but that does not mean we are any less."

"It does not have to do with his money, Mr. Caulfield."

"You do not love him. I have known you most of your life. If you were falling in love with anyone, it would be me." He spat on the ground, and she had a bad feeling.

"My feelings for Lord Edais are not your business, but I did not love you."

His sneer grew. "Think about that while you are being fucked in a house that was used to hold and torture slaves. Think about if it is *you* he wants because he claims to care or if he is looking to get you under his roof where he can treat you no better than the previous owner treated people like you. And have you considered he's just using you to get the trust of those who look like you on this island?"

Coldness swam over her as the gravity of his words hit her square in the face. Fyre hated that she was giving his comments the slightest bit of validation and purchase. But they were insidious and they clawed for a hold on her. She knew Phillip loved her. Right?

"What are you doing here, Mr. Caulfield?"

It had been a while since Fyre had been happy to hear her brother's voice, but when his deep voice posed the question, relief took over and her legs wobbled.

"Just passing along greetings to the future mistress of the plantation." He tipped his hat and rode off.

Turning, she saw Elonne and the kids in the wagon. She realized they had agreed to let her watch them.

His expression hardened and he jerked his head at her. "Get in."

She didn't argue. The kids hugged her and she was grateful for the ride to her house, not that it was far. Without a farewell to her brother, she urged the kids inside and set about making a memorable night for the group of them.

Even so, she couldn't stop thinking about Mr. Caulfield's words and the number of times she had seen Miss Asherford hanging on and around Phillip. In town and at the house party. The one that she should not have been to because she didn't have a business.

Yet she had gotten invited.

Yeah, jealousy was a bitch.

Chapter Twenty-Four

The night sky overflowed with stars that winked down at him, and Phillip paused to look up at them, a small smile curving his lips. Fyre loved looking at the stars.

He had plans to take her out for a night picnic so they could look at the constellations. His smile grew larger as his thoughts drifted to her. She was everything to him and he hated being apart from her.

Marrying her fast was on his mind. He wanted to have the right to say she was his wife, his countess. Have the right to kiss her when he wanted and the privilege of sleeping beside her every single night.

A final glance up and he got back on the trail of the person he followed. He had been working with Archer and Zander to follow Cara and find out who she was meeting. That left Damon and Kolby keeping an eye on Fyre.

Right now, he had taken over the tail from Archer on a guy who didn't look all that intelligent, but they weren't about to count anyone out. The one he followed had received a note from Cara and left. There had been no reading it, so Archer figured he was just the messenger between Cara and the one she was working with.

Something that would make sense as they hadn't seen Cara with people other than the ones she was cheating on Elonne with, but all of those guys gave her money then went back to their lives and wives.

He had learned a lot of hiding places on the island he hadn't known about before. Phillip hated that this was keeping him from Fyre, but he was pleased she understood. Not only that, she was on board with him catching whomever. As well as undermine what that person wanted to do here.

The one thing he had noticed from Fyre however, was that she had gotten quieter since their picnic. She had sent a message she would not be able to come tonight and work on his books, as she was watching her nephews and niece.

While he didn't like that, he knew it was what they had been after. The break they had been hoping for. And why he was out here now, picking up from Archer.

The man he currently trailed slowed and looked around himself more than once before he ducked into the trees a bit more, and when Phillip followed, he saw there was a small shack there.

Moving with more stealth than he'd known he had in him, Phillip paused by the one window that barely let out the light of the lantern inside. It had been covered by some material but he tried to see in.

"What did she say?" a low, gravelly voice asked. Did he know it? He wasn't positive.

"She never speaks to me, sir. Just hands me the note." This voice was thin and reedy but also one he didn't recognize.

"Give it to me then. I cannot be seen here with you."

The voice was familiar but he couldn't see either of the speakers to make a viable identification. Nor could he pull the name from his memory.

"Get moving. I will leave after you."

The man he had been following muttered but left. Phillip watched him from the shadows. Part of him wanted to go after that man, but he had to find out who the one who stayed behind was. So he waited.

And waited.

About fifteen minutes later, the light went out, but he heard nothing. Moving slowly and with caution, he opened the door but didn't see anything. At all. He dug in his pocket for a match and lit it. The small flare of light was enough for him to know that there was no one in the small building.

What the fuck? Not even evidence that anyone had been here.

He had to come back during the day to see what he could find. Backtracking, he returned home in a foul mood. Zander was there and Phillip gave the man a nod as he walked by him into the study to pour himself a drink. After swallowing it, he poured another for himself and one for Zander, who joined him.

"Hate to say it, boss, but you look pissed."

Handing over the drink, Phillip grunted. "I am." Another drink, not the entire glass this time. "I followed that asshole with the message to a shack and he went in, heard him talking to someone. Then the one I followed left. I waited a bit and the light went out. No one left that shack and when I stepped in, it was empty."

Zander leaned against the wall, feet hooked at the ankles as he tapped a finger along the glass he held. "Where is this building?"

Giving him a basic idea, Phillip waited for Zander to say something more.

"Pirates used to run around here, there is a good chance that floor opened into a tunnel that took him somewhere else." A shoulder shrug. "Or…"

Phillip exhaled. "I know, that messenger is not the messenger at all but the one behind it and he is playing Cara as well. And he was putting on a show in case someone, like me, followed him." Phillip placed his glass down and sank into his chair with a heavy sigh.

Zander nodded.

Silence stretched between them for a moment and Phillip opened his eyes to pin a look on the man in there with him. "What are you not telling me, Zander?"

"I did not want to make things worse."

"What? Did I lose more workers? Someone else drop out of this coalition I am trying to get running?"

"It has to do with your woman."

His feet hit the floor as he was suddenly completely alert and focused on Zander. "What about her?"

"I ran into Kolby on my way here. He told me that she had a run-in with Caulfield on the road."

Anger burned in his blood. "Why the fuck did no one tell me?"

Zander just held his gaze until Phillip gestured for him to continue. "Her brother showed up with the children and she left with them."

"So it was today." Did that mollify him? Not in the least. The thought of Caulfield around her pushed him toward rage.

"I do not know all the words of the discussion but I know that she was not happy with whatever he said to her. No, Kolby did not hear it either, as he would have had to have exposed himself to do so."

"Fuck. Why can this man not just get a damn clue and stay out of her life?" He slammed the rest of his drink and wanted another. However, he refrained. Becoming drunk wouldn't do a damn thing except give him a headache.

Kolby didn't speak, allowing him a few moments to get his shit back together. When he had, Phillip sighed and rubbed his temples. Losing his temper at the man who was telling him things he needed to know was not productive at all. Damon and his brothers were doing all they could to help him and keep his woman safe.

"She was fine, but he could see she was shaken up."

He ground his jaw. "Did he touch her?"

"No."

A bit of an easier breath. "How did he know she was shaken up?"

"I cannot speak for my brother, but I would guess because we watch her all the time and have learned this about her."

That bothered him too, but he was the one who had asked them to keep an eye on her and make sure she stayed safe.

"Did he say anything else?" God, he wanted to go to her place and see her, find out how she was doing. Hold her. Kiss her.

Tell her I love her.

That honest admission shook him for a moment and he sat there, staring at his empty glass.

Kolby cleared his throat and stepped forward. "He didn't say anything else. If you draw me a map of where you went, I will sneak back and take a look. If there are tunnels I will follow them to see where they end up coming out."

Phillip nodded and pulled out a sheet of paper to do just that. Kolby didn't stay long and soon Phillip was by himself in his office. He rang for a maid and, when she walked in, he ordered some food and drink.

Not too long after, flipping idly through his books, he gestured for the newly arrived tray to be placed on the end of his desk. He pinched the bridge of his nose and sighed.

"Something I can help you with, my lord?"

He looked up to find the maid lingering. He narrowed his eyes as he took in the expression he had seen on many in England who had been looking for a favor from the lord of the house.

"Why are you here?"

"I am here to serve you, my lord."

"I do not mess with the help. Leave, and if this happens again, you will be out of a job here."

"You messed with *her*." The words were low and overflowing with venom.

Phillip dropped his spoon in his bowl of soup and snapped his gaze back up to her. The ugly expression faded away the moment she noticed he was watching her.

"What did you say?"

The smile on her face was fake, like the simpering flirtation. It wobbled a moment but didn't fade.

"That I am here to serve you, my lord."

"No," he said slowly, drawing out the word. "What you said after that."

She blinked, her smile still not fading away. "I am sure I do not know what you mean, my lord. Was there something you wanted me to say?" A pause. "Or do?"

He nodded. "There is actually. Can you please go get Mrs. Archer and come back with her."

A curtsey. "Of course, my lord."

While she was gone, he took a few deep breaths, not needing to lose his temper. Already so close to the edge, given what Kolby had told him about Caulfield, this wasn't what he wanted to deal with. Not ever, but especially not now.

He ate a bit of soup while waiting for her to return with the housekeeper. When the knock came, he watched them both enter. The maid now had a reserved expression on her face.

"She said you asked to see me, my lord?"

"Yes." He leaned back and laced his fingers on the desk. "This maid," he said, not caring to know her name, "is to be kept away from me and my fiancée. If that means she is let go, fine. However, and I will make a statement to the house after this, I will *not* put up with anyone saying anything against Miss Parker. She is going to be the woman who is in charge here. She will be *my countess*."

Mrs. Archer firmed her mouth and turned to the female beside her. "I will handle this, my lord."

"Of that, I have no doubt, Mrs. Archer." He picked up a pen. "That will be all."

The next time he looked up they were gone, his door closed, and by all accounts he was completely alone. He ate while he went over the books that should have been his time with Fyre tonight.

Despite his frustration at being away from her, it was a late night for him. Even so, he was up early and on his way to her place as the sun crested the horizon. With a brief stop off to Georges, he purchased some morning pastries and continued on his way.

He halted his horse before her home and looked around, knowing that one of the brothers was near, somewhere, watching her, but unable to see them. Phillip swung down and went to the door, where he knocked four times. He knew she had taken the children because of their plan but he wanted to see her.

She opened the door and just like that, his world righted itself. He grinned down at her, loving the look she gave him as well as the view she presented. Her hair had been wrapped in a bright-colored cloth knotted at the side, and it offered him a rare opportunity to see her neck.

"My lord," she gasped, immediately moving the tails of the cloth to hide the scarring. "What are you doing here?"

Leisurely running his gaze over her, he gave a wink. "I came to see my fiancée. I did not know there was a proper time to do that."

"I am not ready to go yet, Aunt Fyre. Can we stay…" The little girl who ran up to her aunt looked at him with big brown eyes. "You'se the earl."

He went down on one knee and nodded. "I am, and I believe you are Isabella."

Her eyes widened. "You know me?"

"You were at my house for a week. How could I not know such a beautiful young lady's name?"

She grinned at him and blinked. "I like him, Aunt Fyre. When are you marrying him?"

He chuckled as he regained his feet. "Very good question," he murmured as he leaned forward to brush his lips against Fyre's cheek.

Phillip noticed the boys standing back, watching when he put some space between himself and Fyre. He gave them a nod. "Elonne and Carlo, good to see you both again."

They both stared until Fyre cleared her throat, then they both gave him a bow and said at the same time, "Good morning, my lord."

"You will be my uncle when you marry my Aunt Fyre, right?" The question came as the little girl slid her hand into his empty one and began bringing him inside the house. "Does this mean you will buy me gifts on my birthday?"

"Bella!"

He tried not to laugh at the shock and embarrassment in Fyre's tone. Once he was sure he could respond without laughing, he did.

"Of course it does. However, I will have to get your aunt's permission first."

Bella patted the back of the hand she held. "She loves me so she will give it to you."

"My lord," Fyre said, drawing his attention once more.

He knew what she wanted. Phillip held up the bag in his left hand. "I was hoping we could have breakfast together. I stopped by Georges' and he provided some things for all of us."

"How did you know I was here?" Bella questioned.

"Georges told me that you three were spending time with your aunt." She didn't need to know they were following her parents.

Bella nodded. "We saw him yesterday evening."

Eyes back to Fyre, he lifted his eyebrows. "Yes?"

When the boys took her hands in theirs, hope in those expressions, he knew he had her. And he hoped they stayed on his side.

I may need them.

Fyre knew exactly what Phillip was doing—using her affection for the children to get on her good side. Not that he wasn't, but still.

He and the boys had moved her table outside and since she hadn't had enough chairs, they were sitting on stumps. Rather, Phillip was, because he was tall enough to do so and still see over the top.

The pasty was a big hit with the children, yet Fyre kept to herself mostly while they talked to him, asking him all kinds of questions—ones he didn't hesitate to answer.

"Do you have nephews and nieces like us?" Carlo asked as he popped in the last bite of his food.

"I have a sister but she is unmarried as of the moment, so no nephews or nieces from her, but my best friends are married and have children. I consider them my nephews and nieces."

"Like me?" Bella insisted, tugging on his sleeve.

He nodded as she climbed onto his lap. "Like you. Keeley is about your age, and I think the two of you would have a lot of fun together."

"Does she look like me?"

Fyre would love to know how he planned to answer this question.

His gray gaze flicked to her as he smiled. "Yes, she does. Your aunt knows her father, my friend Lucian."

Okay, he'd shocked her with that answer, and from the smirk on his lips, he had known she had made her assumptions about his friend's family. He gave her a wink and picked off a bit of his pastry and held it out to her mouth.

That was how they passed the rest of the time, him sharing his food with her while the children carried the conversation.

* * * *

All four of them were in the process of putting her kitchen back together when Cara and Elonne showed up. The air thickened with tension and Fyre hated it, for the children's sake. Her brother had made his decision and she would get over that loss, but the children did not need to be exposed to such hate and anger.

"We need to go." Elonne's words were short and sharp.

It didn't look like he had gotten any sleep, but she kept her thoughts to herself. She wasn't responsible for his actions.

Making sure the children only saw her smiles, she hugged them all.

"When can we come see you again, Aunt Fyre?"

She cupped Elonne II's face. "Soon. I know it has been a while but I will do better about spending time with the lot of you. I miss you all so much."

He hugged her once more. Making sure they had their things, she waved as they rode away in the back of the wagon that her brother used to go back and forth to the fields he worked, picking up a lot of the workers on the way so they didn't get exhausted on the longer walk.

As the wagon went out of view, Phillip slid his arm around her, tucking her close. She didn't fight him on it, just allowed the embrace. He turned her into his chest and rested his chin on her head.

"You cannot just show up early in the morning, my lord. It is not proper."

"Why not? I missed you and I thought you would like to know what we found out last night."

He was right about that. She pulled back and went to make them drinks as he sat at the table. She wanted to change clothes but figured he had seen her in this old dress before anyway.

Once the tea was ready, she placed his cup before him, and he held on to her wrist when she went to move back.

"Yes?"

He cupped her cheek with his right hand. "Good morning, Fyre."

The heat in his gaze melted her resistance. Their lips met and she whimpered as their tongues twined.

"Hi," she muttered when it ended.

He stroked her skin, encouraging her to get closer. She would have been fine with crawling into his lap and going from there, but she refrained. Somehow.

When she took her seat, he pulled her closer to him and turned so her legs were between his.

"What?" he said when she'd watched him for a while.

"The way you look at me." Her words were soft.

"How do I look at you, Fyre? Like you are my everything? My world? Because you are."

Mr. Caulfield's words echoed in her mind, their grip unrelenting and deep, about how she wasn't special and this man before her was using her.

Phillip's words... They were a dream she'd never thought she would hear directed at her. She wanted to believe him so much her heart actually ached.

Especially at the thought of never hearing this man say anything similar again.

Phillip found a way to inch closer to her, surrounding her with his rich scent she loved having around her. "What is going on in your head, baby? Talk to me."

"Why are you doing this?"

He pulled back slightly and she struggled not to reach out, clasp his shirt and yank him closer once more. All she wanted to do was snuggle up into him.

"What is the 'this' you are talking about?"

"Pretending you want to marry me? Are you trying to get the Blacks on the island to trust you more? I am not the best person to do that with, they already think I am different because of my illness, scars, and love of numbers."

Thunder grew in his gaze but he didn't say a word. Just watched her.

She forged ahead. "I see you in town, you know. When you come in. Miss Asherford is always near you, no, not right beside but near your vicinity, and you invited *her* to the party. Yet she isn't a business owner, or married to one."

"Finished?"

One word, cold and clipped.

No, she wasn't.

"No, but if you want to speak, you are the earl. I am nothing in comparison."

"Stop it," he snapped. "Right now, Fyre. What the fuck are you talking about and what brought this on?"

"Mr. Caulfield said —"

He reared back, chair skidding as he shoved away from her. "Mr. Caulfield? You are fucking listening to anything Caulfield says? Why? You know he wants you in his bed and will do anything, say anything, to drive a wedge between us."

Tears of frustration and fear lined her eyes and fought to escape. She blinked them back, furious at their determination to be free.

"I have known him most of my life."

"And because I am the outsider, his words suddenly hold more sway than my *actions* to you since we met?"

"I *see* her," she cried. "How she pushed against you. Touched you. She even sat by you at the meals. That is what you should have as your wife. Your countess."

He righted her chair but didn't sit again, instead he paced. Back and forth, shoving a hand through his hair.

"If I wanted Miss Asherford as my countess I would have pursued her. I do not want her and I will *never* want her." He slammed his hands on the table and she squeaked as she jumped from the loud noise. "Why are you shoving me to another woman? I want to be with *you*, Fyre."

"You do not see this from my position."

"I think I do."

The anger in his words pushed her and she snapped her gaze to his. "Do you? Really?" She rose and put her hands on the table as well, squaring off with him. "You know what it is like to still have to worry they will burst into your home at night and take you away to wake in chains? Or hanging from a tree? You know what it is like to go into a house to work with you or do other things, knowing full well that women and men were held captive there, they were *slaves* and had no say in what happened to them or their families? Do you know what it is like to be ostracized from your own people because you are too weak to work in the fields and help bring in money that way, but to thrive in something that is typically a man's domain? And do you know what it is like to have the richest man on this island ply you with attention, steal your heart and make you fucking scared to breathe because you worry one morning you will wake up and it will have been nothing but a memory?"

He stared at her.

"Because I do!"

"I did not know where I live was such a sore spot for you, Fyre. I do not see a slave when I look at you. I see the woman I will do *anything* to fucking protect. That is why I paid off your brother's debts and put the money back into your account, because you should not have to take care of him at the expense of your own security."

"You did *what*?" Her voice hit a high note.

"I *want* to take care of you, Fyre. I want to buy you things, take you on trips. See the world with you at my side."

"You had no right to interfere in that."

"Yes, I did. You are my fiancée and I will do as I see fit to keep you safe."

"I doubt I was even your fiancée when you did that."

"Not officially, perhaps."

Her heart tripped. "What does that mean?"

"That I knew I wanted to marry you from when we met. I saw you working in the store and my heart was yours."

"How do I know this is not just a way to get my people to see you in a better light?"

"You do not think that of me, Fyre. I refuse to believe you do. For whatever reason you are allowing that bastard Caulfield's words to have meaning. In turn doing exactly what he wants them to do. Split us apart." He walked to the door and out. He didn't slam the door but closed it with a final click that shattered her remaining composure.

She sank to the floor, the tears having escaped, and sobbed at the loss of everything.

Chapter Twenty-Five

Anger pumped through Phillip as he made his way through town to Caulfield's shop. He hadn't seen Fyre since this morning but his rage hadn't lessened. Not in the slightest. Taking two deep breaths before he walked in was the best he could do.

There was no one in the front and he didn't even slow, just marched through to the door leading into the back. Tossing the door open, he paused as he watched Miss Asherford on her knees sucking Caulfield's cock, her breasts hanging out of her shift, red lines over them, indicating they had been caned or something like that.

Caulfield blanched, a feat for a man who seemed allergic to the sun, and gulped. "What the hell are you doing, my lord? This is a private room."

"I do not give a fuck who you are sticking your dick into as long as you stay away from my fiancée. And stop trying to fill her head with lies."

The grin on Caulfield's face was diabolical. Caulfield pumped his lean hips, driving his cock all the way into the woman's face, his fisted hand holding her there as she choked and sputtered around him, but he didn't allow her to move back.

"I only told her the truth. You want the access she gives you to the Blacks on the island."

Did it matter that duels were outlawed in England? Phillip didn't give a fuck.

"I *want* Fyre because I love her and she will make me a perfect countess. The fact it accomplishes you do not get her makes it all the more pleasing for me."

A gasp came from behind him. He whipped around to see Fyre standing there, eyes wide as they looked at him then moved to the sight of Caulfield and Miss Asherford, whose face was turning a fiery shade of red.

"Fyre."

"Leave me alone," she snapped. "Both of you." She stepped away from his touch. "And for Christ's sake, Mr. Caulfield, let her breathe." Fyre bolted.

Phillip turned and went after her but damn, she was lightning-fast. When he reached the front door, she was gone. Nowhere in sight. The heat of the day blistered down and he didn't even see puffs of dust indicating where she had headed.

"Fire! Fire! The fields are burning!"

The chilling cry reached him and he was moving to his horse right away. He rode toward the cries and found a smaller farm on the other side of the town from his property had a burning field.

He hopped off his mount and jumped in to help try to save what they could. As he got into the motion of the shoveling, he thought about Fyre's concerns and realized she'd had a valid point. Something he hadn't even considered.

Where he lived held some harsh memories for a lot of the people on the island. And she was an anomaly, an amazing one, but for a woman doing the work she did, again, he'd looked beyond what doing those things would be like for her.

Christ, he was an idiot.

Add into that a sneaky bastard dropping these lines in her ear about how he was just trying to build up his empire no matter the cost. Apparently that could mean sleeping with her while he was supposed to want a woman like Miss Asherford.

And while that couldn't be further from the truth, he couldn't deny how Fyre could see things. He had some damage control to take care of, after this.

* * * *

It wasn't until later in the afternoon, when they were good with the containment of the blaze, that he stopped working with those who'd come help fight the fire. It was Mr. Colton, a Black man who he had not had at his party but realized he needed to include in the alliance. This island could be a force to be reckoned with if they worked together. Accepting the ladle of water offered, Phillip thought about how he was going to do another gathering, with everyone this time.

"Thank you, my lord."

"Glad we got it stopped and you are welcome. When you have some time next week, I would love the chance to speak with you about your farm."

"I am not selling, my lord. I know there was a fire, but this is all my family has."

He understood the mistrust. "I am not looking to buy you out, Mr. Colton. I want to discuss with you what I have talked to others about. Choice is yours of course. I have to get home. Let me know if you need anything."

Phillip found his horse had been looked after as well. He swung up into the saddle and wiped off his forehead before he touched his heels to his gelding and moved out.

As he reached town again, he saw James bent at the waist, sucking in air.

"James?"

"My lord." He gestured around. "Bad. Very bad."

Phillip looked around and shrugged, not quite sure what James was talking about. Off in the distance, he saw dark clouds gathering, but the rain was too far away to be of use in dousing the heat they were suffering from.

"Are you okay, James?"

"Yes, my lord. I will be. Running messages."

"What kind of messages?"

He shrugged. "Not sure. I do not read them, I just run them."

"Who are you running them for?"

"Mr. Olden."

Shifting in the saddle, Phillip didn't look in the direction of the man's sweet shop. "To whom?"

"A shack. I do not know who. I leave them and pick up the message that is waiting."

Alarm bells rang in his head.

"Where is the shack?"

James' description of the location was close to where he had been and he figured it may be the same place. Digging in his pocket, he pulled out some coins and tossed them to the boy. "Get a drink."

"Thank you, my lord."

He didn't move until the boy had headed off again. Around him wind swirled, reminding him that it was still hot and dry out.

With a groan and an exhausted body, he nudged his mount toward home. Even so, he still swung by Fyre's, needing to see her and talk to her again. He had to explain his comment at Caulfield's to her. But the place was empty, no sign of her at all.

Phillip frowned as the acrid scent of smoke reached his nose on the winds that had been steadily increasing. While there were storm clouds in view, there were all out to sea.

It was dry and crops were suffering. So were the people. His horse snorted and sidestepped.

Without much conscious thought, he brought his mount back under control. He gazed around, unease skipping up his spine.

Something was wrong.

Setting his heels to his gelding, he thundered up the road, and realized as he got closer to Hawk's Cove that the smoke grew infinitely worse.

Keating stood on the porch, issuing orders to all as people worried about.

Phillip jumped off before his horse had fully stopped. "Keating?"

"Crops are burning, my lord. The men are doing what they can but…"

Phillip bit his lower lip, not at all pleased with this. "Where is Fyre?"

Keating shook his head. "We've not seen her all day, since she stopped by after you." He pointed a maid in a direction. "She was not here long, then left."

His gut rolled. "Find her. I am going to the fields."

"My lord."

He shook his head, refusing to budge the slightest bit on this. "Keating. Find her. She is my everything. Make sure everyone is ready to leave if the wind shifts. *Everyone.*"

"My lord, she will not listen to me." A wave of shame crossed his features. "She does not trust me."

Possessiveness hit him but he had no time for postulating. "Are you one of those betraying me?"

Keating looked positively disgusted by the possibility. "Absolutely not, my lord."

"Then find her. I have to help the men. Keep her safe." With that, he swung back into the saddle.

He leaned forward over the horse's muscular neck, urging the creature onward. Men ran, sweating and hauling water as fast as they could. Some were digging. It was organized chaos. Same as before, he was off before the horse fully stopped. Philip tossed the reins to Amand, one of his workers, and strode toward Everett, the man who oversaw the workers.

"Where do you need me?"

Everett finished speaking with another and wiped the sweat from his face, smearing the soot on his dark skin.

"We are losing the far field." A coughing spell for a moment before he got himself back under control. "I pulled the men to try and save the other field. It was my choice not—"

"I put you in charge because I trust you." Phillip realized these words were true. These people were becoming his family. "You would not let it burn for no reason. Are we sure everyone is out of that area?"

Everett nodded. "I sent Otis to double-check."

"Good. Now, where do you want me?" Everett had a horrified expression on his face. "You know better than I, Everett. I just arrived. You have doled out resources. That is what I am. A resource. Use me."

A moment's pause.

"There." He pointed off to the left. "Bernie is heading the trench digging. We hope to stop the flames from jumping."

"Got it."

Long strides took him there and he skimmed the area for Bernie, heading to him the moment he located him.

Sooner rather than later he was once again drenched in sweat as he worked beside his men, and this time the land they fought to save was his own.

* * * *

It hurt to breathe.

Fyre tried to gather some moisture in her mouth but she wasn't able to do so. And she couldn't call out for she had been gagged. She struggled, but that didn't do anything for her.

How the hell did she get here? Why was she stuck out in one of the fields? God, her mind was so muddled. Her head ached and her mouth was dry. Sure, the scratchy burlap shoved in her mouth wasn't helping any. The last thing she remembered was leaving Phillip after overhearing him and Mr. Caulfield.

God, had she gone from one hellish situation directly into another? Considering her plight... Yes, the answer would most definitely be yes.

Someone walked up beside her, she could hear the crunching of their boots against the ground. The covering on her eyes was removed and she blinked to take in Cara standing over her.

Hatred completely engulfed her sister-in-law's features.

"You are such a pain in the ass."

Unable to speak, Fyre just waited for her sister-in-law to continue. Behind her, blackness began to cover the sun and fear struck her. She knew those weren't clouds. That was *smoke*. Which meant something near was burning. And a lot of it.

Memories burst to life as fear took root and held with the force of the sea. Fire. Smoke. Open flames. She'd nearly died from this before when she was a child. It had been a miracle all she had left from that were the nightmares and scars.

Not just the smell, she could hear it. The living, breathing flame. The crackle as it ate anything and everything in its path, insatiable.

Panic grew in her chest, lodging there and making it more difficult for her to catch her breath. Her skin flushed and grew increasingly sweaty. Sure, it could be from the rapidly increasing heat, but she was positive the sweat was from her approaching panic. The tightness in her chest grew with the oxygen fading. She wriggled her fingers and toes, trying to stave off the tingling.

How will I get out of this?

She tried to smack her lips around the sack wedged in her mouth. The air tasted of ash.

"You should have stayed away from the earl." Cara shook her head. "You are not fit to be in his place, at his side. We were born to serve."

"*We were born to serve*"? What was wrong with Cara?

Fyre shook her head and struggled to get into a seated position. Chest aching, she knew wherever the blaze was, it was now heading in their direction.

"I was going to have the life I wanted. Money. Sex. Power." A grimace. "Then you had to turn his head." She jabbed a finger at Fyre. "Your fault. We will not be able to move people to sell into slavery if you and he are on the same team."

This had to be a dream. Or a nightmare. Surely she wasn't sitting on the ground in the middle of a crop field, listening to her sister-in-law talking about selling people into slavery.

Her laugh bordered on maniacal. "You think you knew me? I want sex and power. Being on the inside will get me that. I have no desire to run the world like you do. I know my place, but I also know what I provide. Young people to those who can pay."

Disgust churned Fyre's gut.

"Yes, I sleep around for money. I let old men fuck me and they pay me well for it. I do things for them their own wives will not. Let me tell you when it is dark, or light, they do not care what the color of my skin is. I am the star, the center of attention."

"You are a whore," Fyre muttered from behind the gag.

Cara leaned close and ran a finger along the top of Fyre's cleavage. "I even sleep with *women*." Cara lifted up the chain with Phillip's ring on it that Fyre currently wore around her neck. A low growl slid from Cara's lips seconds before she yanked it off her. "You, however, are too much of an issue. I will do what I can to make sure you are going to be found. Well, maybe. I put you in the path of the fire. It should be here soon."

Another man walked into view and Fyre drew back at the sight of Mr. Olden. She watched the two of them kiss and Cara grabbed his crotch. Revolted, Fyre turned her head.

"Get on your knees," the man snarled.

Fyre didn't want to be here, didn't want to see or hear any of this. Cara listened right away and, from where she sat, Fyre could see a gleam of excitement in her eye.

"Take me out." Mr. Olden settled his feet a bit wider apart.

Struggling to her knees, Fyre moved slowly as Cara listened to the man Fyre used to work for. A man she had seen sleeping with another married woman.

It took her a moment or two to gather her breath — the thickening smoke made it harder. She tried to slow her heart rate as she got ready to lurch to her feet and run.

She stole another glance at the two there. Cara sucked his cock and Mr. Olden had his head tipped back as he enjoyed it. This was her chance. Pushing up, she wobbled a bit but took off, running toward the flames because the other way would take her by the couple.

"Hey!" It sounded like Mr. Olden's voice but with her heart thundering in her ears, she couldn't be sure.

Fyre looked over her shoulder in time to see Mr. Olden put a bullet in Cara's head as she knelt before him, his cock still in her mouth. A sob escaped. Even though the woman had been evil, she hadn't deserved that. No one did. Fyre plunged forward, desperate to get away.

The bark of a gun was the last thing she heard as she sank back to the ground, her head on fire.

"Phillip," she mumbled behind the gag, before her eyes closed.

* * * *

"My lord!"

Phillip looked up to see Keating in a carriage, Davie driving and controlling the horses, who definitely were not fans of the fire.

Readjusting the cloth over his mouth, Phillip hurried to them. "Did you find her?" He didn't like the concern he saw in the butler's expression. "Keating, what are you not telling me?"

"We saw Mr. Olden in town. Davie did."

"And?"

Keating held up the chain with the ring on it. Phillip's heart stopped.

"I saw it and demanded to know where he got it, but he spat in my face." Davie shook his head. "I tried, my lord."

Phillip's hand shook as he took the ring. Fyre would not have given it to that man, which meant she was in trouble. He had to get to her.

"Keating, as soon as this barrier is ready, get the men out of here. The winds have shifted. The flames will be heading back to the house. Get everyone to safety, to town. Find rooms for them. I will pay for it all."

"Where are you going, my lord?"

"To find my woman."

He ran to where his horse was tied up and, instead of putting the saddle back on, he freed him. After that, he grabbed fistfuls of mane and swung up onto his back.

A wry grin lifted his lips as he thought about learning how to mount without a saddle. Ciara had taught him.

He'd never truly believed this would ever come in useful.

But it had.

The gelding, happy to be moving away from the fire, listened to him and ran his heart out. They thundered into town and he sawed back on the reins, bringing the horse to a stop before Mr. Olden's shop. He slid off the sweaty animal. Barely slowing at the door, he kicked it open and stormed inside.

The man was in the back, shoving money into a bag, when Phillip pushed into the room.

"Where is she?"

Phillip didn't even give him a second to answer before he was over the desk and had the man against the wall, his arm along Olden's throat.

"I will not ask again. Tell me where you took this from her."

"Maybe she was with another man? Caulfield? Someone else. Who knows. Their kind are whores, sleeping with anyone." Beyond the hatred and defiance in the man's gaze, he saw fear that lingered in the back. And Phillip decided the fear needed to be in the front.

His own uncertainty of what could be happening to Fyre right now churned his gut. His heart raced with no signs of slowing. Beads of sweat had gathered on his head and dotted the top of his lip, mixing with the day's growth.

Phillip knew he would do whatever it took to find her. If it meant allowing this entire island to burn, then so be it. Fyre was his priority.

Chapter Twenty-Six

It didn't matter how much older than himself Mr. Olden was—the bastard had something that belonged to his woman.

The man's complexion became mottled. Phillip didn't care.

"Let him go."

The voice took a moment to penetrate, and he snarled at the intrusion. Damon tried to force him to release Mr. Olden.

"Back off."

"You do not get answers if the man is dead." Damon's point was valid.

That was enough to get him to listen to Damon and let Mr. Olden slide down the wall he'd been thrust against.

Damon inched in front of Phillip and jerked the man up to his feet. "I will not be able to hold him back long. Tell him what he needs to know."

"My lord!"

Phillip turned as James burst through the door, eyes wide as he took in the scene before him.

"What?"

"Mr. Parker is looking for you. He is outside."

"Send him in here, James. I do not have time to go to him."

"Yes, my lord."

The moment the boy vanished, Phillip snapped back to Mr. Olden and took another step forward. The man's blanche would have been appreciated but right now, he didn't give a fuck if he was scared of him or not. All he wanted was information on where Fyre was.

"You should leave," he said to Damon. "You do not need to witness this."

Damon shrugged. "Witness what? I do not see a fucking thing."

That was when he saw it sink in to Mr. Olden that he had no ally in this room.

"You cannot just kill me."

"Says who? You are a man who went after someone who belongs to me. I can do whatever I want to you."

"We have laws here."

Phillip snorted. "And how did that protect my woman from you stealing a ring that everyone knows is mine and that I gave to her, so do not try to pretend you thought she stole it."

"She is a darkie. Her kind steal all the time."

His blood boiled. "Right, except when they are out whoring around?"

"Exactly. We need to maintain the order. Everyone has their proper place."

"You are very correct. And your place is away from me, preferably in the ground, with your views."

"Where is my sister, Lord Edais?"

Elonne's deep voice broke through as the door slammed against the wall behind them.

"That is what I am trying to find out, Mr. Parker. Mr. Olden here had the ring I gave her, but he is keeping quiet as to where he got that from."

Phillip looked over his shoulder and was more than disturbed by the look of concern on Elonne's face. "Keep him there," he ordered to Damon before striding over to meet Fyre's brother. "What do you know?"

"I saw my wife head away from the house and meet Mr. Olden's wife. I confronted her about that when they began kissing after discussing selling some young girls to a man off this island."

Phillip didn't want to hear this but he had to. He'd not known Mr. Olden's wife was involved, but then again, he wasn't sure of all who were in on this. "Continue."

"Cara yelled at me and rode off, talking about how you and Fyre ruined everything. I thought Fyre was with you but if you do not know where she is and *he* is here with her ring... I do not know where she is."

Phillip hated the feeling of fear that just continued to grow. Like the winds were just flowing under his terror and pushing it along, keeping it moving.

"Mr. Olden," Elonne said. "My sister worked for you, kept your books. How can you know something and not tell us?"

Hatred sparked in Mr. Olden's eyes and the next words out of his mouth were the furthest thing from polite Phillip had heard in a long time, but Elonne didn't blink at the racial slurs hurled at him. Damon slapped his hand over the man's mouth with a growl.

"Shut that shit down."

Phillip hadn't heard Damon sound so dangerous before, and that was saying a lot for a man he'd felt from the moment they'd met he would never want on his bad side.

Elonne just moved closer. "Where is my sister?"

"Dead."

Phillip closed his eyes, unwilling to hear that. Unable to *accept* that.

Elonne's growl matched his own.

Stepping closer, Phillip repeated Elonne's question. Mr. Olden barely blinked. Damon produced a small blade and dug it into the man's body.

"Don't make the earl ask again."

"You can kill me. None of it matters. If she is not dead, she will be soon. Taken by the flames. Like should have happened years ago." The grin that filled his features could only be described as maniacal.

Merciful heaven, she was in the path of the fire. It had taken a while, but Phillip had gotten the truth out of her about the scars she tried to hide. Phillip knew how she feared the beast and how hard it was for her to breathe in some situations because of what had happened.

"Where?" One word. Low. Diamond-tipped. Phillip adjusted his hold on the hilt, waiting.

"I have no clue. I am not with her, am I?"

Phillip pulled the edge from his side and slid it deep in his throat. Blood leeched from his face while more dripped from his neck.

"Try the northeast side of the island. Your property, Earl. Cara was taking her there." A sniff. "Something about reliving the past." The words were garbled and most likely the last this man would ever speak, but Phillip didn't care.

"I know where." Elonne's voice shook. "Where our old home used to be before *that* fire took it."

She never said her old home was on the property I purchased.

Phillip, Elonne and Damon ran out the door. Phillip grabbed his horse and swung up while the other two took the first two horses they could find. All three of them headed back down the road toward Hawk's Cove and the fire that was racing to his house.

All he knew was that Fyre was somewhere in the northeast fields, and he prayed to anyone listening that it was somewhere that the flames had yet to touch. He hadn't known that she used to live on that property.

They split off in different directions when they hit the fields, Elonne pointing toward where their home had been and going that way himself. The winds picked up and Phillip fought his horse until it bucked him off and took off running the opposite direction. He didn't give the beast another thought—he had more important things to worry about.

He could hear the roaring, crackling flames and the wind had him pulling up the scarf that had been tied around his neck earlier to protect him.

"Fyre!"

Despite his belief that it would be hard for her to hear him over the wind and the roar of the fire, he didn't stop. Eyes and lungs burning, he continued moving as fast as he could.

Nothing.

"Lord Edais!"

The sound was faint but he picked it up. Wiping his eyes, he coughed and headed in what he thought and prayed was the right direction. The thought of never seeing, holding, kissing Fyre again was killing him. He fought against his need to scream his rage to the sky and pressed on. He couldn't, *wouldn't,* give up.

They had gone to where Elonne had said their old home had been, which was now nothing but fields of fuel for the hungry fire to engulf. And it was doing a stellar job. Unable to see anything more than the crop, they had split up.

Smoke even thicker, he barely made out the figure that stumbled into his view. It was Elonne, and he had Fyre over his shoulder. The man had no shirt on—it was wrapped around her head—and his pant legs were charred.

Heart in his throat, Phillip hurried to them and dropped to his knees, meeting Elonne there as the man sank down. It took mere seconds for him to understand the situation. Fyre's brother's body had been burned, which meant he'd gone into the flames to get Fyre out. Elonne had placed his shirt there to protect her from even more smoke, and when Phillip moved it he saw the dried blood, the large bump, and the eyes that didn't open.

"Save her. She loves you." Elonne's voice was raspy, like his throat had been singed from the inside. Sweat covered him, but even with the pain that riddled his expression, Phillip could see the love he had for his sister.

"Come on, Elonne. We have to move."

The man coughed, bracing on his hands and knees, blood coming from his mouth. "Take care of her. Love and protect her like I could not do."

And she loved her brother, no matter what the fight between them had made it look like. He had to find a way to save them both.

"Hang on. I *will* come back for you."

"She is what is important. Her and my kids."

The winds lifted again, and Phillip knew his window was closing. Gathering Fyre into his embrace, he pushed to his feet. He just had to get her to safety, then he could return for Elonne.

"Damon!" he called out. Most likely a hopeless endeavor, but he hoped the man was close enough to hear his cry over the roar of the beast barreling down on them.

* * * *

Phillip paced back and forth while waiting for the doctor to meet him outside Fyre's room. Same as he'd been doing for the past seven days. He wanted to be in there, but Mrs. Asher had shooed him out the door, stating that while he and Fyre were engaged, they were not yet married, and she was going to have some proper behavior.

They were at Fyre's small cottage.

Mrs. Asher set down a plate of food on the table and gave him a look. One he recognized as 'sit and eat'. Her smile was small when he listened to her non-verbal directive.

Fyre hadn't woken for longer than merely a few moments at a time for the past week, and Phillip was not happy with the lack of results. Or rather, progress.

He understood the smoke inhalation and the massive bump along with the gash on her head, but why was she sleeping so much? The doctor had said he wanted to keep her quiet and sleeping until her lungs and the rest of her had a bit more time to heal. She had new scars on her arms and legs, from a cheroot, most likely. Who had put them on her, he didn't know.

Didn't care. She was alive, sort of. And he wasn't about to let her go again.

The doctor wouldn't go into detail about her past, but he got the gist of it. She'd told him a tiny bit and he'd pieced together the rest. Her scars were from a fire she'd been in as a child. One that had severely damaged her breathing and also marred her skin. It explained why she wasn't outside in the heat working in the fields. Well, that and her brilliant mind. All he knew was that he needed her to wake up and look at him.

Even if it was only to yell.

The children were crashed on the other side of the room. Personally, he was at the end of his rope.

The moment he finished his food, the doctor walked out and Phillip rose to meet him. "Doc?"

The doctor's eyes sparkled as he reached out a hand and placed it on Phillip's arm. "She is awake. And I am not going to keep her sleeping longer."

He longed to sink to his knees in thanks. "Can she have visitors?" Phillip gestured to her nephews and niece.

"Yes, but go slow."

"Thank you." He shook the doctor's hand, then walked to where the children were cuddled together. He set his hand on Elonne II's shoulder. "Wake up."

All three were watching him moments later.

"Aunt Fyre?"

He went to his knee beside them. "She is awake and you can see her. Just remember she is going to be tired and weak, so be gentle."

They got up and went to the door, constantly looking over their shoulders at him. All he could do was nod that they could go in. He didn't want to share her, but he had to. Especially now. Trailing them, he waited in the doorway while they hugged her.

God, she was beautiful to him. Her hair had been braided and hung over one shoulder, her hands were bandaged, but it didn't take anything away from her. She looked up at him and he gave her a shaky smile.

She touched all three and kissed them before whispering to them. The trio left, albeit reluctantly, and Bella hugged him before she finally went back through the door.

Fyre struggled to sit up a bit more and he went to her side, helping her to get comfortable. Then he lowered himself to sit beside her on the narrow bed, sliding one arm behind her. The moment she was tucked against him, his heart and soul settled.

He rested his lips against her temple, just allowing himself a moment to take it all in. She was awake, safe, and in his arms.

Where she belongs.

"Are you going to say anything?"

He heard the wobble in her voice and swallowed a few times to get his emotions under control or his would mimic hers.

"I love you."

Guess the wobble is still there.

"Phillip."

He turned her face so he could kiss her. "Fyre, I almost lost you. I will not let another day go by without you know how much I fucking love you."

"I—"

"I want you to rest."

"Cara." She closed her eyes. "She is dead. Mr. Olden killed her."

Arms around her, but making sure she wasn't hurting from his touch, Phillip nodded. "I know. *We* know."

She shifted to look at him again. "What happened?"

So he told her while he held her. Told her about the plans between Mr. Olden and Cara with some men on different islands who wanted to bring slavery back to this one. As well as Mrs. Olden. Told her about the loss he'd suffered with the property, and the house.

He fell silent and she rested her bandaged hand on his arm. "I am so sorry you lost everything, Phillip. Will you be going back to England?"

"I did not lose everything. I lost some of the fields and the house, but the most important thing, I have right here in my arms now."

"You are holding me."

"I know, baby." He closed his eyes, hiding the tears that threatened. "Believe me, I know."

Fyre sat there in his arms, never so grateful to have them around her as she was this moment.

Fragile was how she felt. And it wasn't a feeling she enjoyed. The pain was momentary, it came and went, but the thought of never seeing him again…that had been more than she had been ready to face.

She sat still, just soaking up his touch as she ran over everything he had told her. He'd lost it all.

"It was my fault," she muttered.

"No, Fyre. This was not your fault at all."

Phillip squeezed her gently and she knew he was being mindful of her injuries. The doctor had gone over all of them with her. The scar on her head from the bullet was healing but she would always have a mark. The injuries to her hands were from her putting out the flames that had found her skirt as she'd tried to crawl away.

"What aren't you telling me?"

There was a brush of wetness against her skin, but he wouldn't allow her to turn to him. "I am sorry, baby. I tried to save him too, but I could not."

"Elonne." Her heart cried out in pain.

"He got you to me but I was not in time to get him out after you were safe. I can only hope one day you will forgive me for this."

"Phillip," she whispered. "Look at me, please."

He did and she held his face, his tanned skin so much darker than the pale gauze around her hands. "As angry as I know you were with him, you would not have left him to die. You did what you could and I never have to forgive you for any of it." She used the side of the bandage to wipe away his tear and nibbled on her lip briefly.

"Do the children know?"

"I told them."

"I guess I am all they have left now. Both mom and dad gone."

"No. They have *us*, Fyre. You and me."

"No one will say anything when you look somewhere else for a countess."

"I do not have to look anywhere else. I told you this already. You are that woman."

"What about the ruined plantation?"

"There are plans to rebuild the house. Everyone made it out, and they are staying with family and friends or in town in lodging there until they can return to work."

"You did not fire anyone?"

"I am not going *anywhere*, Fyre. Not unless my wife and our family are with me."

She finally understood that she was where she needed to be. He was the only man for her, and he would protect her.

"I love you, Phillip."

His smile warmed her completely.

"Four words I will never tire of hearing from you, my love."

He pressed his mouth to hers, gentle but not holding back any of the emotion she knew he wouldn't show to others. He was hers and she wasn't ever letting him go.

Epilogue

Phillip stood beside Lucien. The men watched the workers as they built his new home. The fire had damaged a large portion of the main house at Hawk's Cove. Knowing about its past and what it had symbolized to the people of this island, people he considered family, he'd had all of it torn down to rebuild anew. This was a new beginning, for him and for Fyre.

They would start over. New home. New lives. Together.

The scorched earth still held signs of the beating it had received, but like him and Fyre, that wasn't all. There was new growth pushing up through the soil, bringing green back to this lush paradise. The salt air had even begun to feel familiar to him. This was where he belonged.

"How did you know to come?" he asked his best friend.

"We got word of the fires here, and there was not going to be any way I did not come to see how we could help."

To their left, the wives spoke to each other, Ciara having immediately calmed Fyre's nerves at meeting a marchioness. Even when he'd reminded her that she was a countess, she'd shaken her head and told him, "*I am just Fyre.*"

To which he'd countered, "*You are* my Fyre, *and you will continue to outshine everyone else.*"

The children were playing, Bella having found an instant friend in Keeley. He smiled and shook his head at the scowl Elonne II was receiving from Hawk, Trace's son, when he spoke to Keeley.

"You know we are putting money into your venture. Myself, Trace, Rafe. Your parents."

"You spoke with my parents?"

Lucien laughed. "Of course. You ignore them, so they come to me to be kept apprised of how you are doing here. You've flourished."

"It was Fyre. She was the spark I needed."

"And how is it going to be to have *four* children?"

Phillip rubbed his face and looked over at his pregnant wife. Their house would be done before the baby arrived and everyone would be where they should be. His fields were taking shape again and the coalition had only grown. "I have never been so fucking scared in my life. I almost lost her once. I have no idea how to be a father."

"Bullshit. You already are. Those three hang on your every word."

Trace and Rafe came over and the four of them stood together in companionable silence.

"I get it now," Phillip admitted. "Took me all this time, but I fucking get it now."

None of them asked him to elaborate, for they knew. And he hadn't lied — he understood now why these men had done what they had for their women, because that kind of love changes a person.

The wind picked up and Fyre turned toward him, the sun highlighting the swell of her body as she carried his child. She lifted one hand in a wave and he returned it, even as his smile grew bigger.

She touched her chest where his signet ring once again rested — her silent way of telling him she loved him. He kissed two fingers in his response. Phillip had never known he could love someone so powerfully and deeply. Never known that sometimes you just needed a spark to get you on your way to being a better person all around. But he *had* found the one for him and *she* would forever be *his* spark.

Want to see more from this author?
Here's a taster for you to enjoy!

Billionaire Brothers:
Saving Rhodes
Aliyah Burke

Coming May 2022

Excerpt

"Sit your ass right there, Bradford. Damn it, I'll get to you and this most current clusterfuck in a second." Livingston Rhodes raked a hand through his short, spiked hair as he paced the wide expanse of his office, wishing he was anywhere but here. And now. Noting his younger brother listened, he focused back on the man he was in the middle of a conversation with at the moment. Gareth Ericsson.

"I can just email you the accountant's information, man. Sounds like you have a few other things on your plate." The man's low, smooth tone slid effortlessly over the line. Gareth was much calmer now and less uptight since he'd found his woman.

Livingston turned his back on the large, polished, handcrafted oak desk to the massive window overlooking his city, New Orleans, and shook his head. "Please." He wasn't in the right space for this, not until he got his brother out of town for a while. And he sure as hell wasn't in the mood for the holiday that was heading to them.

Christmas.

Bah humbug.

"I'll have it to you by the end of the day. I just want to say one thing."

Gareth's tone drew his focus like a shark picking up on blood in the water. "Which is?"

"She's young but don't let that sway you. She's a fucking rockstar at what she does."

Livingston frowned. A woman was why he was in this position to begin with, and the last thing he needed was another coming in to try to fix this mess. At least that was where his gut was directing him. Until he got to the bottom of this, all he had was conjecture.

"Gareth."

"She's not going to be like other women around you, Livingston. Single-minded focus is what this woman is about. She's like you, but cuter, and I have to say, a lot more deadly."

He watched a city worker hoist a Christmas direction up on a street lamp before the truck moved slowly on to the next. "Cuter? Since when do you notice women? I thought Xandra was the only woman for you."

Cutting his gaze to the large flatscreen on the wall, which ran stocks most of the day, he noticed the weatherman talking about an early winter storm wreaking havoc over the Rockies. Dumping ungodly amounts of snow and sleet and taking power from thousands.

"She is. I know Daisy because of my Xandra. Red had her come here and check out our books after we had an accounting concern."

After ensuring his brother still remained seated — he was currently scrolling through his phone — Livingston faced the window once more, needing to do one thing at a time. "How come I didn't hear about it?"

"Not a lot of people did. She came in, worked her magic and nailed down the who, how, when of the problem. After that, *we* handled it."

Livingston grinned at the danger in his friend's tone. They were so alike it was scary. They'd become unlikely friends and, despite their fathers' attempts to keep running their lives and dictating who they could be friends with, they'd endured. There weren't a lot of people that he trusted who traveled in their social circle but Gareth was one. Perhaps *the* one, aside from his brothers and his best friend Eli.

"I'll look for the email. Give that wife of yours a kiss for me."

"Fuck you, man. Your lips aren't touching my Red." There was humor in Gareth's tone. Mostly. "Daisy Wentz is her name, and it'll be in your inbox before the end of the day."

"I appreciate it, Gareth."

"Always, my man. You need anything, you let me know."

He was gone.

One crisis having been dealt with, Livingston pulled the earbud from his ear and dropped it on his desk with a *thunk* as he turned back to face his middle brother, Bradford.

His brother put away his phone and stood. "I swear I didn't do this, man."

"I know. You have no reason to steal from me, you have enough of your own money. But someone," he took a deep breath and forced himself to unclench his fist, "is making it look that way."

Livingston was desperate to know who had fucked not just with his business, but also with his brother.

"Thanks for believing in me. I know it's not easy, especially with Dad being his usual charming self." Bradford pushed his hands in his pockets, rocking back on his heels.

Livingston rolled his shoulders then took a seat. "I think you should get out of the line of fire for a while as the investigation goes on."

A disbelieving snort left his brother. "So after that shit you just spewed, you still don't *honestly* think I'm innocent in this. You believe that this is my fault, that I would actually be dumb enough and assholish enough to steal from you."

"That's not what I'm saying, at all. I'm not in the habit of saying things I don't mean, and I don't think you did this. I *do* think it prudent you take your face out of the limelight for a while."

Bradford's expression grew pinched, full of tension, as he shoved his hands through his dark brown hair. His gray eyes, normally a soft dove gray, were steely and harsh. Anger burned in them, alive and hungry.

"Fuck you, Livingston. Just because I don't want to run a casino doesn't mean I'm a fuckup."

Damn it! That's not what he'd meant, not at all. "Fuckup? No. Impetuous? Yes. And moody as fuck. I'm on your side, Bradford." He rested his hands on the desktop.

"Funny ass way of showing it." Hands up in front of him, Bradford moved back to the door. "You want me gone, fine. I'll be so far gone you can't find me." He whipped around and stormed from the room, slamming the door behind him.

"Fuck!" Livingston banged a fist on the thick desk, wincing at the sting of pain that radiated up his arm.

That wasn't how he'd wanted it to go. He was trying to protect his brother. Did he need it? No, but hell, Livingston had been doing it for both brothers as long as he could remember. Getting between their father and them to take the blows. It was instinctive for him, like breathing.

He could use a vacation.

That shit ain't happening.

His casino, The Empire, flourished here in NOLA, however he was in the process of getting a riverboat one ready as well. This shit with his brother being implicated in embezzlement had put a huge dent in those plans.

And he wasn't a patient man, didn't like delays. But he could use a vacation. Of course, not being a man who indulged in them, they weren't common. He had had one three months ago, but that had been more of a delay in travel.

His lips twitched as he remembered the night he'd spent with a woman in the bar of a hotel before heading up to his room with her. She hadn't known him from Adam, hadn't been interested in anything but sex. Livingston had been all for it.

Waking alone had frustrated him, for he'd wanted to start all over and redo their night together. But it hadn't been meant to be. She had been gone and all he'd had were the memories.

If he had someone like that around, he may me more inclined to not work the long hours he did.

Gareth had just laughed at him when he told his friend about his one-night stand. Reminding him that's how he and Red had met, he'd said to stay positive, she could come back into his life.

He doubted it. Not sure why a woman he'd met in Seattle would run into him in New Orleans. He wasn't in the dating scene, and after seeing what happened to some of the men who traveled in his circles when they did go in that pool, he wasn't ready to go back in there.

Sure, there were *always* going to be people who wanted him for what he could do for them. He was a fucking billionaire. But deep down, in the parts he wouldn't publicly acknowledge, he wanted something like Gareth had. A woman at his side who loved him for him, not his money. Someone who would have his back no matter what.

The circles he ran in didn't generate that kind of people. Not that he'd met anyway.

His computer dinged and he stole another look at the television, shaking his head at the ticker stating how much worse the storm was going to get. Losing power in summer was one thing, but during winter with snow and the cold, he was glad he wasn't there. This Winter Storm Ellis wasn't going to be anything to ignore. He turned away. They had winter storms, he had hurricanes. Everyone had something.

Opening the email from Gareth, he scanned over the information he'd sent over on Daisy Wentz. Whistling at what he read, he immediately picked up his phone and reached out to get her to come here so she could untangle all the threads and the thorns that had wrapped around his business.

* * * *

Daisy Wentz flattened her lips as she stared up at the door leading to her next appointment. The Empire. One of the most popular casinos in New Orleans, or so the rumor went. Men and women, both casually dressed and those wearing their finest moved, in and out of the doors like they were in Vegas.

Hell, for some this was as close as they were going to get. Personally, she had no use for a casino — the odds *always* favored the house and she wasn't on board with tossing away her hard-earned money. On the other hand, she didn't condemn them.

Apathetic.

Turning her right wrist so she could see the narrow face of her watch with its silver filagree arms designating the time, she took a deep breath. Only to immediately regret it. Not that it was horrible, but there were an awful lot of perfumes and colognes intermixed with the city scents.

She would have to do some exploring while she was here. If she agreed to the job after meeting Mr. Rhodes. Smoothing a hand down the curve of her hip over her purple suit coat, she walked to the door, steps brisk and business-like.

The security guard at the door eyed both her and the briefcase she carried and shifted to position himself in her path. His dark gray suit coat fit him and the slacks he wore completed the outfit. If his intent was to both blend and look intimidating, it worked.

"I'm sorry, ma'am, you can't take that briefcase inside."

"I have a meeting with Mr. Rhodes in five minutes. I need the briefcase for that. If you could call up to him and let him know Ms. Wentz is here."

She wasn't a fan of confrontations but she knew her worth with regards to her job. If this man wanted her to help him, he damn sure would let her in with her things.

Blue eyes roved over her and she knew what he saw. And as the case with most men, she was found lacking. She wasn't a beauty by any means. There were curves, not like her adopted sisters had, but she'd spent a few years malnourished and she wasn't ever going to be like some. Not that she was ugly, she just didn't command men's attention by walking into a room. Worked for her though. She'd spent her growing-up years trying *not* to be the center of attention.

Following his wordless gesture, she trailed him to a phone by the door and grasped the leather handle of her Buccio Ragusa briefcase with both hands. A gift from her adopted family, it even had her initials monogramed on the left corner of the flap. Outwardly, she presented calm — inside was a completely different story.

Her heartbeat raced like the horses at the Derby, and she couldn't account for why. Adrenaline kicked through her and she wanted to sit and put her head between her knees. Skin prickling, she scanned the area, grateful for her Transitions, which hid her gaze from the guard and whomever would be watching on the numerous security cameras she didn't doubt were pointed on her.

"I apologize, ma'am. I have a guard coming to escort you to his office."

"You're just doing your job."

He gave a small nod. If it was for thanks, or understanding of her comment, she couldn't be sure. Didn't really matter either. In the next few seconds another man, dressed identically to the one who'd stopped her, appeared. His bright red hair almost brought a smile to her face. *Shredded carrots.*

Great, now she wanted carrot cake.

"If you'll follow me."

She fell into step with him. Neither man had given their name. *Is that common? Are they taking me out back to shoot me?*

Okay, no more late-night horror shows for her.

I should focus on the carrot cake.

They stuck to the edge of the casino and made their way to a bank of elevators. People moved out of this man's way without him having to say anything. A red-and-gray door opened and she stepped in at the man's gesture. Hell, even small talk would have been preferable to the awkward silence.

She didn't do a lot of talking, but this was bugging her. Not even registering the floor they halted on, she walked out and waited for the man to tell her where to head next. At the end of the short hall, to the left, sat a wide set of double doors.

He opened the door for her and gave her a small smile. "He's expecting you. And his secretary is right there."

"I appreciate the escort." The man slipped away and she progressed to the large glass desk behind which a petite woman sat, her golden hair drawn back in a French braid. "I'm Ms. Wentz and I have an appointment with Mr. Rhodes."

Her gaze flickered over Daisy as she smiled. "Of course. Right on time. He'll appreciate that." Nails the shade of soft bubblegum pink flashed as she picked up the receiver and pressed a button. "Mr. Rhodes, your one o'clock is here." A pause. "Right away, sir."

The woman hung up the phone and pushed back from the desk. She walked around the corner and right up to Daisy, who felt dowdy next to this woman in her skin-tight dress and five-inch heels that she walked in so easily.

I have my own problems with heels.

"Follow me, please."

Two knocks on a heavy door before she pushed it inward. Daisy entered right after her. The office was spectacular. Definitely masculine in tone. Heavy furniture. Darker colors. Two plants that were recipients of the sunlight streaming in the window taking up one wall. And in the center, a massive desk taking up a large portion of the room.

Her skin tingled once more and she fought the urge to run away. Either that or squeeze her legs together to kill the ache that had suddenly popped up.

"His bark is worse than his bite," the secretary whispered before she snuck out, closing the door after her.

Skin a living flame, Daisy wasn't positive about that. Shoving down her uncertainty to the bottom of her thoughts, she approached the desk and the man who hadn't turned to face her as of yet.

"Thank you for coming, Ms. Wentz."

That voice.

It couldn't be. Could it?

As he rose from the chair and turned to face her, Daisy swallowed. Sunlight gleamed off the smattering of red in his dark brown hair, so dark it was nearly black. His facial hair was cut tight to his chiseled jawline. Broad shoulders covered by an onyx black suit jacket, with a hint of red along the lapel that matched the kerchief in the pocket. A white dress shirt and a checkered red-and-black tie finished the view. At least until he moved around the desk, tugging on his cuffs.

"I'm Livingston Rhodes."

He stood before her. Far more than a head taller than she was. His pants hugged lean hips and powerful thighs before falling straight down. She wrenched her gaze back up to those eyes. Pewter gray. Unmistakable. Definitely unforgettable.

Thankfully, her professional mind worked even while her fanciful one stopped to take a break and ogle the sexy businessman before her. She accepted his hand and shook it.

"Daisy Wentz."

His brow furrowed ever so briefly before smoothing out. It had to have been her imagination that he didn't release her hand right away.

"Have a seat," he barked as he retreated back around his desk, to his own chair.

He sat after she had. Ankles hooked and slightly to her left, she took a low breath and loosely clasped her hands in front of her. "When you left a message with my service, you didn't go into a lot of details. Could you please explain a bit more to me about what you are looking for me to find."

Livingston leaned forward, hands linked as he held her gaze with an unerring focus.

"There's been some embezzling going on and I want to know the who and how long, and when you tell me that, I'll find the why."

Danger vibrated up from the last part of that sentence.

The way he stared at her had her wanting to fidget, but she'd withstood peoples' examinations for far too long to let this man get under her skin. *Right*?

God, she needed to focus. Not focus on the fact he was the one man in her life who'd ever given her a nickname.

"Please don't take this the wrong way, there are plenty of accountants who could go over your records. I'm sure ones who even live here that could do the job."

Those dark gray eyes heated with a simmering anger. "This is implicating my own brother, and I know he wouldn't steal from me. Not ever. Someone is setting him up and I need an impartial party to dig around and find the answers."

She licked her bottom lip. "Impartial."

A languid blink, removing any and all traces of rage, leaving behind a look almost as if he weren't sure she understood the meaning and he were debating if he should give her an explanation.

"Yes, we have no ties to one another. You are here strictly for business. Not in the area in hopes there will be a discount if you give me the answers I want." He sighed and shook his head. "I'll do whatever it takes to protect my family, Ms. Wentz. Money isn't an object and I want you."

Daisy opened her mouth but he continued on.

"Gareth Ericsson recommended you. He said you've done work for his wife and his company."

The first real smile of her day lifted her lips. "Xandra."

Another minute head tilt before he seemed to shake himself free of whatever spell had gripped him, for however short a time. "I have a suite ready for you in the hotel. All your needs will be comped. Whatever you require to get digging into this, let me know and I'll have it brought up to you."

He stood and she took her cue from him. "You don't think this is improper? Because of the connection?"

Livingston arched an eyebrow, somehow managing to look even hotter even as the thick condescension dripped. "*Our* connection is a business one. I trust Gareth and he trusts you. That's enough for me and there's nothing improper about that. I'm sorry, I hate to cut this short, I have another matter to attend to." He walked to the door. "Monica will show you to your suite and start you with whatever you need. I'll swing by this evening and we can finish going over everything."

She'd been dismissed. All without her actually saying she would take the job. She'd sent a message that she would come *talk* about the work, not that she would take it. He already had his mind made up.

Mind racing, she tried to pull the words she desperately needed to say free from the quicksand that sucked them down. She failed as his broad shoulders faded from her view as the elevator door closed behind him. He never once looked back.

Monica took her to the other side of the casino, walking through the back hallways, and showed her how to get up to the suite reserved for her.

Giving the woman a list of few items that she would need brought up, she sat on the ottoman after she was alone in the opulent space. Without thought, she pulled up two specific contacts and called them, initiating three-way.

"What's going on?" Iris, the mothering one of the three, asked.

"Where are you?" Violet questioned as music was turned down in her background.

"I'm in New Orleans for work."

"What's wrong?"

"Remember I told you both about that night I had in Seattle months ago?"

Both hummed their approval.

"Tall, broody, sexy and the power to go all night and then some. Yes, we remember you saying it hurt to walk the next morning." Iris laughed. "What about it?"

"He's the owner of the company that called me in."

"No shit?" Violet whistled.

"I have to tell him I can't do this." She shook her head. "It's unethical."

"What aren't you telling us." Iris' tone grew serious. "Daisy?"

"He doesn't remember who I am."

"Fuck!" Both women muttered that at the same time.

She had to agree. The man who'd given her a night to remember didn't have a clue who she was.

About the Author

USA Today Bestselling author Aliyah Burke is an avid reader and is never far from pen and paper (or the computer). She is happily married to a career military man. They are owned by six Borzoi. She spends her days at the day job, writing, and working with her dogs.

Aliyah loves to hear from readers. You can find her contact information, website details and author profile page at https://www.totallybound.com

Home of Erotic Romance

Sign up for our newsletter and find out about all our romance book releases, eBook sales and promotions, sneak peeks and FREE romance books!